FALLING

FALLING

Tales from the East-Coast

Erik Van Achter

Copyright © 2021 by Erik Van Achter.

Library of Congress Control Number:		2021911067
ISBN:	Hardcover	978-1-6641-7752-9
	Softcover	978-1-6641-7751-2
	eBook	978-1-6641-7750-5

All rights reserved. No part of this book may be reproduced or transmitted in any form or by any means, electronic or mechanical, including photocopying, recording, or by any information storage and retrieval system, without permission in writing from the copyright owner.

This is a work of fiction. Names, characters, places and incidents either are the product of the author's imagination or are used fictitiously, and any resemblance to any actual persons, living or dead, events, or locales is entirely coincidental.

Any people depicted in stock imagery provided by Getty Images are models, and such images are being used for illustrative purposes only.
Certain stock imagery © Getty Images.

Cover showing Bristol University Students (Medicine) having a Halloween Party. Photograph: Courtesy of William Allison

Print information available on the last page.

Rev. date: 06/04/2021

To order additional copies of this book, contact:
Xlibris
844-714-8691
www.Xlibris.com
Orders@Xlibris.com
827006

I have seen many things in my travels, and I
understand more than I can express.

Ecclesiastes: 34 (11)
New Revised Standard Version- Catholic Edition

For Greet and Vincent – always there.
For Onésimo and Leonor – So far away.

Dear Reader,

All characters in my stories are invented. They do not exist. They don't talk to me, E-mail me or message me. However close they all are to me, what you are reading is fiction and fiction is different from reality. Similarity with real time events may occur, but that was not intended. All has been invented. From scratch.

I would like to thank Pedro Almeida, Daan Peleman, Luke Connolly and Roland Severijns for reading, commenting and sharing their thoughts during the writing process of the present collection. I have learned a lot from these conversations.

Special thanks to Sean Gordon for his in-depth line editing of the scraps of paper I had assembled during my postdoctoral stay at the Portuguese Department of Brown University. Oh … happy days!

Falling, Tales from the East Coast would not exist without the friendship of James Brian Moulder (Clemson University– S.C.) and especially not without the medical expertise of William Allison (Bristol University - School of Medicine – U.K.). William also allowed me to use his Halloween party photograph on the front cover of the present book. Talking to both of you for many hours during a depressing pandemic has been a once -in -a -lifetime experience. Thank you!

CONTENTS

Falling 1
A Wicked, Foolish Lie 13
The Vana Spes Society 25
Paradise Lost 38
Paradise Regained 52
Toys are US 65
Kinderhook 77
Murder at the Boathouse 90
Falling Again 105
Personal Effects 118
Behind the Mask 130
Metamorphosis 143
Acquired Situational Narcissism 156
The Raven 168
A Second Coming 180
Estrangulata Laeta 193

FALLING

Metal leaves were trying to escape from the flowers they had been welded to ages ago. And a bold gilded letter H stared at him defiantly, while the ivies were moving softly to the rhythm of an early autumn wind. Everything in Charlie's mind was urging him on, screaming at him. This was his moment, the chance to see all of his hard work pay off. This was his reward. And yet...

For years, Harvard had been at the center of his dreams. Now standing in front of *Sever Gate*, looking for clues in the meandering artistic ironwork, he remained uncertain about whether he had something more to give. Sobering thoughts were scrambling through his mind. Perhaps literature, once his primary interest, could be combined with his current degree in Economics? Oh, for sure, something never seen before would arise from all this knowledge. He could create something mighty. A Novel! A Musical! A movie! He dreamed for himself an unheard of merger of disciplines. And while these thoughts bubbled up, a subtle smile returned to his face. He was back on track. Oh yeah... he was! Or, wasn't he?

He was handsome and intelligent and seemed to slip into this world as though it had always been his own. It was what you may call a seamless transition. His first class appearance was a testament to his sense of belonging. Everyone flocked to him as he sat down vaguely smiling at the other freshmen pretending to listen to their conversations. He was an irresistible force in his new realm. After the professor had finished his opening piece, Charlie began conversing with the girl beside him. She had come from an expensive private school in Vermont. Conscious of the fact that he would be meeting people from everywhere in the world, he tried not to focus too much as he let his words fly. Everlasting love was not high on his agenda. Not now. As the conversation went on, they discussed Charlie's stellar wrestling career. "Wow, that's so impressive... how did you get so good, Charlie?" she asked.

But there was this bitter note to her words, "Charlie"... That was a name too effeminate. Too childish. The name was not fit for a man. He had always thought this, but never had dared to tell his poor but loving parents. In spite of the girl's clear interest, the sound of his name distracted him, as he looked through her while she continued to speak. His own name disorientated him. Disillusion with the place crept back into his mind. He felt a kind of latent alienation as if Harvard had fallen short of his expectations. When he left the class behind at the end of the period, dark thoughts began to stir. That girl had provoked some sort of nausea within him.

It was more than just the sound of his first name. "Parker" cast another shadow on his consciousness. It had not taken long for her to ask if he by chance had any relation to the notorious Parker Pen Company. Perhaps... and this was a thought that truly scared him: these names he had been marked with, were just a symbol of what he could be, what he was set to be. Even as he stood in these halls of famous high-achievers, the knowledge of another Charlie Parker, a parallel life, blackened his heart. His parents had named him after the jazz musician who had rocked the world on so many occasions. At first, he had loved the idea of sounding like someone famous. The name held an aura. But when he said "My name is Charlie," to the first girl he had wanted to date in junior high, the aura was gone. She smiled at him – "Charlie, you say... Is that not a girl's name?" He would never let her smile at him again. True, that was then; that was Hudson, Wisconsin. But, ever since that moment, he had tried to distance himself from the name.

Falling

There was only one solution to this damnation. He had to make something spectacular of himself. He must become a star that no one could ever forget. Only then would he rest with the knowledge that he had lived up to expectations. Only then would he truly fulfil his destiny. At least, this was how he saw it now. And even though running away had never been an option, his mind relentlessly turned towards Hollywood. Ben Warner would be his name there. He was convinced that this was fitting enough for his character and image, far more than the name "Charlie Parker." He would merge what had inspired him so previously, Ben Hur and Warner Bros, to become a star. A kind of new James Dean or Marlon Brando. No one doubted he wouldn't.

Upon reaching his dorm at the end of the day, Charlie could not help but feel as though an enormous weight had been lifted from his shoulders. No longer would he carry the burden of his former self. His vision of the future was bright. His views of Hollywood would follow him in the coming weeks. Every seminar cloaked a little dream world of potential. Charlie was all too sure of what he would become soon enough. In spite of what distractions such thoughts might have caused, Charlie was performing better than ever in his academic pursuits. He aced every test and paper much to the chagrin of his classmates, who knew his expansionist dreams all too well. "Charlie Parker? What? You mean that sucker who calls himself Ben Warner now? Oh my God!"

The truth was that the knowledge he was acquiring would indeed be a key to connections, to that role he deserved, to greater things. At his enrolment, he had doubted his love for the discipline, but now it was all that mattered, for he knew he would not survive without it. Not in the world he imagined himself living in. Merely starting a futile conversation with the words: "When I was at Harvard... ." Well, whatever they tell you, it would make a difference!

Though she was still in his thoughts through this period, he had all but alienated the girl he had conversed with on the first day. But she, equally full of herself was unwilling to entertain a boy who seemed to care for little else but his triceps and his own future. It was his eyes —mid-west blue and impenetrable - that set her back, the appearance of a stubborn form of expectancy. Now, it would be foolish to say that Charlie had gone without romantic success; he had found someone else without issue. Celia was perfect for his current state of mind. This is not to say that she was passive, willing to let his personality dominate all the interactions. Rather, Charlie picked up on the fact that they were moderately alike. Both were competitive and ready to take on the world outside these walls. A Direct Marketing student, Celia dreamed of a world in which she would create - she avoided the verb *design* - various products, perhaps even develop a brand of her own in the process. Indeed, as they made their way through the autumn-clad campus, they drew themselves into their fantasy once more. This time, it was a deep trance unlike any other before. "Perhaps I could be your manager once you make it," she suggested as Charlie watched her. She looked so beautiful with the early afternoon sun catching her face and saying such precious words. Oh... Charlie was aroused! "Sounds like a plan," he said as he smiled, returning a short expression of gratitude.

"Well, an advert gave me this idea." "An advert? Where? An advert about what? " Celia seemed a little taken aback by the terseness in her boyfriend's voice as his tone had darkened while they descended a flight of stairs, entering Quincy street. "See, this agency here is recruiting," she stated, showing Charlie the ad and refusing to let go of the rush confidence that had got her going. "It's just a minor role, but... I'm sure you could make something great of it." "Oh Yes! To be sure I could! Well... I bet I would," Charlie continued as he let a grin break out. He was anxious to find out more about such a most interesting opportunity. Perhaps his big breakthrough was not as far away as he had thought. She responded, "Well, it's for boys, obviously, boys that can fit a role in a Greek mythology production, you know, guys in robes with big muscles, that kind of thing..." Charlie forced himself to bite back laughter as he heard this. This all seemed perhaps a little bit much and too sudden. After all, he had been expecting something more lowkey. Yet, he felt he deserved this. What an opportunity to showcase both his body and his skills!

"You know, I think that this sounds great. Greek mythology, hmm, Hercules, Icarus, all those kinds of characters... I think I would fit right in." As the couple's eyes met in that moment, both were aware of what was happening: *it* had begun. Even as they were making their way back to the dorms through the courtyard, Charlie could feel the potential in his bones. That evening, looking in the mirror while brushing his teeth, he gave himself a warm kiss on his left cheekbone.

Lying in bed that night, alone and in New England's first autumn cold, he became Icarus in his thoughts. The role had started to consume him entirely. Sometimes he even thought he could feel the beginning of soft cartilage tissue growing on his scapulae. It most certainly one day would mature into a nice pair of strong wings. He felt the wind, the breeze of the air, slide through his fingers as he glided, on and on, through the woolen clouds that scattered themselves around him. He was not complacent, however. There was always the possibility of greater gains, greater successes, and most importantly, greater stories to be told. But this now was a start. His time was here, and he had to make it count. And so, he ascended, higher and higher; he felt himself rise within. It was pure ecstasy, a blast of adrenaline that coursed through his veins as he pirouetted to this hidden level, this isolated paradise, which only he could reach. Could he ever return to life below, knowing what he would have to leave behind? Striding high there, a swift flutter of turbulence made him panic. He shouted: "Not now! Not yet! Wait!" But the air thinned beneath his wings and he tumbled through the skies, falling deeper and deeper into a sound sleep.

Once again, as he sat in class that afternoon, his thoughts pulled him along into unforeseen caverns of the mind. Charlie was stressed in a way he had not been since his first day at Harvard. As he watched the professor's lips move, his thoughts curled at the upcoming audition. He had been informed that he would have to perform a monologue so that the recruiters could check both his pronunciation and dramatic capacity. It would be a five-minute sequence that would indeed decide his future. Despite his shell-like personality as of late, he found himself eager to confide in a nearby peer. Brian, he believed was his name, said "Wow Charlie! Charlie wow!" as his bespectacled face lit up in enthusiasm at Charlie's good news. "What are you going to choose as your reading for the audition?" Charlie's face fell dark for a moment as he heard this query. He had not expected this, and did not appreciate Brian's curiosity anymore. However, he had an idea. Leaning back in his chair, and continuing to ignore the harping professor below, Charlie laid out his plan. "I just remembered a poem, something that would surely be the perfect fit for this modest audition of mine." Brian was eager to hear more. "Well, tell me all about it," he said with a languid southern drawl. "It's a story of myth, that's what it is, I don't wish to impersonate Icarus. That would be too blunt! Don't you think so? I will bring a remake of the classic myth... ." Brian could not help but be impressed as he saw Charlie's drive to perform. He pulled himself forward to his colleague and said, "I'm sure that you'll get it. Best of luck." Charlie turned back and sneered as he did so. He didn't say this to Brian, but he thought that "luck" was for idiots and dreamers. Indeed, he could not afford to ruin a relationship with someone who could be of great help to him in the future. Although he thought Brian a little too innocent, a little too green, he understood fine arts, and that was not to be wasted for the sake of pride. "Could you help me out?" Charlie asked. "I'm pretty confident right now, but it would be nice to run some ideas past you, you and a few others, being part of the drama society and all that. I think that would be really great."

The group, prepared for what Charlie had rehearsed, gathered in the drama hall a couple of hours later. Determined to make the practice run as smoothly as the real thing, he had already memorized the script he had prepared. Looking on at the blank faces of the students, he began his piece:

> *Said the Tailor to the Bishop:*
> *Believe me, I can fly.*
> *Watch me while I try.*
> *And he stood with things*
> *That looked like wings*

On the great church roof-
That is quite absurd!
A wicked, foolish lie,
For man will never fly.

Ready for the applause, he took a step back after finishing his first lines. He truly thought that he could see the committee before him singing his praises and ready to give him the role that he had been born to play. Elevated by this sudden vision, he felt his arms rise also. They were his wings now. His dream slowly transformed into reality. They became light and powerful as he continued his speech:

A man is not a bird,
Said the Bishop to the Tailor.
Said the People to the Bishop:
The Tailor is quite dead,
He was a stupid head.
His wings are rumpled
And he lies all crumpled,
on the hard church square.

But as the words left his lips, he could not support that sinking feeling that had struck him in his sleep, that eventually he too would be falling one day.

Charlie Parker knew nothing of Bishops, but, upon hearing that they resembled Santa Claus, he attempted to add some humor to the performance by snatching a Santa Claus beanie from one of the onlookers before placing it on his head. He was yet to truly stun them with his greatness:

The bells ring out in praise.
That man is not a bird
It was a wicked, foolish lie,
Mankind will never fly,
Said the Bishop to the People.(*)

It didn't matter that his knowledge of the lines was a little shoddy; this was the performance of a lifetime. It only took one look in the spectators' eyes to say so. They were yet to speak, yet to react to what they had just witnessed: such was the magnitude of his words and poise. Oh, it was magnificent.

"Charlie... wow, that was awesome!!" Celia's exclamation rang out through the courtyard as they began their return to their rooms. Charlie had to force modesty in this instance, even though he hated doing so. "Do you really think that I was that good?" he asked, unable to hold back a smile. "I'm sure that there is still a lot of room for improvement." Of course, this was just a test, how was she to respond? "You've got to be kidding! We need to apply as soon as possible! You know you've got this!"

After Celia had settled down from her enthusiasm, she indeed wrote to the recruiting committee and appended all of Charlie's relevant details in the letter. The application was marked by her signature scarlet ink (Charlie had to talk her out of using a sparkling ruby tint).

Only a couple of days later, the two received the response that they expected: an invitation to try out. They had done it! Celia could barely hold in her delight as she came to tell her boyfriend the good news. "I guess you just have to thank my writing ability; I think we both know that this was the reason we were successful," she said as she went on to laugh off Charlie's severe glare. "Jokes aside," he said, trying to cover up the awkwardness that he knew he had created, "this is great news for both of us. I can't wait to get started." He was too determined not to let her silliness overcome him. He had to remain composed and ready to fulfil this role. He was Icarus now. There was no way around that fact, and the recruiters would see this. They would feel it.

"How are we going to pay for the flight?" Celia's words brought him crashing down to earth. He felt as though he had just been stabbed. Had he come this far only to be too poor to audition? He considered quietly, before opening his mouth, words poised and primed, "Could you not lend me the money now? I would pay you back, you know that I would pay you back." Blank eyes were all that faced him from across the room as he settled into his seat, full of the knowledge that his girlfriend was never truly with him. She thought all of this a whimsical adventure. It was never serious for her. What a shame. Charlie knew what she was thinking from the moment that his words escaped, namely that there was no point in pushing her to change the initial decision. He would just have to find another way to LA.

The very next day, the couple decided to catch a Greyhound. They had already settled on their full route. In fact, Celia had been rather cerebral in her ideas for the journey, almost as though she had already conceived a route. The pair had planned on dividing the journey into two parts: they would stay in a motel in Vegas before going to a selection of casinos. They would collect the necessary funds in Sin City. Not stopping for one moment to consider the potential downsides the masterplan, the couple had gone full steam ahead. Sitting side by side in the rattling bus that would take them all those miles up to their destiny, Charlie and Celia began to get down to the details. In spite of his girlfriend's ferocious commitment to solid organization, her arguments just bounced off Charlie as he, too focused on what lay ahead to truly consider them, sat in his isolated silence. All he could see was the other side of his actions, nothing of what came before. That was all far too dull. Those words of hers continued to glide on their way. She would have had equal luck talking to the wind as to her boyfriend, who contemplated his future. At this stage in his trance, all he could see were the dollar signs that would mark his entry. He was too sure that this was the beginning of a fruitful journey. But, of course, Celia had to break the spell. She just had to. "If things don't work out for you, I could always do some dancing. That would be a way to gather up some cash while we're there." He looked at her. A confused expression appeared on his face once more. He decided to leave the suggestion unanswered. No one got hurt that way. It would be smarter to keep things harmonious. Even Charlie was too aware of his pride and its sharp edges.

It did not take long for the other passengers to get a taste of Charlie's personality either. Whenever there was a long break in conversation between him and his girlfriend, he, unwilling to waste these spare moments, would recite his speech. He had to spend his time productively if he was to be successful. The tales of bishops and flying tailors soon found their way to the end of the bus. "What the hell is that kid even talking about?" one older man exclaimed, as he tried to get an answer out of his wife who was just as dumbfounded as he was and equally unable to explain this most uncomfortable situation. The couple who sat a few rows before them heard nothing of their criticism and continued to drift on in their vision. They frequently returned to discussion of their plan until they met their destination.

The flaring lights and colors of the casino would sting the eyes of visitors as they made their way in. Wonderful scarlet and emerald screamed from the ceiling to the floor where they stood. It was everything that Charlie had imagined up until this stage. He thought of himself performing here one day in front of all these people. He projected a new future in thirty seconds with a kick of adrenaline. It would indeed be a fitting place to display all his skills. Perhaps even his body! Why not?

He refrained from reciting his lines in this moment to reserve his vocal chords for the big day that was now approaching fast. The pair then entered a room that was adorned with dozens of sparkling chandeliers hanging above the minds of the big spenders. It did not take long for Charlie to find his rightful place by the slot machines. Now was the time to beckon his future. And just as he had planned, he locked eyes with the screen: he saw it light up with excitement and joy. He spun around as he grinned with glee while money steadily flowed to him. With every successive win that came his way, Charlie reinvested the funds into the machine. Every dollar that was made on the previous go would see itself immediately returned to the previous owner. Flying high on his own wisdom and merits, he was unstoppable at this stage. Until, of course, he began to crash. It was a twisted kind of magic trick: bit by bit, the wins became thinner

Falling

and thinner, and then even thinner still, until Charlie was left in a sorrowful state. In his hand, he held onto half of what he had brought into this pretty little trap. He sat by his girlfriend on one of the green benches that marked the centers of so many casino rooms. Like him, she had a sullen expression. The strip clubs rejected her and sent her on her way in a flood of disappointment. All that potential, all those dreams of greatness and now this.... .

The couple sat in silence as the lights above their heads shone brighter than ever as if to drain them of the little vitality they had left. Just as the pair began to make their way from the grand Caesar's Palace, Charlie, sunken, bumped shoulders with a large, rounded gentleman, who happened to be accompanied by an equally large figure. Charlie, apologizing profusely as he took Celia's hand in an effort to escape a possible nightmare, tried to evade any confrontation as soon as he could. But it was then that the men, stopping him in his tracks, told him of an opportunity that they had come across for young men just like him. Although they did not want Charlie for his acting ability, Charlie found himself drawn by their enthusiastic words. It appeared that, much like everyone else, they loved him for his talents. They could smell from far that his element was air!

An advertising company, this is what he was sure they called their business. Surely, he could find a way to fashion this into a greater opportunity, a greater role that he could then grow into. He was so engrossed in their words that it took a few moments for the young man to slip back to reality. "Anyway, the pay is five-hundred dollars a day for people in this role. It's super easy. It's just that most people are quite scared when it comes to this stuff, you know, being in the air." Charlie kept on nodding as they talked, but all he could hear were numbers, those would be his ticket. The taller man then stood before the couple. Leaning back slightly, he took the chance to explain the business a little more: "Yeah, so publicity parachutes are our main gimmick. They really give us the opportunity to stand out. Do you get where I'm coming from?" Charlie could not help but release a short smile as he made his affirmative reply. Just as he had been planning to give up, fate had stopped him from falling, before then pushing him onward to glory.

It is safe to say that Charlie was very welcome at the company. His fellow workers struggled not to enjoy his loud presence; in fact, it was clear that the factors that led him to such popularity at college worked their magic here as well. Just as he always suspected, he was a hit. The two men that had originally signed him up could barely suppress their laughter as they saw him glide. He was too full on the dream of Icarus and his own wings. Charlie began to beat his arms at his sides, looking up expectantly as he did so. Upon the parachute crest above, the colorful casino names bathed in the gleaming sun. Gabriel was the only one who had really taken issue with Charlie's presence. He simply hated him the moment he saw him: everything about Parker was so predictable. Gabriel had seen this kind of sequence a thousand times. As he set his dark face on the young man that had all but stolen his job, he let his mind wander somewhat while he recalled a scuffle they had had earlier that day following the new payment plans. This kid was taking money just for his pretty face, while Gabriel had fought tooth and nail to be here.

He clenched a fist as he saw the newcomer descend. Screams had already started to ring out below as Charlie's speed continued to build. He wasn't beating his arms anymore. Instead, his face was locked in terror, with eyes fixed to the ground, as he came closer with every half second. The ground met him with a sickening crunch. As the sprawling parachute gathered itself over the corpse, Gabriel withdrew a gloved hand from his pocket and tossed the Stanley knife into the rich bushes. It was about time that someone clipped that kid's wings. He spared himself a grin at the sick thought.

(*) Ulm 1592 - Berthold Brecht. Translation: The New Reasoner, Winter 1957-58, number 322 A Wicked, Foolish L

A WICKED, FOOLISH LIE

I am driving back to New York from Providence, holding on to the steering wheel with one hand, and it seems like the cars ahead of me are falling into the Long Island Sound. It is winter break and I am spending the four weeks with my parents. Well, my father and my stepmother. My stepmother's name is Olga and she's exactly what you would expect from an Olga. She is a full-figured blond woman with a stern face and a large bosom. She is from Brazil like my parents, though she met my father at a convention in Cleveland.

When I reach home, I decide to tell my stepmother about Stephen Costello. I still love him and I am curious what she has to say about him. I am much closer to my father than I ever was to my mother or stepmother, but I can hardly talk to him about someone like Stephen. I tell Olga about the football game and that means I have to talk about Nate too. When I first saw Nate at the game I was surprised that there was a boy at Brown that I had neither seen nor heard of. That's when I realized that he was standing in the Harvard section of the bleachers, which is why I'd never seen him before.

I wasn't myself because I was wearing this Madewell turtleneck sweater that my roommate suggested I borrow from her. I think she did this on purpose in order to hide my beauty. One guy I dated said that I looked like "a tanned swan in human form" and I always thought this was an apt description. But the sweater is unflattering and I'm not in the mood to talk to any guys. I looked away from the

Harvard guys, at the cheerleaders who were doing a formation, and when I returned my gaze to the Harvard section I saw that the guy, who I later learned was Nate, was staring at me. "You should get popcorn," my roommate said, so I squeezed my way out of the aisle and made my way to the concession stand, which was behind the bleachers. I decided to get a hot dog for myself.

When I was done paying for these, I turned around to find Nate standing immediately behind me. Walking away seemed like the best option, which is what I did, but I lost control of a packet of mustard. Of course, Nate picked it up. "You dropped something," he said.

We stood there looking at one another for a few moments and then he said: "I have an idea. Let me guess your name."

"Oh god," I said.

"No, come on. Um. Let me see. Yvonne?"

"No."

"Lola?"

"No."

"Letitia?"

"Getting warmer."

"Dominique?"

I laughed.

"No, it's Patricia," I told Nate. "Dominique was much colder than Letitia."

"I know, I was nervous." And we both laughed. "I'm Nate and I represent the enemy. Harvard."

After a pause, Nate said: "I know this is weird, but would you like to go to a party? Not right now, obviously, but maybe next weekend. It's in Boston, but I can drive to Providence to pick you up. It's a murder party."

Nate told me more about the party and I told him I'd think about it. It's chilly as we walk back to the stands. When he reached his seat, Nate turned to Stephen Costello and I could see them whispering about me, as boys do. Stephen turned around and glanced at me. His eyes seemed a little immature, but they were still unwearied and warm. At least I thought so. Nate and I crossed paths again in the parking lot and I told him I would go to the murder party, but only if he promised that I wouldn't be the one being murdered. He couldn't do that.

I tell Olga about the night of the party. The night began with me sitting on a bench on campus waiting for Nate to pick me up. I was rereading my favorite book, *The Last Unicorn* by Peter Beagle, and I was not wearing anything suggested by my roommate. I watched the wind ruffle the red leaves of a maple tree and it seemed like the leaves were changing color as I sat there. The squirrels were scampering around on the grass. I was a little hungry as I did not have lunch so I took half of a peanut butter and jelly sandwich out of my purse, but I had to put it away after a few minutes because the squirrels can smell the jelly and now they are harassing me: getting nearer and nearer to my bench in circles that cut a smaller swathe each time.

I glanced at my watch and realized that Nate was late. That was all right with me because it gave me time to think about things. In particular, I wondered if Nate could love me in the way that I wanted. He had the look of someone who was safe. Perhaps he tried a little too hard but if you wanted something in life you had to go after it. He certainly wasn't like the boys I was used to but I didn't mind. As long as he was willing to pursue me. I wanted him to find me so beautiful that his mind would never let go of the memory of me. Years later, when he reads in the paper that I have died by falling down the glass stairs at the Louis Vuitton store in New York, I want him to remember me as the woman that none of the other women in his life has ever come close to.

He will not rest until he has me. He should go to sleep at night obsessing over me. When he falls asleep, he sees my silhouette in his dreams. And when he wakes up he is beside himself because I am not lying there next to him. In this fantasy I have of my life with Nate, I do not sleep with him. We just lie there in bed together, in our underwear, and that is enough to satisfy him. That's how in love with me he is.

What's funny about that is that Nate probably would have been happy with this kind of relationship, but it never came to be because

I ended up with Stephen. I had actually forgotten about Stephen when Nate's car finally swung around. He was supposed to reach Providence by 4PM but by the time he got here it was almost 5. He was very apologetic, taking my hand and saying he's sorry and all that, and I tried to act perturbed but I wasn't. The time flew by because I just had so much to think about.

Nate held the car door open for me and I got in. I could tell that he drives around with his friends a lot because the passenger seat is leaned back a little like how a guy would have it. I'm sure he hasn't had a girlfriend in a while, and I wanted to ask about that but I didn't. Later Nate said: "Your hair looks nice." This made me laugh because I wasn't expecting him to say that. Usually guys said something like "So… how do you like Brown?" and it was so annoying because you felt like you were constantly answering the same question.

"Thank you," I said to Nate's remark about my hair.

"You're really going to like this party, Patricia," said Nate. "You'll get to meet some really cool people. And Stephen will be there."

"Who's Stephen?"

"Oh, he's the guy I took with me to the Brown game. He's the tall guy with the brown hair. I'm sure you'll remember him when you see him. I like to bring him with me to things because he's like a puppy. The girls think he's cute and then I swoop in and get their phone numbers."

"So that usually works, does it?"

"Yeah, most of the time."

"What if the girl decides she would rather have the puppy?"

"It'll never happen," said Nate, and we laughed together.

"Tell me about your parents."

Nate said that as we neared the house where the murder party was to take place.

"God, you don't want to hear about them."

"Sure I do."

"Well, they are from Brazil but they're divorced. My mother moved to Washington so now I live with my father and my stepmother. Are we almost there?"

"Yeah, it's just down the street here."

The car pulled in front of a white clapboard house that sat further back on the street than the others. There were already a few cars parked in front and Nate had to squeeze his Suzuki tightly between two other vehicles. Fortunately, it was a small car.

We entered the house through the open door, passing two trees lit by floodlights. We passed a tall man who was wearing a prep jacket like Nate. His hair was dark brown, close-cropped, and in his snug jeans he looked like Clark Kent: someone who is very different from what they want you to think they are. This was Stephen. Stephen Costello... what a name!

Nate and I neared a man and woman standing behind what looked like a hotel check-in counter. As we approached, the man said: "Welcome. Can I have your names please?"

"Yes," said Nate. "We're Nathan Anderton and Patricia."

"Great. Again, welcome. There will be a murder tonight, as you know, so keep your eyes open and your pistols handy. You're up on the second floor." And the man gave Nate a set of skeleton keys.

Nate and I traipsed up the stairs to our room, highly amused. Me more than him, I think. I was holding onto Nate's sleeve and I noticed Stephen watching us as we walked up the stairs. The second floor was completely dark and we had difficulty finding our room, which ended up being the northernmost room of the hall, all the way at one end of it. Nate and I reached the conclusion that we were the only guests on this floor, and as we walked into our room I wondered who it was that was to be murdered.

"Does it have to be a woman that gets murdered?" I asked.

"No, but I think it will be. There's something tragic about that, don't you think? It's kind of modern. Like *woman* represents *earth* or something."

I looked around the room and it was the sort of spread you would typically find at a bed and breakfast. The bed is full-size but it's low to the ground and the bedspread looks like something you would see at your grandmother's house. There are doors to a closet and bathroom on one side of the room and on the other side is a large dresser. There is no mirror.

Nate and I both sat on opposite corners of the bed. After a few minutes, he opened the window and a biting breeze blew in. As I watched him, I was already beginning to think about Stephen. He had been watching us as we walked up the stairs and I wondered why. I wondered if he thought I was pretty and if my butt looked good in the dress I was wearing. I was walking up the stairs and Stephen was standing below so that boded well, at least as far as my butt was concerned. Nate asked me if I was cold and when I told him I wasn't he still took off his jacket and put it around my shoulders. I was wearing a black and white patterned dress by Diane von Furstenberg. Olga bought it for me as a present about a week after I moved to campus. It is the only nice dress that I own.

Nate returned to his corner of the bed and I think to myself that he's nice. Perhaps a little too nice. That's when we heard a loud pop. "What was that?" I asked, turning towards the door. There were several more pops and my body instinctively tensed up.

"That's probably the murder," said Nate. "Those are supposed to be gunshots. Give it a few moments. We'll probably hear a scream."

"Ah!" we hear a woman's voice scream, and it's high-pitched and dramatic, the sort that you would hear at a theatrical performance.

"See," said Nate. "That's the body being discovered."

I couldn't help but laugh and then Nate did the most extraordinary thing. He hitched up his pants like a cowboy about to ride the nastiest bull in town. That's when I noticed that he had this big silver belt buckle that was hiding under the bottoms of his shirt. It still makes me laugh thinking about it. Olga thinks it's funny too. Nate told me he was going to investigate and that he'd be right back.

"Wait," I said. "Are you sure that you should leave me alone? The murderer might still be on the loose."

"Oh, I'm sure he is," said Nate, "but that's how the game unfolds. If you're lucky, the murderer will find you when I'm gone and you'll have a scare. Trust me, Patricia. You'll love it."

Nate left and I listened to the sound of his shoes as he slowly descended the darkened stairwell. I walked into the bathroom, pulling the chain of little metal balls to turn on the light. I wanted to look at myself in the mirror. Olga says this is like me, to check myself out in the mirror even though there's a murderer about, and I let out a soft groan.

My lip gloss is very pale and subdued. I run a few fingers through my hair and I have to admit that I look good tonight. My hair is down, and the auburn shade of my hair combined with the black and white diagonal stripes of the dress make me look like a model. My hair is L'Oreal No. 4R, a dark auburn brown. It's my natural color. As I ran my fingers through the strands of my hair, I tried to picture myself waking up beside Nate and it's harder and harder to do so now that I've seen Stephen. I turned the faucet to wet my fingers, I think my hair has a little too much volume, and that's when I heard the scratching on the wall. The first scratch was brief, but then it started up again and it sounded as if someone was dragging a butcher knife along the wallpaper.

"Nate?"

Obviously, Nate was gone and I felt trapped in the bathroom so I ran back into the bedroom. The light flickered: a low wattage old bulb. The scratching stopped. After a deep breath, I sat down on the edge of the bed. Within two minutes, the scratching started up again and I grabbed my purse and left the room.

The hall was dark but I saw a light at the far end that I hadn't seen before. It crept out from under the door. I took my heels off so I could walk soundlessly, carrying them in my hands. Reaching the lit room, I pushed the door open without knocking. There was a man sitting on the far corner of the bed, his back was to me, and the light bulb was irritatingly low like in the room I had just left. The bed creaked as I sat on it.

"Why are you carrying your shoes?" Stephen asked.

He was looking at me and his eyes seemed very large.

"I was trying not to make a sound. I was scared."

I sighed and instinctively moved a little closer to Stephen.

"You're brave. I wouldn't come to a murder party alone."

"I didn't," Stephen said. He was looking down at the splotchy carpet. "My friends were put in a different room."

"Oh."

"Do you like Nate a lot?" Stephen asked.

He looked at me again and everything suddenly changed.

"I don't know."

Stephen took his jacket off and I noticed he was wearing a really nice watch, the sort that an old businessman would have. I thought to myself that my hardworking Brazilian father would never be able to afford something like that. Stephen rolled up his sleeves and his forearms were very muscular, with just a little down on them.

"My roommate said that I should become a cheerleader," I remark because I feel like I have to say something. "Who goes to Brown and then joins the cheerleading team?"

I laughed, but I made sure it sounded as natural as possible.

"It's a little weird, but not unheard of," Stephen noted.

He suddenly got up and walked to the dresser. The room had the same layout as the one I had left. "Hey, look at this," Stephen said, and out of the top drawer he pulled out lipsticks, necklaces, things like that.

I walk over but I don't feel inclined to join in. It felt wrong, like we were going through someone else's things. "Here," said Stephen. He tested out a shade of lipstick by twisting the stick out and rubbing it on his hand. "This is a nice shade, put this on."

It was actually a really dark, seductive shade of red, like something you would see in an '80s movie about a high-powered woman attorney who lives a double life. But I put it on and when I went into the bathroom to have a look at myself I had to admit it looked good. I was still wearing Nate's jacket and I noticed that Stephen was watching me closely. He had followed me into the bathroom. "You look good in it, but I think you'd look better without it." I started taking the jacket off and then Stephen said: "No, I meant the dress."

I hesitated for a moment and then I removed both jacket and dress, with Stephen standing there, and then I put the jacket back on. Stephen smiled and ran his fingers through my hair. He rested a hand on the back of my neck and it felt good, like I belonged to him. I had no difficulty picturing myself waking up beside him, forever and ever.

We returned to the bedroom, Stephen and me, and we sat on our respective edges. He asked me if he could take a picture of me like that, in only a bra and panties and Nate's jacket, and I said "yes" without really thinking about it. He took the picture, with me leaning on the dresser with a severe expression. Stephen grinned at the result and I could feel the warmth emanating from his body. We went back to the bed and sort of lay back on it with our feet touching the ground. We must have looked like two teenagers who didn't know what a man and a woman normally do on a bed. Perhaps that was true of me, but I'm not sure it was true of Stephen. When I looked over at him, I saw him fingering the cross around his neck. It's old, made of really heavy gold, and he tells me his great-grandfather brought it over from Ireland. I asked him if he was a Catholic and he said that he was. He hadn't gone to Catholic school like me but the connection was still there.

Stephen asked me if I was serious about Nate and I said that I wasn't. "We aren't even really dating," I said. "We just met." Stephen asked if I wanted to go out Tuesday night and I said that I did and gave him my phone number.

Stephen called me the next day and we made plans for him to pick me up in Providence on Tuesday. We drove in his car to a house outside of Boston. It's a much nicer car than Nate's but Stephen admits that it doesn't belong to him. It belongs to a "friend." We met one of these friends on the way to the house. He's an older man with a constantly smiling face. He looks like the kind of guy you would find coming out of one of those naughty shops in New York, the ones with the blacked-out windows, but I can tell that he's very wealthy. His Jaguar was parked in front of the bar and he gave Stephen a fat wad of cash. Just as Stephen turned to leave, the man put a little baggie of pot in the back pocket of Stephen's jeans.

"Who is that?" I ask when Stephen gets back to the car.

"Oh, it's no one. Just a friend."

"What's his name?"

"Mr. Higginbotham," says Stephen.

"You call your friends mister?"

It was a little accusatory but I was chuckling. I'm wearing that Diane von Furstenberg dress again.

"And he looks a lot older than you."

"God, Tricia, why do you care?" And Stephen gives me a hard look. "Look, we can smoke the pot later, all right? We're almost at the house."

I like the feeling of sitting beside Stephen in the car. I don't know him very well, but something about him feels right. It's like he's an attractive man and I'm an attractive woman. He goes to Harvard and I go to Brown, and it makes sense that people like us should be together. But sometimes there's an emptiness behind his eyes that makes me think he could be a serial killer for all I know.

We reached the house and it's one of those big Tudor places with the wooden beams out front and the dark brick like you see in Connecticut. I think to myself that this is such a nice house and wouldn't it be wonderful to spend the night in it with Stephen? To see him coming out of the bathroom in the morning in his terrycloth bathrobe. Stephen comes to me in his bathrobe but I have already awoken: to the nightingales trilling their song, a thing intelligible only to themselves.

Stephen couldn't remember which key opened the door so we were there for a minute or two. Finally, he got it open and we entered the first room of the house, which was bathed in warm browns. There was even a grandfather clock that Stephen called Tiny Tim. "Hey, Tiny Tim," he said as we walked past it, but Tiny Tim remained silent.

The stairs swept up to several upstairs rooms. The master suite was on one end of the hall and that's where we went. The master bedroom had the largest bed I had ever seen and French doors that opened onto the balcony. There was even a bearskin under the bed and paintings on the wall that looked very expensive, like modern art that only people who go to places like Pratt and RISD would understand.

Stephen walked into a huge walk-in closet and started rummaging through the things in there. I assumed that this was his parents' room. The man and woman in the photograph on the end table looked very old. "Here, put this on," Stephen said, returning with lipstick. "You look prettier this way." It's a very dark shade like before. After I put the lipstick on, I returned to the walk-in closet with Stephen. Here we found a fur coat. Stephen put it over my shoulders and we looked in the full-length mirror, which was in one corner of the closet. "Now, you're pretty," Stephen said. "When you're pretty you can have everything." There were other things in the closet too. There was a little bureau where I found many valuable things, like amethyst rings and strands of pearls. As I was pulling out a strand, the string caught and the pearls separated and fell onto the floor. They landed with many smacks against the parquet floor and several rolled into the bedroom. I ran laughing after them. Stephen followed me.

He told me to get down on the floor, on my knees, and when he was done collecting the pearls he stood over me. He spread out his fingers and the white pearls fell on my face, slapping my skin. I looked up and watched them falling.

After that, Stephen took two hundred dollars out of his wallet and left the bills on the table. He said they were for me and then he said he was going for a drive. "This is not your house, is it," I remarked. Stephen didn't say anything at first, but then he said he was going to the gas station for some beer.

So I walked to the French doors, entranced by the graceful branch of a tree that I could see through the panes. As I approached, I realized the branch belonged to a Japanese maple, which I'm familiar with because we have one in the park in my parent's neighborhood, but there was also a *Cryptomeria* tree. I looked back at the couple whose picture was on the table and I laughed. I see that the wife is clearly an Asian woman and I wonder how I thought these were Stephen's parents. The woman is elegant and petite.

I opened the French doors and walked out onto the short balcony. I was still wearing the fur coat, a mink, and the dark lipstick. I looked down where I saw the macadam leading to a landscaped garden. I felt the air kissing my skin. I felt the bristles of the mink tickling my neck. The hairs are long so I know this is not a cheap coat made from the castaway pieces but a high quality item. I thought how nice it would be to have many coats like this and that required money. I didn't have any money, but as Stephen said, when you're pretty you can have everything. If I'm pretty I can get the money. But I can't just be pretty, I must be the prettiest. Since I was thinking this, I hardly noticed the shadow passing behind me. I thought it was the moon playing tricks with the trees. I ignored it. But then I felt two hands against my back. They were soft. A woman's hands. They pushed me out of the window and I fell through the *Cryptomeria* branches until I was lying dead in the back of the house.

Though I was dead, I was able to see the woman who pushed me. I saw her reflection as she passed the mirror in the walk-in closet and then I saw it again when she passed the second mirror in the master bedroom. She is rather lovely, with her hair up like Brigitte Bardot. Her sensuous lips are painted in a dark lipstick and she has a long neck, like a swan. I watched as she tightened her mink coat around her narrow shoulders. Her hair color is L'Oréal No. 4R, a dark auburn. She has my face

THE VANA SPES SOCIETY

Jacob had been named the new chairman and we were all gathered around him. He opened with a reading from Ecclesiastes, which was in keeping with how we opened all our yearly meetings. We would all shed last year's snakeskin and spray new cologne on ourselves to hide our scent. We met in the Cathedral of St. John the Divine. Our vanities were all of the personal kind, but we generally kept those to ourselves. Jacob's face showed his own. Dr. Jacob Loftus was the best of us, with his stoic mien and his well-cared-for goatee. He was primus inter pares and he would be the last to go.

    The doctor made a hand motion to indicate that he was ready for a break and I pressed the stop key on the tape recorder. He cleared his throat and I cleared mine too, though it hadn't been me doing the talking. It was the chief who had asked me to interview Dr. Allison, the only survivor of a secret society whose members were all killed in an accident in 1998. All except for him. There were strange stories told about him, that he was an expert in making things from human skin: shoes, purses and book covers. It was hard to say if any of it was true. Dr. Allison himself appears close to death, with his sunken eyes and his white hair like spider's thread. His eyes look at you through bruises, as if he squared off with the welterweight champion and won. He's not the least bit afraid of you. He has saggy dark skin under his eyes and his complexion is sallow. His eyes also give the impression of an intractable coldness. It is the same coldness my father had in his eyes when he told my mother she could leave if she wanted.

Dr. Allison asked if I minded if he smoked and to my amazement he took out a package of old Cuban cigars. This took me back to Lisbon: the old men sitting outside the cafe and watching the townspeople walking by. Or, just staring at Fernando Pessoa's statue… I remember one day when I was looking for my father. I found him among those men and from where they were sitting it seemed as if the people crossing the square fell right into the Atlantic Ocean. My father's face didn't change when he saw me. He was just smoking and dreaming his life away.

Dr. Allison offered me a cigar out of politeness and when I told him that I had quit smoking years ago, he shrugged. His hands had a tremor and he lit his cigar with difficulty. The cigar smelled as much like its contents as it did like the people who made it. I thought I could smell the sweetness of sugar cane, the biting bitterness of sweating human skin and the salt from the ocean. And heat: unbearable heat.

"I didn't think I would make it out," Dr. Allison said, and I presumed he meant out of the elevator. All of us at the newspaper knew the story, that an accident in an old hotel had caused several people staying there to be killed in two consecutive trips in the elevator. A total of eleven people died. Dr. William Allison was the only one to live.

"It was only after a janitor at the hotel revealed to his wife before he died that he knew who he were, that's when people started to talk," Dr. Allison said. "I don't know how he knew. There was a sensational story in the local paper and now here we are."

But it didn't seem as if Dr. Allison was particularly interested in talking about what happened. He asked me where I lived and why I had chosen this spot for the interview. We were sitting in a cafe on Madison Avenue, a little out-of-the-way place just steps away from the M4 bus stop that goes up to The Cloisters. The latter had always been my favorite part of the City and I told Dr. Allison so.

"I used to go up there all the time when I was a medical student," the doctor said. "I trained as a surgeon but I was a practicing pathologist when the accident occurred at the hotel. Really, the story begins long before this. It is the story of how I joined the Vana Spes Society."

I didn't see how that particular aspect of the story was relevant to our present interview but I didn't interrupt. I laughed it off and Dr. Allison, to my surprise, smiled. The chief wanted the completed interview on his desk in twenty-four hours and as the doctor resumed his story I could hear the loud tick of a hypothetical clock.

"I was a young medical student in New York City when they found me. The members of these secret societies stalk you, observing you closely without you knowing, and when they decide that they want you they make their move. It's a form of hunting, a type of group predation. Those who play with fire get burned, I suppose. I was living in an apartment on West 86th Street at the time, with my roommate and his girlfriend. We didn't want to live in the dorms because we wanted to be hip New Yorkers."

We were briefly interrupted by the honk of a horn.

"I've always had a fear of elevators. That apartment was up on the fourth floor and I always walked the stairs rather than take the lift. There was something about the building that gave me the creeps. It looked like something out of *Rosemary's Baby*. You know, the people smiled at you but it was like their canines were unusually sharp or their eyes stared at you too long or something. Besides, I've always been superstitious and I figured one can never be killed by an elevator if one doesn't get into one."

"So it was the elevator that killed your colleagues?" I asked. "Not something inside."

Dr. Allison paused for a moment, looking at the traffic on the street rather than at me. "Inside or out, it doesn't matter."

The good doctor turned to look at me again and I dropped my Parker pen. "It was Bernardo Soares who brought me into the society. Bernardo was also one of the eleven that died in the elevator. Bernardo and I were friends for a long time. In medical school we both wanted to be neurosurgeons so we would argue about synapses. You see, we didn't know as much then as we know now about neuroplasticity so we used to get into long discussions. He thought it was possible that one day a surgeon could repair a single neuron."

"You saw Bernardo die?"

"I did," said the doctor. "One minute we were raising our glasses and the next I was watching Bernardo bleed to death."

His look was a challenge, challenging me to be bold enough to continue but there was an amity there as well.

"We raised our glasses at the hotel of course. By then we had already left the cathedral. We were in the hotel about to start the meeting when we got a message that we needed to go to the hotel lobby immediately. There were two elevators in the hotel, but one of them was out of service so we had to use the other one. That's the one that killed them all."

"There's a story here," I began, rifling through the various articles and newspaper clippings that I had brought with me. "A story about a woman who worked at the hotel and she says she saw a man getting out of the elevator after the accident. And, if you can believe it, this man was actually getting out of the elevator that was said to be out of service."

"Yes, there was an 'Out of Service' sign on the elevator," said Dr. Allison.

"So how do you account for the other elevator?"

Dr. Allison laughed and it was not the laugh of an elderly man. "My roommate had a girlfriend, I told you that, didn't I? Her name was Juliana Braga. I would always find her in the apartment alone, without my friend, and I didn't understand it at the time. Bernardo always said Juliana was bad news, but that's just because he wanted to sleep with her and she didn't like him. He could tell that she wasn't interested. Well, one day when Brian wasn't home, that was my roommate, she asked if I wanted to share a glass of wine with her and I said that I would love to. I got drunk on Azorean wine with Juliana and we fell asleep on the couch. I wasn't forward enough to push matters and Juliana seemed to vacillate. It was the very next day that Bernardo asked me to join Vana Spes. I thought it was silly but I agreed."

"Do you think that Bernardo had been stalking you all that time? That he was never truly your friend?"

"That's something I have often thought of. I believe Bernardo had been hunting me but I do think we were friends. At least that we became friends. You know the fox can befriend the wolf because they have the same nature. It's a little strange that it was the fox who died first. Bernardo was the fox."

I heard the honk of 18-wheelers on Madison and then a delivery man bumped into our table.

"Bernardo was in the second elevator with me and four others. By that point, we had already seen the bodies of the first six but we got into the elevator anyway. It had been Bernardo who initiated me, him as well as a person in a hood who I never saw. I drank from the wine glass, my arm linked with Bernardo's. He also drank and that was the beginning of it all.

"When I returned home that night, Juliana was waiting for me. She was wearing a skimpy top and a gauzy silk wrap around her tan legs. There was some sort of syncretism to her, like she was a little bit of Europe, a little bit of the Americas and a little bit of something else. There was an ease to her, a sexual freedom that didn't seem European to me even though we think of Europeans as being freer in that way. It was like sex to her was something you simply did, you didn't have to think about it. You didn't have to talk about it. You just did it. And we did it that night. When I closed my eyes, I could feel her legs and her arms wrapping around me. It was like she had eight arms and eight legs and the supple skin of each was touching mine. She was two women, three women. Four… Five. It was like her body was a vessel filled with fluid, coming from a third yet to be invented circulatory system that ran through her body parallel to blood and lymph.

"I think what they had me drink when I was initiated was chicken blood." Dr. Allison laughed quietly as I scribbled on my notepad. "I have always thought that. It was some manner of blood. You know, there are rituals in South America and in Africa where they drink chicken blood or smear themselves with it after a sacrifice. When we met at the hotel in New York all those years later I thought it would be chicken blood in the glasses again but it wasn't. This time it certainly was wine."

"So now you are at the hotel."

"Yes, it is twenty years later and we are at the hotel," said Dr. Allison. "It's the Nancy Astor Hotel, right across from Central Park. On 59th Street. Dr. Loftus is there, sitting at the head of the table, but it's Bernardo who is doing all of the talking. That was his nature, to always try and put everyone at ease. Bernardo is telling us to raise our glasses as he wants to get started. "Vanitas vanitatum," he says and he adds: "et omnia vanitas." We all respond eagerly with our most favorite line: "Vana spes et mendacium viro insensato: et somnia extollunt imprudentes."

I look around the table and I think it'll be an interesting meeting this year. Dr. Ma is doing better than all of us and I have a feeling that he's going to try and steer us more his way. You know, he was always the type to sit and wait patiently for the rest of us to make a mistake. That's how we were, having little wars with one another while working towards a supposed common goal. Dr. Ma had purchased a pharmaceutical startup and he was doing very well. His chest was puffed up but I knew he wouldn't say anything about it. All of us already knew.

"Then there was Dr. Ando. Tadahisa Ando. His laboratory worked on surgical techniques to improve hearing, especially congenital and early childhood hearing loss, and he had also had some success this year. His team had developed an experimental drug to regenerate the hair cells of the inner ear. Ma and Ando were like warlords fighting over a little patch of territory. I think it was Ma's secret wish to wait for Ando to make a big discovery, have someone encourage him to incorporate and then covertly buy all the stock so he would own Ando's invention."

Dr. Allison laughed, a thing that was both rare and terrible.

"After we toasted, Bernardo suggested that we break bread to start the meeting but Dr. Loftus said that he had something to say first. Out of all of us, Dr. Loftus was the one who looked the least

Falling

like a surgeon. There was something very physical about him. He looked like a prize fighter or the ringleader at the circus, it's hard to describe him. He had this theatrical quality and these snake eyes. Anyway, Jacob said that he had an announcement to make. We sat silently waiting for him to say what it was and that's when Jacob chuckled and told us he was getting married.

"Then Jacob did something very strange. He took out his cellphone and showed us a picture of him and the woman he was to marry. This was strange for Jacob as he was a bit of an anti-technologist. Oh, he knew all about computers and the latest medical techniques like the rest of us, but he always said that if he had children they wouldn't be allowed to watch television or have mobile phones. There was something about all that he didn't like. They would all be reading books all of the time and wearing homespun clothes, I imagine.

"Well, I look at the photo and I see a shirtless Jacob and a beautiful woman in a bikini standing on a startling, secluded beach. Black, volcanic sand. I imagine it must have been the island of Pico, the Azores. Or perhaps Porto Santo. The woman is Juliana Braga. Part of me knew it would be her before I saw the picture. Well, Jacob takes his phone back, he politely nods as he listens to all of our congratulations and then we are ready to get started with our meeting. That is when we hear a knock on the door."

"Just ignore it," Bernardo said. He was hungry and he wanted Jacob to get on with breaking the bread. Jacob appeared to be of a like mind because he signaled for the platters of bread to be passed around. Our cheeks were already flushed with the wine and the scent in the room was of rosewater as well as wine. The bread would also be dipped into the wine.

Jacob said that the last year had been a good one and there was a better one to come. That's when Bernardo said: "Yes, it was a good year for Dr. Ma and the upcoming one will be even better for Dr. Ma." A few of us chuckled, but most were busy eating. "Aren't we bringing in someone new this year?" Bernardo asked. "It was always intended for us to be at thirteen but we're down to twelve. There should be a replacement for Callum. Don't we have one?"

Jacob sighed deeply, not looking at any of us. "I've been hard at work looking for Dr. Maxwell's replacement. We need someone to increase our influence among the trustees. And it would help if they could steer the university to invest in our portfolio of holdings. That was always the goal. Dr. Maxwell wasn't the most successful at that."

"Then we'll find someone who can be successful," I said. I took the nods of the other members as a form of tacit agreement.

Jacob said that no one had yet caught his eye. He didn't want to be hasty with invitations because he thought we should treat our society like the university treated its student body. We should remain as exclusive as possible. If the society was thrown open to just anyone the character of our organization would change. We all knew how important it was to keep our meetings and our actions a secret. It was a testament to how well we had done this over the years that our society had escaped mention in the papers, even though other groups that were ostensibly similar to our own hadn't been so fortunate. Our society had been successful both in its secrecy and in its individual objectives, even though those objectives were not always clear to all. Indeed, I think it was the role of the chairman to keep much of the true intentions of the society obscured. Obviously, our goal was rooted in the teachings of the Old Testament, we all understood that, but it always seemed to me that there was something else, something hidden: not just in the objectives of the society but in the nature of the group itself.

Only the twelve of us were privy to the secrets of the society. It sat in the heart of Columbia University in New York; most of us were part of the faculty at the Columbia School of Medicine and had admitting privileges at Columbia Presbyterian and other hospitals in the city. Our influence was steadily growing both in the school and in the wider network of power in New York and the United States. Part of our power lie in our control of decision-making at the university, but we had influence beyond that, like the old Roman *patronus* who had clients outside of the city of Rome as well as in.

It was important that who we were remained a secret. In fact, I sometimes thought that who we were was a secret only to ourselves.

Only Jacob seemed to know everything, which seemed natural as he was the chairman. There was a part of me that resented him for his power as I thought I was smarter than he was and a better surgeon, but I had to admit that he was my better in other ways. He had the look of power and authority. We may not want to admit it, but some men just have a quality that makes others want to follow them and Jacob had that quality. Human beings are followers after all.

And we would follow Jacob. We'd follow him right into the elevator. We'd leave our perch in the penthouse suite of the Nancy Astor Hotel and climb into a deathtrap of metal and wires. Even after we saw the severed bodies, we followed Jacob. At this specific moment we were eating in great solemnity. I think that's what most of us liked about being members of this particular society. There was something old fashioned about it: all of us men commiserating with one another at secret meetings in swanky hotels and knowing all the steps of the intricate male dance that was power. We might as well be doing a war dance on a Polynesian island. We knew when to talk, which was sort of like strutting our feathers like a bird, and we knew when to be silent and listen. That was the dance.

That's when I heard a knock on the door again. "We might as well just answer it," I said. I figured whoever it was wouldn't go away until they had told us what it was they wanted. Jacob frowned but he agreed. Dr. Ando got up from the table and opened the door; that's when a member of the hotel staff came in. She was a young woman with severely arched eyebrows and her hair pulled gently into a chignon at the nape of her neck.

"Please pardon my interruption, but your presence is needed downstairs immediately," she said.

Jacob asked her what could possibly require us at that moment and she said: "I'm afraid I cannot say, sir. I merely convey a message. You are asked to come down at your earliest convenience."

And with that the woman retreated and shut the door behind her, leaving the twelve of us in silence. One of us remarked that the whole thing was odd and Jacob was still frowning, which cast ominous shadows over the contours of his face. He didn't ask what we thought we should do. He stood and that was our cue to go. We were all curious as nothing like that had ever happened before. In my twenty years in the society our meetings had never been interrupted. As we left the suite and walked to the elevator, a few short feet away, I thought that the problem was this particular hotel. We had never chosen to meet at the Nancy Astor and it perhaps was the wrong choice. We met in a different location each year, which we always said was to keep our movements hidden but it was also to please Jacob, who liked that air of the mysterious.

"I wonder who knows we're here," Jacob whispered to himself. It was out of character for him to say something seemingly without a purpose. He hadn't intended for us to hear it, he merely said it in passing and allowed us to overhear.

"It's one of Dr. Ando's girlfriends," said Dr. Ma.

Dr. Ma didn't laugh but the rest of us did. We all knew that Dr. Ando liked to hire women for company and we had heard stories about his predilections. "Men shouldn't engage in idle gossip," I said. Dr. Ma said it wasn't idle gossip if it was true and salient to the present moment. Of course, it was debatable whether it was actually relevant to the moment, which made it gossip to me. It was Dr. Ando who made the important observation that we wouldn't all fit into the elevator. He suggested that we take the stairs but when we reached the stairwell we found that it was barricaded. There was a sign mentioning that the stairs were closed off. So the elevator it was.

We returned to the elevator. As I mentioned, there were two but the second had an "out of order" sign hanging from yellow tape. Jacob hit the call button. "Sam and the five of you can go first," he said. "The rest of us will go in the second trip. Wait for us at the bottom and don't speak to anyone until we get there."

Sam nodded and the elevator soon arrived. It seemed to shudder as the doors opened. The air inside was stale like the inside of a mausoleum but Sam and the others stepped inside. The doors clamored closed and the elevator hummed as it descended. We watched as the numbered floors ticked down and we all groaned when the elevator paused at the sixth floor. I wondered if someone else was trying to

Falling

get in the elevator on that floor, but then the numbers descended again until finally the ticker reached one. Jacob hit the call button to summon the elevator again and we watched as the numbers ticked back up.

Jacob sighed when the elevator finally arrived. The doors parted painfully, spilling shadows across Jacob's Salvatore Ferragamo shoes, which he seemed particularly proud of. A metallic scent crept from the shadows. The scent was also sweet and I recognized it instantly. It was blood.

Jacob stepped inside the elevator, caking the soles of his expensive shoes in blood and burning the image of blood on his retinas. "We won't say anything," he said. "We won't call the police and we won't call security. We'll just get in."

"You must be joking," said Dr. Ma. "I'm not getting in there. You test it out first."

"Whoever did this could be coming up the stairs now to finish us off," Jacob said. "You saw how the elevator stopped at the sixth floor. That must have been where the killer got in."

"We don't know it was a killer," Bernardo asked. "It was probably just an accident with the wiring."

"An accident with the wiring doesn't sever limbs from bodies and split torsos like that," said Jacob. "We need to get out of the building as quickly as possible. Let's go."

We felt a collective unease but we all crept into the lift: Dr. Ma, Dr. Ando, Bernardo, Jacob and me. Jacob's steps were steady, stepping fearlessly into the pool of blood. He pressed the lobby button and we waited in terror for the doors to clatter shut. They finally did, and as the lights had gone out in the calamity we soon found ourselves shrouded in a cloak of darkness and blood. Nothing happened at first and then the elevator suddenly jolted as if it was going up, but we were on the top floor. But then, as the dusky lights fluttered on and off in the recesses of the wood-paneled elevator walls, like shuttered window panes, the elevator began to plunge. It plunged like the final descent into the abyss, like one's sins finally being called into account. In the mirrored metal of the elevator doors we could all see ourselves. The elevator gained speed with each passing second until it finally crashed.

It was late and Dr. Allison suggested that we resume the next day. I didn't want to as I needed to have the completed interview on the chief's desk by close of business the next day but I could see the old man was tired. It seemed wrong to make him stay.

So after bidding the doctor goodbye I walked up to the F train and rode it down to Brooklyn where I lived. I could already smell the dinner that my fiancée cooked when I emerged from the subterranean inferno that was the MTA subway system. Of course, I couldn't smell anything but that was how famished I was. My fiancée and I had been engaged for ten years but we never took the step to marry. I think there was a part of her that believed that if we finally tied the knot it would ruin things; that she wouldn't want me anymore.

As it stood, the interest was still there. And I held out hope that she'd change her mind. I expected to find her in her apron when I opened the door into the apartment but I found another woman instead. The woman was lying face down on our large couch and she wore a pair of skintight jeans and four-inch black stilettos. She was reading a book, one with an apparent spelling error in its title: *The Adventures of the Seefarer*. She was like a black swan lying there, waiting to do whatever it was that black swans did. As soon as I saw her I knew it was Juliana. She hadn't aged a day. I put my coat up on the rack and knocked over the duck-head umbrella in the process.

"Oh, it's you!" my fiancée called from the kitchen, which was about twenty feet away. "Come smell this, dinner's almost done."

I took one last look at Juliana, squirming seductively on the couch, and walked into the kitchen. My fiancée was well-known in our building for her lasagna and her pasta sauce. She used fresh garlic for both. Today she was making spaghetti, a quick meal as she had had to work late, like me. She held the wooden spoon up for me to taste. It was oh so good. I licked the last of the sauce from my lips, waiting for my fiancée to introduce me to Juliana. I would wait in vain. "Oh, this is a friend I made from a project I'm working on," my fiancée said.

Falling

The woman came into the kitchen. Clack-dap-clack-dap rang the sound of her heels on the parquet floor. "Hello, I'm Adriana," she said. She had what I thought was a Brazilian accent.

My fiancée had Adriana try the spaghetti sauce as I had done and her praises far exceeded mine. I suppose Brazilians weren't known for their spaghetti sauce so she was especially sensitive. My fiancée said that she had to go to the restroom and I was left alone in the kitchen with this woman who was as tall as I was in her heels. As the sauce pot gurgled, the woman maneuvered herself behind me. She slipped her tan, taut arms around my waist. There might have been five or six of those arms for the way she made me feel. Seven. Eight.

PARADISE LOST

As soon as the doorman opened the door, I was ushered into the dark interior of the apartment building, which was warm and rather unlike the chill of late winter outside. The walls of the lobby were entirely obscured by branches of wild pimento, palmetto, and by blooming camellias and magnolias. There was also dwarf convolvulus, even then climbing up the bits of wall between the elevators.

The doorman directed me to the elevator, and he told me that Mr. Hale was awaiting my arrival. It was not until Peter brought me into the living room that I got the view of Riverside Drive that I was anticipating. Indeed, this thoroughfare on the West Side of Manhattan seemed like an afterthought when one saw the Hudson River, whose gray-blue waters were made apparent by the jutting cliffs of New Jersey on the other side. Of course, this is intended as a record of my investigation of the disappearance and possible murder of Evan McDougal, but every man has his place, and an investigation into what happened to Evan would not be complete without describing his own.

Peter Hale, Evan's roommate, immediately offered me a seat in the living room, which had walls that were practically floor-to-ceiling. On either side of the living room were two small bedrooms, and closest to the entry door were a tiny kitchen and a minuscule bathroom. I wanted to let Peter do the talking as I perceived there was something curious about him, but I could not help but express my wonder at how two poor medical students had obtained such a nice apartment overlooking the river. "Not so poor," said Peter. "My father is the chair of Pediatric Surgery at Weill Cornell. "Oh, that's how you got in…" I thought…

Peter and I were sitting across from one another by the river-looking window. I was on a low gray couch and he sat upon a ghastly wicker chair. "It's a little strange that a student would want to live on the other side of the city from the medical school," I remarked.

"It isn't too far," said Peter. "Evan and I both ride our bikes. I'm sure you know that Evan was a football player, but he was a mountain biker too. And he was pretty good too. We both bike through the park to the school. It maybe takes 15 minutes. At least we used to."

Peter was tall and thin, and there was a childish precocity in his totally smooth, smiling face. One might even call it an androgyny. He looked the part of the contented fraternity president, ever-ready to torture the plebes. I asked Peter to tell me about Evan and he said: "Evan is the smartest person I've ever met. He's one of those guys who you can tell right away that he's got an incredible head on his shoulders, like the professor in *A Beautiful Mind*, but that doesn't always work out. Like my dad says, sometimes you can be too smart for your own good."

I thought this was an odd thing to say to a private investigator so I asked Peter to elaborate. He said: "Well, didn't you see the movie?"

Peter directed me to Evan's room and I took my investigation there. It looked like the room of a student, with its small desk and computer and its narrow bed, but there was a methodical cleanliness that I was not expecting. Evan was a medical student after all, and it was safe to assume that he would not have much time to keep to a high standard of cleanliness. Indeed, from what I had learned about him Evan was part of an important research team that was using gene therapy to bring about breathtaking leaps in cancer treatment. The cancer lab was on the other side of the park, like the school, and here I was looking at a blanket that was tightly tucked under the mattress military style. Not a piece of fabric out of place, not a crinkle.

"Did you believe that Evan was honest?" I asked.

"What do you mean?" Peter inquired.

"Did you believe he was who he presented himself to be?"

"He seemed true enough to me," Peter remarked. His long legs were set in a wide apart yet relaxed stance. "There was nothing false about him that I could see. He was a football guy, sometimes a goofball, but like I said, he was smart. Appearances can be deceiving."

"What did you know about the research that Evan was doing?" I asked Peter.

After a long sigh and a long look at the river, Peter said: "I knew that Evan was an important member of the team. They were doing really critical stuff. I think something had happened recently because Evan seemed distracted. But really I didn't know anything about it. Nothing."

A woman joined me in the elevator down from Evan and Peter's apartment. She got off at the mezzanine and I decided to join her as I was not in any particular hurry. My meeting with Evan's parents and the dean of the medical school wasn't until the following day, and I didn't have any other gigs on my caseload. I would spend the rest of the day writing down my findings and following leads, except I didn't have any leads.

The first thing I felt as I approached the landing was heat, like one might expect in a tropical country.

From the top of the stairs, I might imagine that I was descending from the heights of Manhattan to the Amazon rain forest for all the fern-like plants and trees. In addition to the ferns, flowering bushes and creepers, there were irises and roses, and I noticed for the first time a pool in which were the characteristic wide, flat petals of Indian lotus. I descended the stairs, attracted by the novel scent of this area, and soon I had reached the doors. "That's $18.50," said the cab driver to a man getting out near the door.

The subway dropped me at my favorite bagel spot in Chelsea. I really wanted a coffee but it had taken me longer to get downtown than I had expected so now I was hungry too. I was immediately met with the melting pot scent of New York; that is, a scent of a million body odors from around the world and mingled together like the ninth circle of Hell. The street was treeless and my boots struck against the hard concrete pavement. On the news this morning, the hosts were talking about the City's plans to repave many Manhattan sidewalks because of cracks, and I pictured the city growing higher and higher into the heavens from all these layers of concrete. It had to happen eventually.

Just as I opened the door into the bagel shop, my phone buzzed and something told me it was the McDougals: Evan's parents. I went back into the street and answered the phone. It was Mrs. McDougal, and she was breathing heavily, as if she had just walked up a flight of stairs. It seemed that our meeting with the dean of students at Weill Cornell had been rescheduled for today as the dean had to go out of town tomorrow. They wanted to know if I could get to that side of town in the next twenty minutes. I didn't think I could but I would try.

The dean was a middle-aged woman with a face that had been plumped and smoothed into an angelic infancy by collagen injections and Botox. She was still beautiful, albeit a beauty from a different time. Our own. There was no Peter Paul Rubens or Anton Van Dyck in that face. "I'm Dean Morris," she said to no one in particular. "I am here to represent the school as regards the situation with Evan. Mostly to discuss our perception of events. What we know and what we don't."

"If you could get on with it," said Mrs. McDougal. Her voice faltered at the end and she turned away. I heard a choked sob, and her husband rubbed the fingers of her hand with his own.

"Of course," said the dean.

The woman swiveled her chair in her office, which was surely as large as my apartment on the Lower East Side, until she faced a tall file cabinet of brazilwood. The parents took turns looking at her and looking down at the floor.

The dean handed the parents a file that I knew contained the police report of Evan's disappearance as well as typed statements from pertinent students and faculty. As the parents reviewed the file, the dean looked at me, which I took as my cue to speak.

"At this juncture I'd like to review my own findings," I said. "As you know, I've met with several of Evan's classmates, including his roommate and Evelyn, his girlfriend."

I cleared my throat and continued. "Although the general impression I've formed is that it is unlike Evan to up and vanish, I don't have any proof that he was abducted or that he's hurt."

"That doesn't mean he hasn't been abducted," Evan's father noted.

"No, it doesn't."

"So how do you plan to proceed?"

Mr. McDougal was a tall man. He gave sort of a Jesse Ventura impression, like a man who had been strong and powerful in his youth and perhaps still was.

"What I'd like to do next is spend some time at the lab with the researchers Evan worked with," I remarked. "I was told by independent sources that something was going on at the lab that might have disturbed Evan. The team was said to be on the cusp of a big breakthrough, but something went wrong."

"And go talk to that girlfriend again," said Mrs. McDougal.

"I'm sorry?" I inquired.

The lady sighed and said: "If you have some downtime it might be a good idea to talk to the witnesses again, especially Evelyn."

I nodded although I was not entirely in agreement. It was common that when someone disappeared and was presumed dead that their relationship partners were immediately deemed suspect, especially if that partner was a woman. It seemed natural to me that Evan's mother would point a finger at Evelyn, even though the impression I had gotten was that their relationship was not particularly serious.

"Is there something wrong?" Mr. McDougal asked.

I told him there wasn't, and I immediately jotted down a note to schedule to meet with Evelyn again.

"I sometimes think the world wasn't made for people," Evelyn said.

It was my second time meeting her, and this encounter was quite different from the first. Indeed, Evelyn suggested that we meet in her dorm room. Unlike Evan and Peter, Evelyn lived on campus: in a well-appointed 1920s building that looked no different from any other pricey Art Deco building on the Upper East Side. There were even gargoyles with ogreish canine teeth standing watch at the corners.

Evelyn had come down to meet me wearing a heavy wool coat, which was not surprising as it was still technically winter. But when I followed her into the apartment, she took off the coat to reveal that she was wearing a sheer nightie. Her short hair came down to the middle of her ears and was raven; it framed her model-esque Eastern European face. Not many women could pull off the pixie look, but with her sharp Czech features, Evelyn managed to.

"I am not feeling well today," Evelyn said, stopping her nose with a quick squeeze of a tissue. "I'm coming down with something I guess. Do you mind if we sit in my bedroom so I could get back under the covers? My roommate isn't here."

I signified my tacit agreement with a slight bow, and Evelyn began to jaunt to her room so I followed behind. Her legs were long and white, and they moved rhythmically and with a methodical languor through the apartment, which did not have the appearance of a dorm to me. The bourgeois bones did not have the dormitory feel, but the floors were strewn with this and that, and the room itself was cluttered with academic bric-à-brac.

Evelyn's room was quite narrow, forcing me to be rather close to her even though I was in a chair and she was on the bed.

"You didn't tell me that Evan was having problems with his research group," I remarked, removing my notepad from my over-the-shoulder bag. I clicked my pen so the ballpoint was sticking out.

"Yes, that's true," said Evelyn. "I knew that the others would tell you."

"They were on the brink of a big discovery," I said. "Colon cancer. That was the cancer they were working on, and they had singled out a gene from *Amaranthus caudatus* that might be used in gene therapy in familial colon cancers."

"I know. Evan told me about it when I met with him for lunch a week and a half ago. I can't believe he's been missing for a week," and Evelyn looked around her as if searching for something.

"What did Evan tell you about his research?"

Evelyn shrugged, and one of the straps on her white nightie slid down her shoulder. "He told me that he had been chosen to do the therapy on the test cells and he mucked it up," she said. "Evan was smart but he was better at the theoretical stuff than the actual lab techniques. That's why the head docs wanted him to do it, so he could get better. They expect him to be the lead in his own research lab one day. Everyone has high expectations of Evan."

"And you? Did you have your own expectations?"

Evelyn looked at me with a woman's eyes. Hers were green.

"No," she said. "I wasn't planning on marrying him if that's what you mean. He was a good lay, which you wouldn't expect from such a smart guy, but I'm not one to talk as I'm a medical student too. Evan was supposed to meet me for dinner last week and he never showed, that's how I knew something was wrong. Sometimes he didn't respond to texts, sometimes even for a day or two, but when he didn't show at the restaurant, that's when I knew there was a problem. He always kept appointments."

"Which restaurant was it?" I asked.

"We were supposed to go to Horde, this Mongolian-British restaurant on 10th Street. They serve yak burgers with curdled milk or something. They serve them in these yurts, and all the waiters are dressed in traditional Mongolian attire."

"I don't know how I'd feel about paying $100 to be served curdled milk by a guy in a Speedo."

Evelyn's laughter was restrained but virulent. "No, it's different. Evan actually loved to travel, though he didn't have much time for it since he went straight to medical school from undergrad. He was MD-PhD, you know. He did do a year abroad in Scotland, but I think he wanted to go somewhere more exciting."

"I talked to Evan's teammates in the cancer group," I said, looking down at my unintelligible scribbles on the notepad. "They seemed more angry that Evan was gone than anything else. They barely took their eyes away from their work to talk to me."

"It was all sterile white coats and white subway tile walls, I'm sure," Evelyn echoed.

"I didn't get the impression that they were particularly close to him."

"They weren't," said Evelyn. "There was one guy on the team named Babak that Evan really liked, but the rest of them, well. They were the sort you sometimes meet in the scientific community. They were more concerned with their future accolades than befriending this person or that. And I think there was something about Evan some of them didn't like."

"What was that?" I wondered. My chair legs scratched the floor as I had sat up straighter.

"You never met Evan obviously but surely you've seen pictures of him," Evelyn said. "He was a prepossessing man. He sort of looked like a '50s stereotype of the All-American boy. He even had the red and white collegiate jacket like in the movies. And these people are all researchers, you know? You might call them nerds. Some of them might've felt that the gods had given Evan a little too much. Babak wasn't like that, but the others…

Well… And I think Evan knew that. I really think Evan liked the way people looked at him. All those admiring eyes on him, he drank it up. He flourished in that kind of light. He grew in it." Evelyn pulled the covers over herself tightly as if suddenly frightfully cold.

"But there was still some bad feeling," said Evelyn. "Here was this handsome jock, for lack of a better word, an MD-PhD student at Cornell. He had people in the back pulling for him, family members and friends in high places who liked him. And we were all cast into his shadow."

Some can thrive in the shadow of others, I thought, but certainly not everyone. I did get the impression that at some points Evelyn was speaking of herself, but I said nothing. She pointed to a guitar that rest on a chair in her room, which she said Evan gave to her. I asked her if he was a musician, and she said that he was. He loved guitars and rock music, especially English bands like The Clash and The Cure. Evelyn informed me that Evan was the owner of several guitars. This surprised me as I had not found any guitar in Evan's room, and no one had mentioned his love of music before.

"Do you think anyone would hurt Evan?" I asked Evelyn.

"No," she said, and closed her eyes.

So I left Evelyn and entered the hall of the apartment where I passed many flowering plants. There were small specimens of oleander and *Cascabella thevetia*, and clawing its way up the wall the vines of blue bindweed, also known as bitter nightshade, which, like the others, was poisonous. As I pondered these plants, the power in the building went out, leaving the entirety of the hall shrouded in black. There was no natural light entering the apartment as it had been a dark and dreary day throughout. I thought I heard the sound of a sleepy moan coming from Evelyn's bedroom. In the silent and ephemeral space of time that followed this sound, I felt what I thought was a touch of a hand, Evelyn's hand. It was soft and warm, but when I turned I found that it hadn't been Evelyn's hand at all. It was a tendril of love-lies-bleeding, also known as *Amaranthus caudatus*: the only plant in the apartment that was not a known poison. Evelyn was, I assumed, sound asleep in her bed, surrounded and protected by her toxins.

I returned to Riverside Drive feeling a powerful sensation that I had forgotten something. I tried to connect all the pieces that together form the fabric of Evan McDougal's life, but instead of a quilt I was presented with a Dali or a Chagall; it's something that I not only do not understand but which seems to bear little resemblance to the picture of friends cheering in the football stands, cheerleaders slowly pulling down their red pleated skirts beneath these stands, and fawning professors and alumni. A man wearing a black leather vest races down Riverside on a Schwinn, his boom box blaring: "We all look so perfect as we all fall down..." like a dirge.

I see a woman sitting in the narrow park between the street and the river. She was cast into shadow by ordinary temperate trees, and she was not looking at me but I approached anyway. I asked if she lived in the building, and my official demeanor and the deepness of my voice probably suggested to her that I was a plain clothes police officer, a mistake which I don't mind. Deep in thought, the woman did not hear me so I asked again if she lives in the apartment building across the street, and I indicated Evan's building with a nuanced toss of my head. She answered no, but said that she has a friend that lives there. I asked if she knew Peter Hale. "No, but I know his roommate Evan."

I asked the woman if I could take a seat on the bench beside her. I sat before she could answer, dwarfing her small-boned body and her tiny, feminine feet. She said that I was welcome to sit, but that she had to leave to meet a coworker in a minute. I told the woman that I was investigating the disappearance of Evan. This admission was met with silence.

"Do you mind if I ask you a few questions?" I inquired. "I would like to know how you knew Evan, what you knew about him."

The woman, named Maria, said that I could meet her at eight, a few hours away, in a quiet church in Midtown, a proposition to which I agreed.

The church of St. Julian is located in the middle of a busy street near Times Square though most visitors to Manhattan leave the city without ever getting a whiff of it. It lies down the street from a busy Broadway theater, fifty yards away from a typical New York Irish bar, and between two busy hotels, yet when I entered upon this holy ground the only denizens I found were the hundreds of lit candles lining the pew aisles on stands and surrounding the altar. There was no priest, though I could smell the incense of the thuribles from that morning's mass. The church was hidden from the hectic clamor of New York, and Maria Hasegawa too was hidden in the dark masonry of its walls, which seemed to slope inwards like the boughs in the understory of a forest. She was arrayed in black, and her lovely porcelain face was shrouded by her night-shimmering black hair.

"I didn't think you would come, Miss Hasegawa," I said, unbuttoning the top button of my coat.

"You can call me, Maria," said the woman. Her face was small and cherub-like, but her eyes were large and full of feeling.

"You said you were a friend of Evan's?" I asked.

"I was," Maria said. "We've only known each other for six months or so, but we became friends quickly. Evan came to me for guidance. He wasn't happy with his life: his friends, his family. He was on the road to perdition and he didn't think anyone around could help him."

As Maria spoke, I realized that in spite of all that I had learned till now I hardly knew Evan at all.

"Perdition?" I asked.

"The world is filled with sin," said Maria, "With the sinful nature of humans, and some people feel it more than others."

I could hear the characteristic trill of a Mercedes engine outside.

"You might say that Evan was like a fish out of water," Maria continued. She looked at me and I suddenly felt the intense heat of her stare. "Like a big, spotted fish. He enjoyed the research side of his studies but everything that happened there, every little thing, took on a huge significance. Every stumbling block he met with in the lab was devastating to him. And then there was his girlfriend. Evelyn."

"What about her?"

"He had been having some sort of problem with her. He didn't say what the problem was, but even that I think took second place to his work. He had recently suffered a setback in his research, the whole team did, and Evan felt responsible. He felt that he was being castigated."

"Evan doesn't seem like the sort of person to be castigated," I remarked.

Then the wind came in through the church door and rustled the pages of the bibles.

Maria didn't answer my unasked question, but she said: "Evan's parents are Presbyterians. Everything is either a punishment to them or an indication of some preordained fate. Evan had an uncle who lost everything after an accident and the family turned their back on him. They thought that he had been marked with suffering from birth. Evan thought maybe he was marked too. He came to me because I work with the chaplain's office at the medical school. I'm Catholic and Evan was thinking about converting. I took him to several Roman Catholic churches, and he met several priests who discussed the conversion process with him. It isn't as easy as it is in other faiths. Being a Roman Catholic is rather a big deal." Maria looked away, at the pained face of Christ pierced by his crown of thorns at the altar. The blood streamed down the sides of his face. "I was born a Catholic in Sapporo, Japan. There are not many of us in New York but there are some."

A candle beneath a painting of St. Julian triumphing over a dragon flickered and then went out.

"I didn't know," I said.

"No one knew," said Maria. "Only Evan and me.

When I got out of the taxi, everything suddenly felt as dark as if Maria had actually brought sin into the world when she had spoken those words to me in the church. "The world is filled with sin," she had said, but one wouldn't know it if one had only the face of the maître d'hôtel to go by. I had made a reservation at Horde that morning, a day after I had spoken to Evelyn and Maria, and I was just being led to my yurt when I remembered that I was supposed to call Peter. He would have to wait.

"This president will certainly be the last one," a man was saying from the yurt next to mine. Yurts are big, shaggy things so I couldn't see him and his voice was like an echo. "The world is ending. A friend of mine is into prophecies and Nephilim, Nostradamus, things like that, and he says there's a prophecy that there won't be any more presidents."

I turned to the waiter, a burly man dressed in Mongolian wrestling garb, and he suggested I might like the haggis with stir-fried yak or, if not, a meat pie smothered in yak butter, chives and roe. That's when I got a text from Evan's mother.

"Just got a postcard from foreign country," the text read. "Probably from the killer."

I couldn't help but chuckle and I ordered the second option – the meat pie with the yak butter – hoping to be able to finish it quickly and get uptown before it really started to pour.

It seemed like I reached Evan's apartment building in a matter of minutes. It was Evelyn who met me at the door. "Peter, it's Mr.

Murphy!" she shouted. She walked back into the apartment and left the door open, which I took as an invitation to follow.

A dining room table had been pushed from its corner of the living room into the center, and here I found Peter seated in front of a plate of freshly-cooked food. Haggis smothered in a very greasy butter. There was a plate and place setting for Evelyn on the other side of the table. "We'd ask you to join us but there's only enough haggis for two," said Peter, grinning.

I took a seat in the wicker chair near the table and turned my gaze to Evelyn.

"Yes, and you probably wouldn't want to join us anyway," she said.

Evelyn tossed her head back in laughter and Peter's eyes gleamed.

"I don't know," I said. "I was at Horde when I got a cryptic message."

"Evan's mother, I bet," said Peter. "What? Did she tell you she got a postcard from Evan? She probably said it was from the strangler. I got one too but it definitely wasn't from a strangler or a homicidal lunatic. It was definitely Evan. I could tell because the scene on the postcard is clearly in Havana, and Evan and I talked about going to Cuba and then Paraguay next summer if he could get away from the lab. I guess Evan knew what he needed to do."

"You never told me that," said Evelyn, her voice suddenly sweet and natural.

"Oh yeah," said Peter. "A guy who graduated from Weill Cornell last year was from Paraguay and we always said we would visit him."

"Ernesto?" asked Evelyn.

Her hair was pulled to the back of her head in a neat chignon, and she was wearing a white evening dress by Lanvin. I recognized her teardrop earrings as Van Cleef and Arpels, as my ex-wife had wanted a pair (and never got one). Evelyn was prettier than I had ever seen her.

"Yeah," said Peter. His air was free and easy, not a care in the world. It was more old money than anything else.

"My father has a ranch in Paraguay," said Evelyn.

"He also has a private island in the Chesapeake. Did she tell you that?" Peter asked.

"No, I didn't tell him," said Evelyn. "An island that's just a hop and a skip away from Dad's office at the NIH. My dad just loved Evan. He basically promised him a spot in his lab when he graduated, even though he wasn't really one of us. You know what I mean."

"My dad loved Evan too," Peter said, but he was laughing hard. "Sorry, Evan. I guess you knew what you had to do. My God, Evelyn, where'd you get this recipe?" Peter wondered.

"From the chef at Horde. Duh."

Peter armed himself with his serrated steak knife and looked down at his plate. The haggis, the ugliest thing I had ever seen on a plate, might have moved or winked at him for all I knew. Peter's other hand was resting on the table and this hand Evelyn took into her own.

PARADISE REGAINED

I hadn't seen Evelyn for several days. Her arrival in a low-cut dress was sudden, though she said she had been thinking about me and that we should have dinner. She tossed the flowers she brought into the sink, quickly forgetting about them, and then she started talking a mile a minute about this and that. We watched television as we waited for the Thai food to arrive, the usual pad thai and a couple other dishes. Evelyn was happy about that, that I remembered her favorite Thai place was right around the corner. As she fumbled for my hand to hold and then fumbled for the zipper of my jeans, I looked toward the kitchen where I knew the flowers, they were forget-me-nots, were. They were like something you'd bring to a kid's birthday party.

I'd seen her bring these kinds of flowers for Evan before and it was more than a little irritating that she couldn't even think of something different to bring when she saw me. Evan had been gone for three months and I really just felt like I'd had enough. Enough of the false starts with Evelyn. Enough of Evelyn. Period. I had been lying in bed for an hour or two, staring at Evelyn as she slept, when I finally decided that that was it. She was sound asleep. I had satisfied her fully, surprising even myself. She moaned herself right to sleep. Why wasn't I sleeping soundly like she was? I shifted my position in the bed and tried to fall asleep again. By then it was 5AM. I used all of my medical training to meticulously describe her body as I saw it, an exercise to help me fall asleep again. A whole course book of anatomy, learned by heart: the tissues, the blood vessels, the visible bony prominences of her leg, her hand. I knew the names of the various tissues of her body, invisible to the naked eye. Several weeks' worth of feelings were now becoming clear. I couldn't stand Evelyn. I couldn't stand being near her. I couldn't stand the smell of her expensive perfume. There was part of me that wanted to take a match to her to be honest. The truth was, I hated her and I was jealous of her.

I might have convinced myself that I loved her. There was something about her that made it seem natural for a man to want a woman like her, but it hadn't really been about that. It wasn't really about Evelyn at all. What I really wanted was to become a part of Evan, and Evelyn was like this thing that just happened to be there mucking everything up. I had made love to Evelyn, but I had never wanted to become one with her. I had made love to Evelyn in the way that I thought Evan would: licking where I thought he would lick and smiling at her displays of excitement. I had mentally exaggerated every little facet of the act of love that Evan, when tipsy, had unwittingly provided me with. He could not have imagined then what I would do with all that he had told me.

When I pulled Evelyn's hair or nibbled at her skin, that was Evan, not me. He had a way of tucking the loose strands of her hair behind her ear, showing off his class ring, and I began to do the same thing. I began to whistle when I entered the room like he did, even though that had irritated me at first. I began to leave the laces of my sneakers undone. I would notice something up on the ceiling and laugh; that was Evan too. I did this subconsciously, in fond memory of Evan, and soon it turned into habit.

I couldn't get it out of my head that Evan wasn't here anymore. The smell of him was in the apartment still and sometimes I would wake up in the middle of the night expecting him to walk in and kick his sneakers off. It made me angry. He wasn't coming back. He had sauntered right off the edge of the earth, without notice and without a care. He had sauntered right off to Latin America, as the postcard suggested, and he hadn't thought about me at all. Why hadn't I been invited? Why hadn't he taken me like he usually did? Where was the complicity that had always existed between us? He could have said something like, "Listen Peter, I am disappearing for a while. Play along, okay?" He could have said anything.

And then there was Evelyn. If Evan's behavior was a surprise then hers was an even bigger one. She had jumped from Evan's bed right on into mine. As long as she had a man's body to keep her warm at night. Really, she was nothing more than what I had always thought her to be: a slut on the fast track to an MD. And she would be an MD married to another MD that would certainly make daddy happy. I suppose one medical student was as good as another. If Evan's gone we can just slide Peter in, hardly worth losing any sleep over. I suppose I was a healthy substitute for Evan. Maybe that's why we had been so close. Did she compare my body to his?

It was easy to hate Evelyn thinking like this, but maybe I was wrong. She was just doing what I had done. She had put her little Evan action figure up on a pedestal and when that action figure was gone she had to find a substitute. Perhaps that was her way of coping with grief, but I still think she's a whore. God, I was really starting to loathe her. She could have had Evan every day for the rest of her life, fucking him into eternity, and he hadn't been missing for a day when she picked up the phone and called me. Evan wasn't stupid; he must have gotten a whiff of what Evelyn was really about. She must be the reason why he didn't want to live here anymore. She drove him off. But had he really wanted her? Evan told me once, "I want Evelyn forever and ever, for better or for worse, richer or for poorer," but perhaps there had been something else lurking behind Evan's smile. I remember watching Evan smile as he put down that bottle of gin.

Fine, I told myself. Peter, you've had enough of the bitch. Just get dressed and go. So I got dressed, grabbed my backpack and left.

When I got back home, Evan's father was in the apartment. He still had the key. He was with another woman I didn't know though I'm sure I've seen her somewhere before. They were cleaning up, putting Evan's stuff in clear plastic boxes. They were the transparent boxes you see in those dirty storage facilities. It was like they were taking Evan apart and putting each piece in a clear box.

"Peter," Evan's father said.

He said my name like I was a child coming to his house to play but his kid wasn't there.

He stood in front of me and handed me this antique-looking leather-bound book. "You'll get a kick outta this," he said. "It's an early edition of Grey's Anatomy. Evan said you were into old books, so."

I nodded. Mr. McDougal said Evan had other books that he would give me: *Mademoiselle Giraud, ma Femme* written by Belot, and something called *De Humani Corporis Fabrica* by the Flemish surgeon Andreas Vesalius.

Mr. McDougal and the other woman walked out and I was left alone.

It was time to go again. I needed to go for a walk, a longer one this time. Just get away from everything. Honestly, it felt like Evelyn's spirit was creeping back into the apartment again. "What are you gonna do with that book, Peter?" she said and laughed.

So I was walking along the Hudson, following a path that didn't make any sense, veering this way and that. It didn't make any sense at all, not to me at least, but I convinced myself that this path would lead to Evan. Oh, it would all right. All I had to do was walk. Somewhere at the end of this path, I would find Evan and he'd be sitting on a bench and he'd say: "Oh, you found me, buddy." And I'm sure he'd smile. He might even whistle. "Peter, why is it always *you* who finds me? Come and have a sit-down buddy, right beside me."

He'd laugh out loud, just lean his head back and laugh like a kid.

And then I started crying like I never had before. It was hysterical crying, the kind you do when you're suddenly birthed into the world or when a woman like Evelyn suddenly leaves you even though you hate her. But this was different. I was crying with a new awareness: the awareness that I was Peter, he was Evan, and that, in the end, one had nothing to do with the other. I would never be Evan and I would always be far away from him. I would have to build a life for myself, even if it was the shittiest life on this shitty little rock called Manhattan. And I would do it with no further ado. That's what everyone does, isn't it? Why hadn't I done so before? I had eight years to do it.

And there I was crying over Evan's death, or so I thought. No one ever said he was dead. Maybe I bawled over my own death. Weren't they one and the same? Something in me had slowly and assuredly died, right along with Evan. I had become obsessed with Evan and his death had meant my own. There were lots of ways two men could become one, it didn't have to be through sex. We were two spirits and everyone knew that two spirits could become one. Why did everyone always have to make everything about sex? Why did people always think about this type of closeness as something that had to come about in a carnal way? It was animalistic.

I stopped to rest against a shack that sort of leaned against this old apartment building. The building looked half empty; honestly, this part of the block looked mostly abandoned. I had a feeling that this might not be the best area. It could be dangerous here and, honestly, I wasn't exactly sure where I was.

And then I heard Evan's voice. He was talking about religion, and I remember this quality his voice had and the idiosyncratic pronunciation of certain words. It was like I was piecing together events and creating a reality because the things he was saying now he had said at different times. It's strange. It's like putting a tape in the VCR and pressing play. I was sure it hadn't happened like this: this teleplay of Evan talking about converting. It was none of my business really. He could become a Hare Krishna for all I cared, but I did care. And he didn't want to become a Hare Krishna, he was talking about becoming a Catholic. I really wasn't interested in that- a Catholic! - and I certainly didn't care for the implications that this change meant. Everything just seemed old and wrong, those Latin words and expressions, and it baffled me that someone like Evan could buy any of that shit. Maybe Evan was struggling with his ideas about God as he grew closer to becoming one: a paternalistic God toying with all of us in his big hands. Evan must have realized that I wasn't really onboard with his thinking so he started couching it all in medical terms: healing wounds, taking away cancerous tissue and replacing it with patches of new tissue, exposing the new epithelium and allowing the diseased organ return to normal functioning.

Evan told me once that his problem was that he was obsessed. "Yes, I'm obsessed in the etymological sense of the word," he said. He told me that it ran in the family. "Obsession is a disease just like inflammation of the pericardium." And then he told me the story of an uncle who had gotten in over his head in various enterprises and eventually had "completely lost himself like" and had become lost to the family. I smiled because Evan loved to use the word "like", ending almost every sentence with it. "It runs in the family like," he would say and then he would smile.

I could see him now. It was like he was resurrected; he was standing next to me, in effigy. It wasn't Evan, it only looked like him. Evan the effigy stood right before me, smiling and saying like in every sentence. He was close enough and real enough that I could touch his cheek and feel its warmth. There was something religious about that… that transfer of minute skin cells through touch. To touch and not to touch, to be carnal and to not be carnal. Was this what Evan's conversion had been about? The spirit? The soul without the flesh?

I couldn't understand my own train of thought so I had to move on. I fell to the ground and looked around. I opened my backpack and unscrewed a water bottle, that's when I caught the sight of a red and white jacket floating on the surface of the Hudson. I thought I was imagining it; it couldn't be the jacket that Evan always wore when he biked to school. The funny farm was in my future if that's what I was seeing. I got up from the sidewalk, turned away from the river, and starting mulling over my present state of mind. *Acute depression. Viral meningitis. Simple Grief.* When I looked back at the river, the jacket was still there, ballooning as the wind had crept under it. It was now closer to the embankment. It was Evan's.

Curiosity dragged me along for a closer look. It wasn't just a jacket, there was a body attached to it. It was Evan's. The body rolled a little and Evan's face was turned towards me. He was smiling. It was like he was asleep and having this killer dream. I couldn't help but think that this must have been how Evan looked after fucking Evelyn.

Well, I knew what Evelyn would do. She would go into the water and see if it really was Evan so that's what I did. I leaned over the embankment with the help of these metal rods on the side, diving my arm into the water and pulling Evan closer to the river wall. I pulled him out of the water. As the sun shone over the Hudson, I lay there next to him.

After a few minutes like that, I dragged the body into the shack and put the dead Evan to rest. The Late Evan. Evan-That-Had- Been-But-Was-No More. I left him there, his muscular form visible through the thin polyester of his Cornell jacket. His face was slightly cyanotic and a little bloated, but he still had that sharp jawline and even his hair looked perfect even though his body had been in the water for weeks.

I took my Swiss army knife and I cut a square out of Evan's Cornell jacket, just a little bit of Evan to take with me. I put the piece of fabric in my pocket and I watched the red-blue sun through the metal planks of the shack. I didn't know what to do after that so I stood guard over Evan's body. That was the last time he'd run off without me.

I read a story about Evan in the newspaper, something about how a rising medical student had vanished to South America, but I knew better. The article was so ridiculous that I actually crumpled the paper up and threw it in a trash can on the Upper East Side. That garbage can was a few blocks away from Dr. Allison's office at the medical library, where I was headed. I figured I should call first so I rang his office and left a message since he didn't pick up. I waited in Central Park for an hour or so and then I went to Dr. Allison's office, which was in this old limestone mansion right off Fifth Avenue.

Dr. William Allison was well-known among the student body, partly because we had a lecture from him in our first year but also because he was known to be the last survivor of the Vana Spes

Society. He was on the faculty at Columbia and he divided his time between that institution and the library where he had an office and saw private clients.

I stood in the waiting area, waiting for Dr. Allison's secretary to call me back. She didn't do it right away as she was chatting on the phone and that gave me time to look around as I had never been there before. There was a specimen of a fetus with an elongated skull in a jar from Peru, a perineal area of a woman with two vaginas from Ancient Egypt, preserved in jelly, and the usual fully-conjoined Siamese twins in a jar that was sort of like the centerpiece. There were books too. I honed in on one in particular. It was called *The Narrative of James Allen* and I let my fingers run over the thick yellow-brown cover of the book, which I knew had been made from human skin. Mr. McDougal may not have realized it, but the books he had given me also had covers made out of skin. The Belot book in particular was wild because its cover was so soft and yellow, as if the person whose skin it came from had been fattened up first. I knew that yellow color probably came from a high level of adipose tissue in the skin. Mr. McDougal may not have known about these books but I'm sure Evan did.

I rubbed a finger over the book, appreciating how well the epidermis had been preserved and how the connective tissue had contracted perfectly. Whoever had made the book must have known to use a little more skin than was necessary to account for the way the skin would shrink as the water dried out with age. It was interesting to think how these sorts of medical considerations could be applied to something as routine as making a book. That's when the secretary, Jessica, called me back. She was a hardbody and I made a mental note that I should get her number before I left. We could meet up after I found a way of getting rid of Evelyn.

"Dr. Allison will see you now," she said. "Just go back."

He was standing by a bookshelf when I saw him: a tall person with a wisp of gray hair standing up and forming a sort of a magnetic field around his head. He turned around and with a hand directed me to take a seat. He told me that he had originally been trained as a neurosurgeon and had only become a pathologist after many years practicing neurosurgery. He said that most of his students didn't know about his past as a surgeon. Doctors could do that back in the day, he told me, sort of jump around from one practice to another, just as long as there was someone to vouch for their training. We couldn't do that anymore. Dr. Allison said he thought the world was turning against us doctors.

I told him that I had heard about his training when I had visited Edinburgh.

"Oh," the man said. "After I finished my medical training, I did some studies in medicine at the University of Edinburgh, before I started my residency," he went on. "You could do that, too, back then. Edinburgh's an old city with a very dark history when it comes to the human body."

Dr. Allison placed a hand on my shoulder and I guessed he was determining how my skin would hold up for a book. He was an expert, he could probably make a pair of traveling suitcases out of me. Use my femurs to make the handles.

I told the doctor that I had heard stories about grave robbing, and then I chuckled in that easy way that Evan used to do. There I was imitating him again.

"Yes. They're all true," he said. "Some of the people used to fornicate with the cadavers. You hear stories about women who became pregnant and no one knew who or where the father was. Well, all they really needed to do was take a stroll through the graveyard and see which men had been dug up," and Dr. Allison's laugh was so long and giddy that I thought he was intentionally trying to make me uncomfortable.

He told me that there were various considerations to take into account when making things from skin. First of all, there was the question of which area of the skin to use and how to prepare it. He said the scalp was a good area to use because the skin was thinner and more compact and would therefore give a refined quality to the book cover made from it. The suitability of the scalp was in part due to the dual areas of connective tissue just below the dermis and above the periosteum. But then one had to consider the scalp was usually covered with profuse hair, which would have to be removed with chemicals, and then many people had diseases that impacted the scalp like psoriasis, or the scalp might tear as you removed it from the skull. I just didn't think the scalp was the best idea because of all the prep work it would need.

Dr. Allison moved on to the various methods of preparing the skin. There were masters in the Renaissance days who would prepare their victims like the Japanese prepare Wagyu beef. They would feed them only the highest quality foods, massage them to make sure the skin and flesh were nice and tender. Dr. Allison made a massaging motion with his hands in the air which gave me the impression that if he hadn't himself made a book out of a human being he had at least thought about it.

He said that in Edinburgh he had learned how the old practitioners of making books from human skin made a point of trying to preserve the skin, or the entire body, in water, so as to keep the three layers of the skin hydrated. Everyone knows that corpses found in water are usually in a remarkable state of preservation. Water also helped to keep the skin just a little stretched, which I noticed when I took Evan's body out of the water. He was clearly bloated but the beauty of his face and body was still there. The water had given his skin the alabaster hue you'd see in a Calvin Klein ad. The water kept the microtubules in the connective tissue layers of the skin from excessive contraction due to drying out. You didn't want the skin to stretch pathologically with hyperpigmented striae like you see in corticosteroid abuse, but just a little bloating to give the skin a fattened, pristine look. Like Wagyu beef.

The benefit gala with Evelyn didn't start until 9PM so I had plenty of time to make my way across the park to the other side of town. I hated wearing the dress shoes you have to wear to these things so I decided to wear sneakers with my suit but I carried my shoes in my over-the-shoulder bag and I'd change into them when I was maybe a block or so away from the venue. As I was changing into the shoes, this guy in a dark coat started working towards me which pissed me off because on the news that morning they were talking about how there was a resurgence in crack abuse in the City and I figured he was probably a crackhead. I braced myself for a fight but then the guy gave me a strange look and I realized it was Neal who is an MD-PhD student that I met a couple times before with Evan.

I apologized to Neal and ran across the busy intersection at Columbus Avenue to reach Lincoln Center. There were blinding lights everywhere like in Evan's lab. I had never been there but he had shown me a picture of him and his colleagues huddled around a Petri dish as a stupid Christmas joke. Evan could really be a fucking nerd sometimes but I still have the picture hanging up on the cork board in my room, behind the laptop. There's a picture of me, Evan, and Evelyn there, too, on a day we had gone to Montauk, and you can see Evelyn sort of resting the heft of her breasts on Evan's shoulder as he's holding her up. She's wearing a bikini and her nipples look all perky and sweet like tiny lollipops. I'm taking the picture with my left hand and I'm closest to the camera. Evelyn isn't even looking at me, she's making googly eyes at Evan. Her skin looks soft and Evan's just loving the shit out of it, holding her up like that.

When I get inside Lincoln Center, I see my dad, my dad's hot secretary, this other woman, Professor Bruckner, and all these other people I see all the time. It's the yearly Pediatric Surgery Benefit Gala and my dad is the head of the department so it's no surprise that he's there with the woman he's sleeping with. I remembered that I probably shouldn't bring my over-the-shoulder bag with me into the gala so I ask the attendant up front if I could leave it in coat check and he looks very confused about what I'm asking but I leave it there anyway. I feel like I need some space so I sort of hover around these students I don't recognize. They look young and doe-eyed like they're in high school or something.

That's when Evelyn walks in. She's wearing the black pant suit from Alexander Wang that I've seen her in once or twice before. It basically makes her look like sex, which I now understand is all she thinks about so it makes sense that she would wear it. But she looks good. As she walks in, a lot of the older guys turn to look at her and it

Falling

even seems like the lights in the foyer grow brighter. We're basically all standing there waiting for the classical music performance to start. Evelyn is wearing her hair up.

Evelyn is basking in all the attention she's getting but when she sees me she walks straight up to me. She puts a soft hand on my waist and it actually feels good having Evelyn touch me like that in front of all these guys ogling her. It's like she's claiming me in front of everyone else. I start thinking about how Evan must have felt when he went out with Evelyn and now she's here with me and it's like a small victory. I realize that maybe I was wrong about her and that I shouldn't give her the thing I was planning on giving her that night. It's been a few weeks since I found Evan in the river. I even start to wonder how we're going to screw later, Evelyn and I, how Evan would go about it, and that's when I hear laughter behind me: a man's laughter.

Evelyn sees someone she knows and I know him too. It's that idiot John Muller and Evelyn immediately goes up and starts talking to him. And just like that Evelyn's at it again, ready to jump into another man's bed. I began to size John up; no, not his size, but his face. His skin. He had the thin skin of a Northern European, very thin, to absorb as much of the sunlight through the skin as possible. It had to do with Vitamin D. That was something I knew without Dr. Allison having to tell me. He hadn't said whether thin-skinned people like John were suitable for making book covers and wallets. It seemed like a challenge. And though he was young and in pretty good shape, there was just enough bloat to him to make him right for it. He might even be better than Evan.

John walked off and I was left with Evelyn again.

"John was just telling me about going to Uruguay next year," Evelyn whispered. "God, what if we run into Evan?"

Her laugh was cruel and it amazed me that after all this time I'd known her I had never seen her for the opportunistic slut she was. I figured that was the right time to give her the gift. I told her to follow me back to the coat check and she was suspicious but she came along. She had a smile on her face when I took the little black box out of my over-the-shoulder bag. "Oh my god," she said. "Is it a bracelet?" I didn't say anything to that but I watched as she carefully opened the box and took out the contents. It was a purse and Evelyn's eyes widened in excitement. She clearly thought it was a nice gift and it was. The purse had that wrinkly, bumpy look, like an expensive Hermes bag. Evelyn actually clutched the purse to her breasts in joy, rubbing it with her greedy little fingers. There was no way she could have known that what her fingers touched was Evan's scrotum. I wondered how she'd feel if she knew.

TOYS ARE US

The machine hammers out the last toy and then powers off with a bang. The toy falls into a bin and stays there because the workers have all gone. On a far wall hangs the picture of a man who looks older than he is. This is my father. The lights all go out in the factory after the last machine shuts down, but the picture is still lit up because it has galley lights right above it. From where I stand, the toy-making machines are like gray behemoths walking on all fours. It's ridiculous that their only purpose is to spit out plastic toys for children aged 6-12 but a man has to make money somehow. That's what my father told me before he died. He told me: "I know you don't want to be president of a toy company, but a man has to make money somehow." Right now, I'm walking past the wall display where my father has every award-winning toy the company has ever made displayed behind glass. I'm naked and I can see my flawless reflection in the glass.

My aunt, Rosalba, came to the factory today for an inspection. She also came because there's a rumor that my father planned to shut the factory down and open another one in the Philippines. Honestly, Aunt Rosalba came because, at twenty, I'm too young to represent the family to the employees even though I inherited control of the company. It's mine. My family decided that I should focus on my studies at Penn and on lacrosse, and Aunt Rosalba will run the company until I'm ready. I think that's a good idea. I don't particularly want to be the president of a toy company, just as my father suspected.

As I'm heading to my first class at Penn, the dreaded statistics for business and industry, I notice that I have a message from Rosalba. She tells me that yesterday the toy-making machines spit out one or two extremely defective toys. The toys have disfigured heads or something, and the superstitious factory workers think it's a sign. Something bad is sure to happen to Rosalba or to me. We're doomed. Rosalba tells me "not to worry. I'm handling it."

January thinks this whole story with the defective toys is hilarious. January is a blonde (not her natural hair color) and she's wearing a wool sweater, but the fabric can't hide the regular rise of her breasts as she talks to me. The rhythm of her breasts is fast, like she's running a race. I wonder if she got her breasts done because they look bigger than last time, but it's only been a few days and I don't think that's enough time to recover from breast implant surgery. January's face is a narrow oval, the perfect shape for her 36F breasts. She's very beautiful and it's hard for me not to stare at her as we look for a table in the coffee shop after statistics.

January pretends not to notice the haircut that I got that cost me $200. My hair, practically black, is swept over to one side with a deep part and lots of gel. I guess it's a thing in my family that the guys all wear lots of hair gel. My father always told me that when you go outside every morning you see the world, but the world also sees you. For me, it's hard to imagine going outside without gelling my hair first. I'm drinking my black coffee, but I'm also looking at my reflection in the coffee shop window. My shoulders are getting wider, with perfectly round deltoids, and my legs look good in the lacrosse shorts, especially the teardrop formation right above my knee, but I don't think I put on enough gel this morning. "Do you think I need more gel?" I ask January.

January grins and says: "No, Dom, I don't think you need more gel. You look great."

She says this without looking at me. January's very WASPy and unperturbed by everything, but I think I'm already falling in love with her, even though it's only been about three months since I stole her from Aaron, another player on my team.

I stole her just like a child would steal a toy from behind the counter of the toy shop. The child takes the toy while the owner isn't looking. January is staring at her bagel, as if the very idea of a bagel is obscene. I'm not eating a bagel and I'm actually surprised that January ordered one. If I remember correctly, the bagels from this shop are 337 calories of which only about 52 calories are from protein. That's 13 grams of protein. That means there's somewhere in the region of 66 grams of carbs in this one bagel, and January is too smart and too pretty to not pay closer attention to her macronutrients. One bagel in the morning hardly seems worth the 66 grams of carbs.

"Rachel wants to know if you plan on going with us to her dance performance," she says, looking down at her phone. "Remember she's doing that African dance thing."

"Yeah. Yeah, I remember that. That's not tonight, is it?"

"Yeah, it is. It's okay. We can go some other night. They do these performances every week. But I think the guy who does the drums only comes on Wednesdays."

I don't know what to say to that because I never met the guy who does the drums, so January and I just stare at each other. I can't tell if she was being honest when she said I didn't need more hair gel, so I start to look around for the tube.

I find the gel and I'm just about to get up and go to the bathroom when I notice three guys in windbreakers coming into the coffee shop. I noticed Aaron right away, and then I saw Taylor and Toby. Aaron stops to look at me while the other two guys walk to the counter to order. Aaron stands with his back against a column, and he looks like he's posing for a spread in *College Lacrosse Monthly*. He's a tall guy with close-cropped blond hair. I can see the veins snaking down both hands from where I sit. He has really long legs for his body, and they look especially long the way he's leaning against the column. He always looks very presentable in his crisp khakis and spotless white tennis shoes, like a Southerner, even though he's from the Mid-Atlantic region like me. Right now, he looks like an action figure.

I wonder what Aaron thinks about me sitting here with January, with her sultry bottle blond hair, but he doesn't even look at her. She could be any bimbo from Pennsylvania for all he cares. January doesn't notice Aaron either. She looks at me like I'm the last piece of chocolate cake on the cake stand. The cake stand is circular and has a glass cover. January's bulimic and she'll probably throw me up after eating me, but right now she's starving.

I glance at Aaron. I can't help but wonder how he would look walking naked past the display of award-winning toys. If he would look better than I did. Aaron pulls up a sleeve of his windbreaker and points to his watch, and this signifies that we're supposed to meet up later. The fact had completely slipped my mind so it's good that we ran into him, even though I'm sure by now that Aaron would look better walking naked in the toy factory. I can see the defined mass of his calves in his khakis and I can't stop thinking that Aaron has better calves than I do and I really need to work my calves more and he's got the perfect ratio of calf width to quad length. I'll have to call Rosalba later to tell her that I can't meet up for a late supper since I have to go to Aaron's family's house in Lehigh Valley.

Aaron's parents and sister look like they were produced in the same factory where Aaron was made. They were all standing around in the kitchen as my car pulled up in the driveway. I could see them through the window, but I don't think they knew I could see them. They looked burdened with something, as if the same horrible secret occupied their minds, but as soon as I came in they were smiling and they were perpetually smiling the rest of the night. Aaron's father even stood behind my chair at one point at dinner and gave me a friendly back rub. Aaron and his sister Justine chuckled at that. For dinner we had a not-so-bad meatloaf, au gratin potatoes and lightly seasoned asparagus. Although I could tell the potatoes were prepared from scratch, Aaron's mother referred to this dinner disparagingly as WASP food and they all laughed.

Falling

"We went to that new Italian place on Fifth, it was great," said Mr. Gebhardt, Aaron's dad. "We both had the veal and I hear the fettucine is really good," but he doesn't look at me, which I think is weird because this is all a polite way of pointing out that I'm Italian and I'm theoretically used to better food.

"Oh, I loved it. Even the wine was the perfect accompaniment. It was suggested by the chef, Dominic."

Aaron's mother is a woman with small hands, hidden breasts, and very expensive looking brown leather boots. They made a clack throughout the night.

"This is a new recipe," Mrs. Gebhardt added. "I got this from that woman's website. What's her name, Justine?"

"Gwyneth Paltrow."

"That's right. Gwyneth Paltrow. I'll try a different recipe tomorrow."

Aaron is looking really happy as he asks his parents, looking from one to the other: "What's Patrick having for dinner?" And then Aaron turns to me. "Patrick's my younger brother. He's not feeling so hot right now."

A look of momentary panic appears on the face of Aaron's mother, an anonymously beautiful woman with short hair, but then she says: "Oh, you know about Patrick's special diet. He's sticking to that. He won't get any meatloaf. Well, not this kind of meatloaf," and they all shake their heads in amusement.

It's hard for me to believe, but we spend so much time talking that I don't notice how late it is. When I look at my watch, it's almost midnight. I have an hour-long drive back to Philadelphia, and I need to make it back to my dorm early because I need to make some edits to an essay that has to go out that morning. When I glance up from my watch, everyone at the table is looking at me with menacing eyes. But then they smile and Aaron says: "You know, Dom, you could always spend the night. You could sleep in my room. It'll be all right."

"I think that's a great idea," Mr. Gebhardt says. "There's no need for you to drive all the way back this late, all those crazies out on the road. You sleep in Aaron's room, Dominic, and we'll make sure to wake you up bright and early tomorrow so you can get to class on time. That's if the star lacrosse player doesn't mind spending the night with a bunch of weirdos. You don't mind, do ya, Dominic? I promise, we don't bite."

Aaron has two beds in his bedroom. He's sitting on one of the beds and watching me undress. I'm taking off my blue slacks before I put on a pair of shorts that Mr. Gebhardt gave me to sleep in. These shorts belonged to Aaron when he was in high school and there's something personal about putting them on as I prepare to spend the night in Aaron's room. As I fold the slacks and place them on the floor, Aaron looks down at his hands, which are calloused from years of holding a lacrosse stick. He flexes the fingers and does a wave with them as if he's playing an invisible piano. "I don't mind that you're fucking January," he says.

After I put on the shorts, I lie down flat in the bed, on top of the bedcovers. I'm not wearing anything else besides the shorts and my crew socks. I'm shirtless, and I can't help but notice how good my abs look from this angle, with my neck and upper back slightly higher than the rest of my body. I can't see my short black hair, but I'm sure I have the right amount of gel. I probably look like the Zedar the Conqueror action figure that my father released back in 1980. Aaron doesn't lie flat in his bed like me but he continues to sit on the side of the bed, talking. At one point, I tense my abs, which rise up like little mountains of muscle between the rivers of ligaments that separate them into squares. I look over at Aaron and the pupils of his blue eyes are dilated. I wonder if he thinks I look like an action figure. "Do you think I look like an action figure?" I ask.

"Yeah, man, you do," Aaron says. "You look really good right now. You deserve the Whitey Tomlinson Award. You deserve everything good that happens to you."

A brief moment of connection between Aaron and me passes. Later that night, I hear an angry growl. I'm sure it's coming from the Gebhardts' house but I imagine that it's one of the toys at the factory. One of those defective, devilish toys that Rosalba told me about.

Falling

He's walking through the factory. He's naked and he has another young man with him who is naked. The two young men walk past all the displays along the hall that leads to the president of the company's office. One display has the photographs of all the employees that have been named Factory Worker of The Year. The workers wear canary yellow helmets with white chin straps because a toy dropped from high enough can cause a traumatic brain injury or death if it hits a worker on the top of the skull. There are plaques that have the names of the employees that have been named Factory Worker of The Month as these employees do not have their photographs taken. The names are engraved in gold on a dark wood background. Stabbed to a board outside the president's office are photos of past presidents doing things with their families, such as opening public parks on the sites of shut-down factories and riding dolphins in the Florida Keys. There are glass displays of prior successful toy models.

A toy stands up inside the bin that it has fallen into. This toy has a misshapen face and one of its arms is longer than the other. It hops out of the bin and lands on the polished concrete floor of the factory. From where it stands, the toy can see the mezzanine floor of the factory where the offices of the president and factory manager are, and where there are displays of prior successful toy models. From where it stands, the misshapen toy can see the Zedar the Conqueror action figure. This action figure has close-cropped black hair and wields a club that he uses to fracture the skulls of alien snake-men. Zedar has a powerfully muscular physique, which surpassed the sleekly muscular physique in the 1990s to become the most popular action figure build. In advertisements for children in comic books, Zedar the Conqueror was described as residing in the jungle and having the ability to communicate telepathically with animals. He wears a brown Speedo over his pelvis and thigh-high animal skin boots. He has a wolfskin thrown over his head and shoulders.

From where it stands, the misshapen toy watches the two young men walking down the deserted halls of the factory. Their mouths laugh and sometimes their eyes and their mouths laugh together. The misshapen toy sees how the blond young man gazes at the display of the Zedar action figure. Beside the Zedar action figure is a female figure. She has no name but is referred to as The Concubine. The Concubine has long blonde hair tucked beneath a Valkyrie-style helmet with wings. She wears a metallic bathing suit that forms a V in the middle of the chest to draw the eyes of the potential buyer to her deep cleavage and 36F breasts. The Concubine has long legs and a very attractive thigh gap. A woman can only achieve a thigh gap like this through a particular type of liposuction. When the blond young man, Aaron, watches the other young man walk naked into the office of the president, he opens the door of the glass display with hand outstretched.

It's funny how I can't remember what Rosalba smells like until I see her face-to-face. Sometimes she smells like kerosene, but it's kerosene beneath an expensive perfume. Her doorman lets me into her condo, which sounds strange but that's always been how we do it. The doorman knows me and he knows Rosalba. Later, I'm sitting in Rosalba's living room when I hear the clack of her four-inch heels on the polished concrete floor. I can see her out of the corner of my eye and she's holding a black leather folder. She sits across from me and begins talking without looking at me. "Everyone's freaking out over these deformed toys," she says. I know that by *everyone* she means the workers at the factory. "To them, it's like a portent of disaster or something." She laughs, which is her way of saying that she finds this idea, this idea of portents, totally absurd. Rosalba graduated from the Wharton School of Business, the school at Penn that I am currently attending. I can imagine her saying: "But it *is* important to understand the beliefs of the workers if you plan on effectively managing them."

"I thought you wanted to talk about the Philippines," I remark, reaching for the glass of water I poured from the top-of-the-line water filtration system in the kitchen.

"Well, that too," says Rosalba. She crosses her tanned, shapely legs. "Look, I don't want you to worry about these takeover bids. I don't even want you thinking about them. As you know, we've got the bid from that Danish company and then we have the bid from Asia.

Falling

If I'm being honest, your father *was* planning on opening a factory in the Philippines, but he didn't have definite plans on what to do with the US factory. Did he tell you that?"

I sigh, but not because I'm irritated that my father didn't tell me. "No," I say. I glance at Rosalba. She's got long, beautiful brown hair. She's tall. She's a little too thin, but her thinness chisels her face so it's acceptable. If I'm being honest, which is something people in my family love to say… If I'm being honest, Rosalba is more my type physically than January and it'd be nice to find a wife that looks like her.

"I thought Dad wanted to make sure all the toys were made in the USA," I said. "I thought it was important to him."

"It was. He wanted to partner with an Asian distributor to sell the Philippines-made toys in Asia. The toys for the US market would still be made in the USA. Your father was a very intelligent man, Dom. He cared about his family. He understood that times were changing. A company that confined itself solely to the US, with all the problems we have here, a company like that would probably go the way of the dinosaurs. But I don't want you think about that. I just wanted you to have a basic idea of what's going on. You're Domenico Abenante III, obviously, and that means something, but don't worry about any of that right now. I want you to focus on your lacrosse."

I want you to focus on your lacrosse. When you're charging on the field, tossing your stick from one hand to the other to fool the guys chasing you, and you can see the goal twenty yards off, I don't want you to think about the Abenante Toy Company. Just focus on getting the ball into that goal. And if you can get the Whitey Tomlinson Award like your father wanted that would be great too.

Rosalba goes to the kitchen where, to my amazement, she makes breakfast. I know that because I hear when she turns on the stovetop, and when the scrambled eggs start to sizzle, I hear that too. She makes some forgettable comments to me while she's in the kitchen: about this cousin or that. She doesn't ask me where I was last night and I don't plan on telling her. She looks elegant from this angle, from behind. She's wearing a business suit, the old-fashioned type with the wide, power shoulders, and her pink skirt comes down to just above her knee. That's the proper length for a skirt when you're wearing a suit like that, at least if you're thinking about it from the standpoint of the attractiveness of the woman. I don't know what that area behind the knee is called but the areas behind Rosalba's knees are truly amazing. She makes a sort of dance with them as she scrambles the eggs. In the living room, I turn on the high-definition plasma television, and on VH1 Robert Palmer's Simply Irresistible is playing. I turn up the volume. Rosalba hears it and laughs.

Rosalba's laugh is deep and enthralling, and it's still on my mind as I drive back to the Gebhardts. Apparently, they enjoyed the dinner we had earlier in the week so much that they wanted to repeat it. We had to wait until Sunday because Aaron and I were both busy with lacrosse practices and events the rest of the week. Aaron said he would meet me at his parents' house, and as I drive up I can see him standing on the porch. The house is a long brick colonial and it has two white porch columns. As I step out of the car, Aaron walks down from the porch. He's smiling. He offers me his hand and we shake. I can see the dark figures of his parents and sister in the window.

Aaron and I walk into the kitchen where we find the smiling faces of Aaron's family. Everyone immediately sits down to dinner, and though everyone is smiling I feel like the Gebhardts are avoiding making direct eye contact with me. Dinner feels rushed as well. Tonight, we have grilled scallops seasoned with garlic and stir-fried Asian vegetables. This dinner is much better than what we had last time and Mrs. Gebhardt tells me that she didn't get this recipe from Gwyneth Paltrow but from some other woman's website. I notice that Justine, Aaron's sister, is wearing a nice dress. I glance over at her to make a compliment, but she immediately looks away.

"It's probably best if you spend the night in Aaron's room. Like last time," Aaron's father says.

I look at my watch and it's only 9:30PM so I decline. I don't have anything to do, but I decline anyway.

Falling

"Oh, it's okay if you don't have anything else to do," says Mr. Gebhardt. "We can find something to do. Do you like chutes and ladders, Dominic?"

"Or what about charades? Or musical chairs?"

Mrs. Gebhardt suggests these and she's speaking very rapidly.

"It's fine," says Aaron. His smile is broader than usual. "Dom doesn't have to stay if he doesn't want to. I'm sure he wants to get home and watch lacrosse tapes. I can just take him upstairs and show him the thing I wanted to show him."

"Are you sure?" asks Mrs. Gebhardt, beside herself.

"Yeah, Mom. I'm sure."

I follow Aaron to the stairwell. He walks up the stairs very deliberately. I think that maybe he trained lower body yesterday and he's just tired, which I understand completely. I don't know why, but I thought then about how I first met Aaron. I first met him at the Penn Club in New York before we matriculated. He followed me into the bathroom. "It looks like you're my competition, buddy," he said. He was already wearing a Penn collegiate jacket, even though we were both still seniors in high school.

When we reach the top of the stairwell, I notice that the steps to what I assume is the attic are pulled down. "Hey, Dom, do you mind following me up here? I want to show you some old pictures real quick."

I agree and follow Aaron up the steep, old steps. I hear a low moan, which Aaron laughs away. Once we are both settled on the attic floor, Aaron sweeps behind me and pulls up the steps. The steps close with a loud thud. After that, I listen as Aaron rifles through a box. "Those pictures are in here somewhere," he says. There are action figures scattered on the floor. Some are standing, but many are not. A dark figure creeps out of a corner of the attic. I watch as it approaches me and I lose all concept of time. When I turn around, I don't see Aaron. The figure stands before me now and around its neck is a chain that has a name inscribed on it. Patrick. Patrick is about the same height as Aaron, but his entire body is blanketed in lurid blond hair, the same blond hair that Aaron has on his head. The features of his face are all in the wrong place and one arm is longer than the other. Patrick launches himself at me with an ear-splitting growl and I scream. As Patrick's teeth viciously tear my limbs, I think to myself that he looks like Mondo the Marauder, a toy that my father released in 1985.

KINDERHOOK

It was on the evening of Halloween that I decided to travel home to see my father in New York. He had been behaving rather strangely lately. Ever since my mother had passed away in that impossibly hot summer of last year, I had the impression he was slowly losing a connection with the real world. And although ours was a silent and strong relationship, I could not call us partners in that necessary art of small talk. Yet, he had begun to call more often than he used to. I interpreted this greater frequency as a sign that something perhaps was not going as well as he pretended it was in his unexpected late afternoon calls full of artificial excitement about his latest golf game. When I told him, "I am paying you a visit on Halloween," he hesitated and paused, a silence which implied gratefulness, and then he laughed. "You or the ghost you pretend to be?"

I am afraid I have to admit that my visit represented my own egocentrism more than any real concern over the well-being of my father. Or, perhaps it was a combination of both. At this stage, I was a bit fed up with Yale: watching the lives of the students pass by in an endless, repetitive cycle. Every year the same: Commencement, Halloween, Thanksgiving. Every year the students were younger and more excited. Sometimes it even seemed I met the same students over and over again, year after year, though I knew they must be different. After twenty years teaching, grading and living in fact a small town life it all had started to weigh on me. I yearned for the cosmopolitan lifestyle of my youth. If you had grown up in Lower Manhattan, you would understand.

I was in New Haven Station trying to find my way to the track. This meant avoiding the students dressed up as characters from *Dead Man Walking*. Judging by the price of the Amtrak ticket, I had a feeling that the train might be fuller than usual. I feared I would not have the comfort to re-read the paper I had prepared for an upcoming conference on the nature of the short story.

To my surprise, there was only me, and I started going over some of the latest post-modern theories on short fiction by a friend and colleague whose name does not matter here. I discovered an oversight and just when I was making a note, the door opened with an eerie sound and a young and flashy gentleman entered, concentrating on his ticket. He looked for his reserved place, pretending not to notice me.

Vincent van Houden.

The man stretched his hand so as to shake hands with me. "Vincent Van Houden," he repeated. Yale Law School. Now, associate of the notorious New Haven law firm, Hutchinson, Dale and Vanini. He presented his card.

The young man smiled to conceal the fact that he was actually carefully examining me. "I know," he added. "The family name is a bit difficult to pronounce. But, please, call me Vincent! Or even just Vince. I did my undergrad at Berkeley, and there everybody just called me Vince."

As the train started moving, we talked very casually about the difference between East Coast and West Coast life. Vincent was convinced that life on the West Coast was simpler, less conventional. But yes, sometimes a bit shallow. "Plastic and fantastic," he said and he laughed a ghostly guffaw. He added: "That is how they say it there. It's not exactly how I see it." Again, a loud chortle to complete his sentence as if nervousness had overtaken him. Whether it was this laughter or certain features of his face, especially when he swept over it with a hand in tiredness, I had a vague impression that his visage was not new to me. I had seen it before.

"Are you by any chance a relation of the famous Van Houdens from Kinderhook?" I asked.

I cannot recall now what precisely triggered the question, but I had to ask it, as if something gnawed at me. Vincent gave me a look that was both new and familiar. This look was followed by a droll silence that gave the impression that it would last forever.

Vincent turned pale. "No." And he looked at me suspiciously. "No, not really." He was contrite. "No, no, no," he finally concluded. He had never heard of such a family. In fact, and he stressed this vehemently, he knew practically nothing about the New York Dutch. And after all that time in the US he had never sought contact with the Dutch community, if such a thing really existed. His identity had vanished in the melting pot called California; he had hesitated for a while on whether he would go to Yale. He liked the sun, the beach, the girls and Santa Monica Boulevard. He might have mentioned the amenities in a different order but it was all the same.

Vincent seemed inclined to prolong this conversation on the wonders of the West Coast and the hustle and bustle of LA, but he must have noticed that I still had an unanswered question lingering on my mind. I brought up the Van Houdens again, and Vincent took the conversation another way. He said with a light sigh: "But tell me all about it. I am quite surprised there are people with my family name. It is very Dutch, that is true, and yet you still have the Van Houdens in Amsterdam on the one hand. By the way, you can translate Van Houden in two ways. To hold firmly in a grip or to love." He fashioned the fingers of his right hand into a simulated vice grip. "That is bizarre, isn't it?" he inquired. "Perhaps one has to do with the other. But, all right, tell me all about it."

The reason I asked was because a few years ago I had an odd encounter in the Van Houden Mansion in Kinderhook. Looking back on it now, I wonder whether it really happened or whether it was just a dream. The incident was so unprecedented that I never told anyone. I intimated all this to Vincent.

"Well," said Vincent, "it is Halloween. It's the time of year to tell a ghost story." And he unleashed on me again that ferocious laughter. "It is the season, I'd say, when dream and reality merge." And he pointed at an enormous pumpkin lumbering somewhere in the streets of New London, a Connecticut town the train was now slowly passing through.

It was one of those rare fine days in New York. Everyone was up to their daily routine, and everyone had the impression overtly or subconsciously that they were "making it." I would say it was a normal day for me too. I was sipping my morning brew while flipping through the paper. I typically read the serious news stories and, of course, the book reviews. I had just received the good news that I had been selected by the Yale search committee to be a senior lecturer in the field of literary theory. By coincidence, as it were, I had stumbled upon an article in the paper which reported the disappearance of a man in the small town of Kinderhook, New York. The article suggested that the disappearance might have something to do with the supernatural, and, in particular, had introduced the existence of a haunted mansion. As this story reminded me too much of a fake story cut away from a collection of stories by Washington Irving, my interest was piqued, especially as I had a friend named Max Hollbrook who was living in Kinderhook. If I knew Max, he would deny the paranormal in the strongest language as he wasn't a believer, and so I thought it would be neat if I paid a personal visit to the town. I could explore the mansion and see for myself, furnishing proof that nothing extraordinary was passing there, and all the while catching up with a friend I hadn't seen for some time. I had loved and admired Max much in childhood. So I packed my bags and took a Greyhound bus from Lower Manhattan to Albany, from whence I would take local transport to Kinderhook.

Upon arrival, I was of a mind to pay a visit to my friend first. Max had been a junior investment consultant with a major hedge fund on Wall Street but left the job to pursue his passion for state archives. He had accepted a lower paying job in Albany. He moved to Kinderhook, deciding to live even further away from where he was posted.

"It is never a good thing to live too close to your workplace," he had said once.

Falling

I reached Max's address by late afternoon, and I felt the cold winds as soon as I got off the local bus. Given the weather, I was glad that I had packed my Shetland wool sweater and a warm scarf. I soon noticed something peculiar about the neighborhood. Max had only had the job for six months, yet, to my surprise, I was met with a large house, practically a mansion, looming over the street. Max's success pleased me, and I would have been happy in his place. He had always dreamt about old houses like these.

I knocked on the door, feeling a mélange of excitement and restlessness. The door opened, and Max's eyes lit up. He was surprised by my unexpected visit and welcomed me warmly. I followed Max into the house and saw another man sitting on the couch. Max introduced me to the man with whom he said he shared the mansion. He then took me to his drawing room and we began chatting, just like old times. Max asked me what had brought me to Kinderhook without any prior notice. I told Max about the stories I had read in the *New York Times* and how the place reminded me of him. I had been overwhelmed by a sudden feeling of nostalgia. On hearing this, Max grew curious as he too had heard rumors about that strange disappearance. One of us changed the subject, and we continued our banter.

The train plodded on.

"Who was that man?" Vincent asked.

"What?" I asked.

"That man on the couch. Who was it?"

"Oh, he was a gentleman. He had sort of a distinguished face. The sort of face you see in Upstate New York and New England. I don't remember his name."

Well, we lost track of time talking to one another, and before we knew it it was almost 9 o'clock. Max was tired, he said, but I was excited at the prospect of staying in this strange yet mysterious and extraordinary neighborhood. I asked Max about the town. It seemed to me so lonely and quiet. Max told me about another house that residents claimed was haunted, but it scared most people away. He laughed and brushed it off, claiming that no one appreciates the beauty of houses like these, and he would do something to change that. He wanted to publish an article about Kinderhook in the *Journal for Early American Architectural Heritage* and make the place a tourist attraction, for the better-informed tourist. It was a project Max spoke of with enthusiasm.

"Ah," I said. "Now here is the New York banker I remember."

Max mentioned that the mansion was only a couple minutes' walk from the house. I thought that it would be a great place to start and that it might be the house he was actually looking for, for which he had come to Kinderhook in the first place. Max refused my suggestion that he accompany me and even tried to stop me from going. I laughed it off and told him that he was being a coward. I would go alone if I had to. Max didn't take well to that and, to counter the argument, made a bet that if I was such a courageous man I would go inside the house, the "castle" he called it, and take a selfie from inside and send it to him.

Vincent stared with gray eyes wide. "A selfie," he laughed mysteriously. "And… And did you take up the challenge?"

I looked out the train window, breaking eye contact with Vincent for a moment. The scenery of Connecticut could be dreary but there was something hopeful in it. "Of course I did!" I said.

It was a lengthy yet somehow very short walk from Max's house to the mansion. The lengthiness I attributed to my own excitement about this little adventure. I already envisioned myself finding a hitherto unknown Washington Irving manuscript I could publish. They'd be floored at Yale. And, soon, I'd be a full, tenured professor of Early American Literature. Oh, the pangs of ambition in an age where all has been said and done!

I smiled at Vincent Van Houden to see if he followed my philosophical meandering, but his eyes were fixed downward, at his iPhone.

He seemed to notice the short pause, and he looked up from his phone. He feigned full attention but something told me he was busy with something else.

Falling

    I reached the mansion and felt uncommonly eerie sensations and yet the wind was calm. The place didn't seem abnormal except for the fact that it was rather ancient and was mostly a wreck as no one was there to tend to the place. I entered. It was dark and forbidding with only the natural light for guidance.

    I felt some fright, but I reminded myself why I had come.

    I proceeded to snap a selfie, and I sent it to Max. I called Max to tell him to check the picture but he didn't answer. I tried again and this time the call was answered but Max wasn't speaking on the other end. I asked whether Max received the photo but to no avail. I chocked this all up to poor network reception in this part of town.

    I turned around to walk back when I felt a push from behind. I turned to check who was there but, to my horror, the place was just as deserted as when I had arrived. Perfectly deserted. I was now more horrified than I would like to admit. I finally walked out the door and didn't look back, though I was tempted. I soon made it back to Max's.

    Max and his housemate were awaiting my return. I felt relieved as soon as I saw them. I asked Max why he hadn't answered the call. Max was confused and told me he hadn't received any calls. "Ha!" I smiled wryly and told Max that that's exactly why he has an answering machine on his phone as it prevents people from telling fibs like he was doing. We both listened to the message in which I repeatedly asked for Max to respond but there were weird noises in the background, almost as if someone was having a conversation with someone else on a fast train. You could not really hear what they were talking about due to the bustle of passengers and the clattering of the train on the rails. Now and then there was the shrill *hoot-hoot-hoot* as if a speeding Amtrak train was approaching. However hard we tried, we couldn't understand the conversation. At one point, Max's housemate even thought it was not English but something which sounded like Dutch.

    At the end, just when I was about to switch off the device, we heard a slow, quiet voice saying, "You should not have called here," and the call ended with a malign laugh. The three of us were now quite bewildered and a little scared but I assured them that this wasn't a big deal as I had already made it back home safe and sound. Max apologized for having made such a bet. "I really put you in danger," he said and sighed. I laughed it off, saying that he had actually won the bet.

Suddenly there was a beep on Max's iPhone, telling us a message was coming in. It was the selfie. At the back of the selfie, to my left, was a man in archaic clothing, knickerbockers and all, and to my right was a woman in matching old timey garb. In front was a child who was similarly attired. The three of them seemed to be a family, and their faces held neither mirth nor sadness. All that was visible to the naked eye was anguish and anger. I thought it must be a practical joke concocted by Max and his housemate, and I posted the photo online with the caption "Ghost caught on camera."

It was almost midnight when I awoke dying of thirst and went for a drink of water. I checked the picture I posted online, which now had almost 500 likes and the same number of shares. But something had changed. Something that made my hair stand on end. The woman in the picture, who had been on the right, was now in front, the child was now on the left in the back and the man at the right side in the photo. Just as I was processing all this someone rang the doorbell. I had no idea who it could be at the door, and I was the only one who was still awake. I was in the kitchen.

I was nearest to the door and figured that I should go and check it out. I glanced through the peephole and felt a surge of astonishment and horror. The family from the photo was on the other side of the door. I shrieked with terror. It was so loud that Max and his roommate came running to check what was amiss. I told them how the family had changed places in the picture and was now standing outside the house. Max forced a laugh, but I could see that he was frightened as he went to the door to check through the hole. He did not find anyone standing there. Despite my warnings, Max opened the door where we all saw that there was, in fact, no one. Stewart, Max's housemate, tried to show him the altered picture online but it had changed back to its original conformation. Max tried to calm me down, telling me that he was sure I was just frightened, suggesting essentially that I had imagined it all. He said I should get some rest and that this would make it all better.

I was sleeping peacefully now, but before long my rest was disturbed by a voice. I opened my eyes to check the source of the sound, and I became aware of something that made me freeze with fear. The sound was of someone knocking on the window. My hands and legs were now tremulous with fear. I gazed at the window and there they were again, the family from the photo: the man, the woman and the child. I ran to Max's room to wake him but, to my horror, instead of finding Max I found the family from the photo, and all three of them suddenly turned their faces toward me with a wry grin. I looked towards the window and saw Max tapping from outside. When I looked back towards the bed, I saw Max sleeping soundly next to his roommate; I again looked towards the window and there they were: the family.

I woke up with labored breaths, soon realizing it had all been a nightmare. I was relieved and returned again to the kitchen for a drink of water. On my way back to the bedroom, I saw Max's roommate now sleeping in the opposite room. I tried to go back to sleep again and this time I fell asleep as soon as my head touched the pillow. I began to dream once more, and this time I saw that I was back in that mansion where I had taken the selfie. I could hear the same sounds as before, and I felt the same sensations. The dream continued, and it was as if I knew what was about to pass, when someone pushed me just like when I was in the house, except this time when I turned around it felt like my soul left my body as the person I saw standing there was none other than Max's housemate. I awoke again feeling anxious and restless, and this time I was truly scared. Now more than ever.

I woke Max up and I told him about everything, that I saw the ghost family knocking on our window in my nightmare and how it had been his housemate that had pushed me. Max was clueless and confused. He asked me who I thought had pushed me in the mansion. I reaffirmed that I was practically certain it was his housemate who did it. On hearing this, Max began to laugh, but soon his laughter turned to anger and frustration. He shouted that I was being ridiculous and childish because I was jealous of his housemate. I paled on hearing this but remembered that I had seen Max's housemate sleeping in the other room. I took Max to that room but, to my horror, there was no one there. Max asked me about the person I thought I had seen. Had I spoken to him? Was there ever any sort of exchange with this so-called housemate? In all sincerity I didn't know how to react to this as I couldn't even remember the housemate's name. Max was adamant that he lived alone in this house and there was no one in the house before I arrived but him. He himself. Max!

I was confused, feeling an odd mix of irritation and fear. I truly didn't know what to do. Max, on the other hand, decided to do something. He would put a stop to it once and for all. He told me that we were going to the castle together and we would end this thing where it had all started.

In the dark and quiet night, we now found ourselves standing in front of the castle, as Max called it. I tried again to convince my friend that this wasn't the best idea he'd ever had and that we'd better return, but my pleas fell on deaf ears. Max wanted to go inside the mansion with me, but I wouldn't go so there we were standing outside the gate of the mansion waiting for something to happen. The night was calm and nothing extraordinary seemed to pass. The roads on both sides of the mansion were empty as far as I could see.

Max finally decided to speak up. He turned towards the mansion, took my hand and spoke in a fearful yet loud voice, addressed to the family. He began by apologizing to them for trespassing on their property and promised that neither of us would ever come back to the mansion and wouldn't ever lift our eyes in the mansion's direction. He apologized for disturbing them by coming and requested them to let him and his friend go. He told them that it was not our intention to disturb their afterlife on Earth. Before Max had the chance to say anything further, someone pushed him from the front and he fell down on his back, screaming in fear. Before I was able to help, someone grabbed Max by the legs and pulled him right inside the open maw of the mansion. I heard Max screaming for his life for a moment and then the night was again quiet. I was close to losing consciousness and was about to fall to the ground too but somehow I held myself up and decided to run from the place as fast as I could. I ran towards Max's house and, once inside, locked myself in.

I wept about all that had happened and I thought that I had lost Max when, all of a sudden, I heard something. What could it be? I heard snores coming from Max's room. I went to check and there was Max sleeping peacefully as if nothing had happened. I was unable to process what I saw and realized that I might still be in the dream; I didn't want to wake Max as I knew that once I woke him after all that had happened I would be faced with the thought of what might happen next. I had these negative thoughts for a while, feeling restless and helpless about it all. I went to the bathroom and turned the tap for some water. I began splashing the water on my face in panic but I soon realized that I couldn't feel the water on my face. I again thought that perhaps I was still in a dream. I began slapping myself on the face with full force and tried every way I could to wake myself up. There was no change, and I sat down in the bath crying and screaming with no idea about what perhaps I should have done or shouldn't have.

On hearing me scream, Max came running to me and in anger lashed out at me; he asked what in God's name had gotten into me. He commanded me to stop acting like a petulant child and to cease this ridiculous behavior. I told him in a fear-stricken voice that I couldn't grasp what was going on and that I had no idea what I should do, and I started crying again. I told him that I couldn't even discern whether I was asleep or awake. I was seeing people that don't exist. Appreciating my situation and condition, Max realized that I probably suffered from an acute depression. He tried to console and calm me. He had seen me in many varied states but never had he seen me like this. Max, in a very calming tone, told me that everything would be alright and that I was just dreaming about things. I was only confused, that was all. He lied to me in a slow and soothing voice, saying that he too had been as confused as I was when he first came to the mansion. Max's face slowly morphed into that of his friend and housemate, and slowly his voice also changed from a calming tone to a sinister one; his face was now awash in a devious grin. He went on saying that he was initially as puzzled as I was but that things would soon to return to normal, that is, as soon as Max hanged himself.

I laughed uncomfortably. "Hanged himself?" I wondered aloud. "Hanged himself?" I asked again. "As if Max would ever do that."

I left the mansion the next day and we never spoke again. Perhaps I was too ashamed to call in the weeks that followed. Max was probably busy. And then a few weeks later in the newspaper there was a report of the death of another man in the town of Kinderhook. This man was found hanging from one of the smaller turrets of a Kinderhook mansion. Police had interrogated the victim's housemate, a younger man with a strange accent who had studied psychology at Berkeley and who had been.

I ceased my narrative at this last sentence, waking up from my trance, and I continued on slowly as I saw that Vincent Van Houden was staring at me with a face full of expectation. With a dignified, cynical smile.

At that very moment, the train jolted to a sudden halt with a screech and a shock. A voice said: "Pennsylvania Station. Final destination."

Without looking at Vincent, I quickly took my belongings and disembarked from the train. I had the urge to start running as far and as fast I could, but I controlled myself. Standing on the platform now, I looked through the windows of the last carriages of the train to see if Vincent Van Houden was following me, but I couldn't see him. I saw other passengers, but not Vincent. I tried to remember his face: noble and unique, but also one that I had seen before. I scanned the cars for the man, but he was nowhere to be found. With a face like that, with a character like that, he should be easy to be found, but his presence eluded me.

I thought about what had happened to Max, but stopped myself as I knew that this was neither the time nor the place. I must find Vincent. All of a sudden, as if the train conductor had pushed the wrong button, the train started pulling back, and then it lurched a bit

Falling

forward and stopped. It stopped in such a way that I found Vincent Van Houden standing in the carriage facing me, right where I had left him. Our eyes met but his look was unfathomable to me. I had begun to walk towards the exit of the track when I heard a voice shout: "Sir, that housemate, it was me!" and this declaration was followed by a horrific laugh.

MURDER AT THE BOATHOUSE

Tall men were huddled in front of the Yale boathouse, shoulders together like Spartans. That alone was not a strange sight but the sun, still coming up, seemed darker today. One member of the crew team broke the circle, and I saw in the center a pair of long legs lying on the concrete: Adam's legs. I saw James, one of Adam's teammates, and he said: "You should go. It's bad, really bad." James tightened the blue crew jacket over his shoulders.

Statement of James Skipton, student, Yale University, 22nd November, 2019

I knew Adam from heavyweight crew but I actually met him before that. We lived in the same residence house in our freshmen year. I was recruited to be on the crew team but Adam walked on. Honestly, he was better than all of us and should have been recruited too. I think it bugged him. He was not the happiest person, and he always looked like he had a lot on his mind. I saw him injecting himself with testosterone a lot last year, but I think he stopped. I think he just wanted to look better. He said he felt like his stomach was too smooth, but I think he also wanted to be slimmer. I heard he took erythropoietin too, but I think that's just a rumor. People were saying that Adam owed dealers steroid money for a long time but I don't believe it. I just happened to be walking past the boathouse this morning, and that's when I saw the guys.

Statement of Ana Dos Santos, student, Yale University, 22nd November, 2019

I saw Adam Quigley trying to get into the boathouse last night. He was stumbling, and I didn't think he would make it up the curb. I live across the street from the boathouse, and Adam lives next door to me. I knew it was Adam because he's big, and he was wearing one of the blue jackets that have Yale Crew on the back. He walked into a garbage can but picked himself up. After that, I don't know, but he couldn't have made it into the boathouse in the state he was in. The phone rang and I went to answer it. I figured I should just leave him alone. Adam was a quiet guy. I think people were intimidated by him because he looked strong, but I also think he didn't feel comfortable with other students. Some girls I know said that he had gotten into a fight with a guy in his senior year in high school. He put the guy in hospital, that's why he had to take a year off between high school in California and Yale. But I never had a problem with him. I only learned Adam had died when the groundskeeper knocked on my door. I went outside, and I saw Adam face-down across the street, lying in a pool of blood.

The picture of Adam that Chantal gave me was a newspaper cutout from last year's Crew Supplement in the Yale Daily News. The touch of Chantal's hand was soft, and her fingers smelled like salt water. "It's the only picture I have of him," she said. "The only picture where he's alone."

We were walking in the grass.

"I'm surprised you kept it at all."

"I always keep 'em," she said. She put her hands in her dark green Barbour jacket and nimbly avoided stepping into an ominous puddle in her leather boots. "The Crew Supplement, I mean. My dad always had us following the crew team, ever since we were kids."

It had been night when I arrived at The Burn, and Chantal let me in as Jack wasn't home yet. I'd been here with Adam before, all 6'4 and 220 pounds of him. The paper had published a picture of the police officers hovering around the boathouse, and the photographer must not have noticed that you could see Adam's strong legs and his size 13 shoes in the background. The photo ended up splattered right on the front page.

Actually, Chantal hadn't let me in. She told the guard to buzz me in as the house, sitting on 60 acres about an hour north of New Haven, was gated. Gate or not, this rambling house in the middle of pitch-dark woods was a dream come true if you were a homicidal maniac. I didn't have to ask why Chantal was in the house alone without Jack, whose house it was, as I was smart enough to put two and two together and make four. After the gate opened and I drove up the driveway, a police siren could be heard speeding down the street behind me, which startled me. Adam had only been dead two days.

"Dinner will be served now," the maid said, sliding the French doors apart and calling to Chantal and me.

"Jack's always late to dinner," said Chantal.

"I don't mind waiting," I said. "I had something before I came."

"I don't know how you have an appetite after what happened. Did you see what they published in the paper?" Chantal brushed her blond hair away from her face.

"Yeah, but it's been two days."

Chantal continued to play with her hair as we sat at the table. She looked at me with the same hesitant interest that I had seen a year ago in much the same setting.

Jack arrived not long afterward.

"God, Adam was an ugly guy," said Jack, taking the small rectangular picture of Adam that I handed him. We all understood that he meant the opposite. Even in the black and white newspaper reproduction from the crew roster it could be seen that Adam's hair was a masculine almost-black, his head was nearly a perfect square, his nose was aquiline, his eyes were large, and his cheeks had the flush of youth.

Falling

"Adam Quigley," read Jack from the text below the picture.

"I never thought him the type to do that," Chantal remarked.

There was a pause, and the knell of the grandfather clock was like waiting for the doctor to tell you what the prognosis was for your cancer. Jack took his fork and ate a garlicky green bean off of Chantal's plate, and then he put his arm around her, pulling her close and grazing her right breast with his fingers. I shifted in my chair.

"Yeah, I know it's weird to see your former professor with a classmate," Jack said with a laugh

I grinned. "It's more the age difference," I said, "and those manly, hairy hands you got goin' on."

Jack laughed but he shot me a challenging look. Jack was about twenty years older than Chantal and me, he was already tenured, and he occupied that liminal ground between older alpha male and lecherous creep. It was one thing to lose Chantal to someone like Adam but Jack...

"You know everyone thinks that Adam and I were dating but, honestly, he was really quiet," said Chantal. "I mean, I don't think he was the type to ask someone like me out."

"Someone like me," Jack said and laughed. He looked away dramatically.

"You know what I mean," said Chantal. "Loud girl from the bush who was rumored to have slept with half the crew team."

"But not Adam," said Jack, rubbing his salt and pepper beard with his finger.

"No, not Adam," said Chantal.

"It's good that you are on sabbatical, Jack," I said, "because a couple guys on campus were talking about you and Chantal."

Jack laughed and pulled Chantal closer to him. "Yeah, you know, I'm not going broke or anything so I might not even have to teach anymore. Old money and all."

Touché.

"Actually, they brought the coach in for questioning," I said, changing the subject. "The crew coach. Someone saw him coming home with bloody hands that night, and they're holding him in custody."

"Oh my God," said Chantal.

"The guy came all the way back to New Haven and didn't wash his hands?" Jack asked.

"No," I said. "Adam's body wasn't found at the new facility in Derry but the old boathouse in New Haven. It's like a frat house for the crew guys."

Jack chuckled. "I'm picturing a bunch of dudes in a circle jerk at the boathouse."

He made air quotes with his fingers to show the derision in which he held the word "boathouse".

Chantal glared at Jack, but there was laughter in her eyes. "Jack, a boy is dead," she said. "You know, you should talk to that girl Tonya," and Chantal glanced at me.

"Tonya?" I asked.

"Well, if Adam did have a girlfriend it would have been her."

"The world may never know," said Jack.

"Well, I'm sure Tonya would know," said Chantal. "Oh, Ken, I found some more pictures." She handed me a short stack of four or five. "There's one of Adam and a couple other guys from crew. There's one of the coach and Adam. There's one of me and Adam. There's the MacDonald twins. And, duh, that one is just me."

"Wait," I said, honing in one of the pictures with a dog-eared corner. "This one's not Adam. This is Romulo."

"Oh, that's right," said Chantal.

Jack was blowing in Chantal's ear but I couldn't take my eyes off his steak. Jack's steak was bigger than mine, and it was juicy, with bloody bubbles forming a delicious pool on the bottom of the plate. Chantal leaned in towards Jack, and the weight of her bosom rest against Jack's chest through his open shirt.

Statement of Tonya Wang, student, Yale University, 22nd November, 2019

I met Adam at a party last year. He had a nice smile, and he was different from the other guys. There were all these stories about him, that he was on steroids and such, but he was really nice and treated me, I don't know, like a lady, I guess. He didn't make any of those stupid remarks that college guys make. I think he tried to be a gentleman because his father was such an asshole. I never met Adam's father, but I heard him screaming at Adam over the phone once. Adam had a scar over his eye, and he told me that when he was fourteen his dad hit him in the head with a golf club. I think Adam tried to be nice so he could be different from his dad. I don't know why they didn't get along. Adam and I were what I would call friends with benefits. I mean, we had sex regularly. He was a little clumsy, but tender. I wouldn't say I was his girlfriend though.

Tonya lived on the third floor of her residence house. I didn't know anyone in the house and she didn't know I was coming so I had to wait for someone to leave in order to get in. But when Tonya answered the door after I knocked she was pleasant. She was wearing a tight purple sweater and her hair was curly black. She was definitely Adam's type.

"So you're writing for the paper or something." said Tonya. "About Adam."

"No, I'm writing something but not for the Yale Daily News," I said. "I always thought you were a graduate student."

"No," said Tonya, and she laughed. "People always say that. It's because I look older."

"I wouldn't say older, just more mature. Actually, I've seen you before."

"I know," said Tonya. "I've seen you too. You were at that crab thing, at that bar downtown."

"Yeah, that's it."

Tonya was sitting at her desk. She had turned her chair to face me, so her computer was behind her. Her screensaver was of a bunch of leggy women standing in a ballroom from an anime. "So what did you want to ask me?"

"Did Adam ever talk to you about killing himself?" I asked. "I mean, did he ever give you reason to believe he would do that?"

Tonya avoided looking at me. She turned around, reached for a pack of cigarettes and then fumbled in a drawer for her lighter. "Who says he killed himself?"

"What do you mean? The newspaper called it a suicide."

And after she lit her cigarette, I said: "You're not supposed to smoke in here."

"Yeah, I know," said Tonya. "I live here, Sherlock. I know the rules."

After a few puffs on her cigarette, Tonya cracked open the window. Then she looked at me. "So you didn't hear about his eyes?"

"In the paper it said that Adam's face had been severely wounded."

"My sister works in the medical examiner's office," said Tonya. "When the groundskeeper turned Adam over his eyes were sewn shut. And that's how the ME's Office found him."

My heart began to thump.

"None of the crew guys saw it because the cops wouldn't let them touch the body once they reached the scene," Tonya added. "Adam was lying face down."

"A neighbor said she saw Adam stumbling home last night," I remarked. "She said he never made it into the boathouse."

"Well, maybe she lied." Tonya crossed her legs. They were shapely in a pair of tight, faded jeans. "Do you know Stavros?" She asked. "Go talk to him."

Statement of Milt O'Keefe, groundskeeper, New Haven, 23rd November, 2019

I had seen Mr. Quigley many times before so I knew it was him when I see him lying there. It must have been 5 or 5:30 in the morning. He was lying there and I thought he tripped and fell. I says, "Mr. Quigley? Mr. Quigley, are you all right?" But he doesn't move. I thought just to leave him there as I am responsible for the grounds, not for the students who pass out drunken upon them, you see. A man owns the land this boathouse is built upon as well as the houses across the street, which he rents to junior and senior students mostly. Well, I was stepping over the boy's legs when I saw the blood. I decided to turn him over. He was frightfully heavy. But I managed to turn him, and that's when I saw that he had a bloody wound and that his eyelids had been sewn, sewn as with surgeon's thread.

Stavros had been the RA when Adam and I were freshmen so he knew both of us. He graduated two years ago and was in his second year at Yale Med. I had texted him the night before, and we decided to meet at a cafe across from the hospital at about six. I saw Stavros standing outside the hospital building as I neared but just when I noticed him I heard the unmistakable clack of high heels approaching me. I turned around, and I saw a woman in a fur coat a few steps away. Her dark sunglasses were large and shaped like two bugs' eyes. Her dark brown hair shimmered. I wanted to speak but I couldn't find the words to say. "You're Ken," said the girl.

Stavros had crossed toward me, and as I walked away with her, he shouted: "Ken, really?"

The girl suggested we go to a different cafe, which had several outdoor tables. The tables were lit by candles as it had grown dark. The entire time we spoke, she never took off her bug eyes.

"I'm Ana," she said.

"You live across from the boathouse," I stammered.

"Yes," she said. "I am also Romulo's girlfriend."

I was stopped dead in my tracks. The only person who saw Adam come home was the girlfriend of one of his teammates. "Do the police know that?"

"No, and I would appreciate it if you wouldn't tell." After a pause: "I was in the neighborhood to visit Romulo at the hospital."

"Is he all right?"

"The psychiatric hospital."

"Oh."

"Romulo hasn't been doing well since Adam died."

Her Brazilian accent was a lot stronger than Romulo's. She crossed her legs, and that's when I noticed she was wearing a leopard-skin skirt and wasn't actually naked under her coat. She didn't look like a college student at all. She was entirely Adam's type.

"God punishes us for our sins," she said.

"You mean that Romulo is being punished," I remarked.

"No, that isn't what I meant at all." Ana looked away, at the cars hissing by on the road, and I saw her in profile. Her head was small and girlish, but when she turned to look at me there was something predatory in her black eyes.

"I have to go. I have to meet with my advisor about my thesis," said Ana. "I'm studying this mass murderer in Scotland in the 19th century. I want to be a medical anthropologist."

"Oh.... That's cool."

"Would you mind meeting me at the boathouse, say 9 o'clock?"

"I would love to," I said. "I mean, I wouldn't mind at all."

Statement of Charles Goluchowski, security personnel, New Haven, November 23rd, 2019

I reviewed the CCTV footage from 9PM the night of the 21st through to 7AM of the 22nd. The camera is able to catch the sidewalk and the boathouse across the street. I saw a man in a Yale Crew jacket come into view in front of the boathouse at exactly 10:06PM. Based on Adam's size of 6'4 and weight of about 200 pounds, it could have been him. This man tried to get into the boathouse unsuccessfully, sat on the curb, and had left by 10:25PM. I saw another man in front of the boathouse at exactly 1:03AM. This man was about 6'3 or 6'4 but he appeared much older and was wearing a dark coat and a hat, which he tossed in the water. He paced for a while and then he left after five minutes. At 4:13AM, I see a blue or black truck pull up in front of the boathouse. A hooded figure steps out of the driver's side of the car, which faces the camera. Occasionally, a hooded figure is seen in view but the truck blocks the view directly in front of the boathouse. At 4:16AM, the hooded figure gets back into the vehicle. When the truck drives off, a body is seen resting face-down on the ground, which was not present before the truck pulled up. The groundskeeper is shown to arrive at 5:15AM.

"The Dufour's gland was discovered in France, in 1841, by Monsieur Dufour. It developed in the Hymenoptera over 100 million years ago, and is present in bees, ants, wasps, and related species. The gland serves many purposes, which depend on the species. The secretions can be used to alert males to female fertility, as a warning signal, or as a marker."

The professor droned on in his smooth Italian accent, and I began to wonder why I had chosen to major in the biological sciences. It had been Adam's major too, but Adam's father had wanted him to be a doctor. I didn't plan on being a doctor, and I certainly had no intention of analyzing the scent markings of wasps.

It was an evening class, so after grabbing a bite to eat, it was time to meet Ana. It was 9:01 so I didn't know if I was early or late. There was no sign of Ana so I walked towards the door of the boathouse. The door had a glass window that had become so caked in dust that it could barely be seen through, but I could see the rowing boats in the back. I heard footsteps behind me and I turned, but didn't see anyone. I turned back around, looking for something, I didn't know what, and that was when I felt the first whack on the back of my head. I fell to the ground, more because of tripping over my feet than anything else, and a man in a black mask started punching me in the chest and kicking me in the legs. He was big, but I managed to kick him right in the left knee. He turned, reeling over in pain, and he groaned. He had the voice of a man in his 50s or 60s. I clamored up to my feet. I looked for a minute, deciding whether to fight or to run, and I decided to run. I had made it to the curb when I felt another whack on the bag of the head.

Statement of Roderick Quigley, venture capitalist, New Haven, November 24th, 2019

I hadn't seen Adam in four months. He spent the summer with his mother in Greece so I didn't see him before he started his senior year. I had a lot of trouble with Adam when he was a boy but he really seemed to flourish at Yale. He wasn't hanging out with any rough or lower class types, and he wasn't getting into fights, not that I heard of. I did beat Adam when he was a child but only when he misbehaved. He used to wake up in the middle of the night and eat all the food in the kitchen. He was 150 pounds by the time he was 12. His mother and I would wake up to find most of the food in the kitchen gone, as if our house had been attacked by raccoons overnight. Only it wasn't raccoons, it was our chubby kid. Adam was a tall child but he was still fat. But Adam did well at Yale. He grew into a handsome guy. I did fly into Hartfield the week that Adam died, but I didn't get a chance to see him. Adam was my oldest. He wasn't as smart as his sisters but he was the oldest.

When I woke up, Chantal was standing over me. "Oh god," she said. I lost consciousness a second time. The first thing I remembered after that was being pushed out of the ambulance in a gurney and then a doctor asking me a series of questions. Chantal followed in her car, and she was there when the doctor told me the results of the head CT: no hemorrhage. I had some superficial bruising on my head and scrapes on my face. I was stitched up, cleaned up, and the ER doc told me that I could go home if I wanted. I could either wait for the police to show up and take my statement, or I could go down to the station later. Everyone's attitude seemed a little too relaxed after what happened at the boathouse with Adam but I decided to go home. Chantal drove.

I was lying in the bed when Chantal turned the lights down and turned on a playlist on her phone. I don't know why but I laughed and she laughed too.

"I can't believe you ended up with Jack," I said in the whiniest voice I could muster.

"I know," said Chantal, who I had first seen in a production of The Cherry Orchard freshman year. "He's kind of gross, but his house. And, you know, the money. If I get a good job after I graduate, I'll dump him. Then I'll have my own money."

"You know, the English say it's bad manners to talk about money."

"Oh, screw the English," said Chantal.

"Did you hear about Adam's dad?" I asked.

"Yeah," said Chantal. "He was ID'ed on camera as being at the boathouse the morning Adam's body was found."

In that moment, Adam was forgotten. Chantal sat on the edge of the bed. She helped me take my shirt off, and then she softly rubbed my bandaged forehead with her hand. *Thou shalt not covet thy neighbor's wife.* I definitely knew that one, but Jack wasn't exactly my neighbor. And if I could not covet his wife, was it all right to covet his house, his money, his freedom?

I woke before the sun came up. I saw a woman's silhouette in front of the mirror that sat on the dresser. This woman wore a black bra and panties, and one of her hands was touching the mirror. It was Ana and I sat up in surprise. I gazed at her face in the mirror's reflection and she looked at me too. She smiled at me. I got out of the bed with difficulty and went to the mirror. I put a hand on Ana's shoulder and her tanned skin was warm as a thousand suns. I turned her around only to find that it was not Ana at all. It was Chantal. She had a tear in her eye. She hugged me and I held her.

Chantal left while I was in the bathroom. I found an imprint of her forearm on the glassy sheen of the dresser top. It was the kind of cheap furniture you find in a residence house or in an already furnished room. I also found a letter. On top of the letter was a note in Chantal's writing, which read: "Adam gave this to me when he was drunk."

Handwritten letter by Adam Quigley to Phillip Quigley, August 4th, 2019

The first time I saw Ana it was like I had dived headfirst into Lake Phelps. Remember when Dad took us to North Carolina when we were kids? She was like a backflip in Lake Phelps. I knew she was with Romulo but I didn't think much of it. He said his family thought her family was trash because they were poor and from Northern Brazil, but he loved her anyway. He said she was good in bed, and that's when I started to wonder. I started to hang out with Romulo more. I think people noticed when I started dyeing my hair jet black to match his but no one said anything. Mine was already dark to begin with.

Well, I'm sure you're curious what she looks like but she's hard to describe. She looks like that Victoria Secret model Adriana Lima. She has the sweet and innocent act down pat but she's a panther. Typical naughty Catholic girl. Every time I look at her, I imagine Romulo fucking her. It doesn't make me mad though. I stay over a couple nights a week at her place. I get up early just so I can watch her eyes open when she wakes up. Sometimes I see Romulo jogging past outside her window. You don't know Romulo. He's about the same height as me but he has visible abs. Year-round. I guess he's better looking. He also has a better watch, a Breitling that supposedly cost $100,000. I was thinking about trading in my TAG Aqua-racer for an IWC or an Omega but maybe Mom can lend me the money for a Breitling?

I don't know why, but when I was well enough I went to Ana's house, across from the boathouse. She didn't open the door, but I saw someone looking at me through the window of the house next door, Adam's house. Adam's house was not closed off by the police because Adam hadn't died there and, besides, other students lived there. The front door was unlocked and I took the central stairs to the third floor, passing Adam's apartment which was sealed off with police tape.

The guy who opened the door was painfully thin, pale, and his sandy hair was slicked back. I thought he looked like the guy in the slasher film who turns out to be the killer. Then I realized that he was more like the recluse next door who caught all the murders on camera and has all the MP4 files on his computer. I sat in a chair by the door while Ron, that was his name, sat by his computer. "I only met Adam once," he said in a noticeable Boston accent. "He asked me what an Audemars Piguet was."

"It's a watch."

"I know that," said Ron, "but Adam had never heard of it before."

"Do you know Ana?" I asked.

"Not really, but I took a class with her. A pre-req for my major. I used to hear her and Adam fight all the time."

"Ana and Adam? No, you must mean Ana and Romulo."

"No, Ana and Adam. Adam used to come over, I could see him going into her room from my window. Then I would hear the sound of crashing, of throwing things, and I would hear her saying things like: 'You're crazy. You always wanted me'."

Ron had the television on. It was playing softly in the back.

"I'm sorry Adam's gone," said Ron. "He didn't talk much but he had the kind of face that made you feel like you could trust him. I also felt like he had a hard time. An unfair time, you know, in life."

"Adam was rich," I noted.

"And?"

"What do you think of Romulo?"

"I don't know Romulo."

"Well, what about Ana?"

Ron, chuckled, finally giving his flat, old fashioned face some character. "She's something else," he said. "One of those insects that mates with the male and then eats him."

Ron turned to look at the TV.

"James Anderson was last seen entering an all-you-can-eat Chinese buffet in Stamford, Connecticut in March," said a man's deep voice from the television "He was declared missing after not reporting to work for 48 hours. Local detectives called off the search when a resident discovered tracks that led to a stream behind the restaurant, tracks matching the Caterpillar boots that James Anderson was known to wear. A team searched the area, looking for any clues as to the whereabouts of Anderson, at this point missing for two weeks. Until one night when the search was declared over. James Anderson had been found and, according to the medical examiner, his body was in a remarkable state of preservation due to the temperature of the water. Forensics attributed the cause of death to a blow dealt to the back of the head, but they were unprepared for what else the examination revealed. Anderson's mouth had been sewn shut, and a strange fluid of undetermined origin was found on his abdominal skin. Anderson's wife could not be notified as she had disappeared. After she attempted to withdraw $50,000 from her husband's life insurance policy, Mrs. Anderson was found and brought in for questioning."

FALLING AGAIN

She told me it was love at first sight. She even called it everlasting love. In fact, that's what Patricia would say any time she was invited to talk about Khalid. When she said these words to me, she uncrossed and re-crossed her legs, looking off down the tunnel that led to the waiting area: a black space that seemed to go nowhere. It had been a tough experience for her, perhaps the worst that a young woman from a school like Brown could be expected to go through. She had not committed any crime, but she found herself marked with a scarlet letter. It might have been my feeling of the injustice Patricia had been subjected to which drew me to her.

I met Patricia on a Sunday morning at Brussels International as I was awaiting a flight to New York. So was she. I recognized her from television, and I knew that she had recently opened a high-end fashion boutique on Avenue Louise near the European Commission. I believe she sold expensive handbags and well-made leather goods like belts and wallets. She was making quite a name for herself. At present she was waiting for her flight in the silent inferno that is the boarding area, and I felt somehow drawn to her.

Perhaps it was her perfume. I could smell it as I approached: Chanel No. 5, but beneath a scent all her own. She was looking at me out of the corner of her eye I thought, though I did not have much time to ponder it, as soon after I joined her my attention was distracted by a group of marathon runners who had arrived in the airport and were being very noisy. They must have been Boston marathon competitors on their way to the States too. I had noticed Patricia watching me before I had drawn closer; she was sizing me up as women are wont to do.

I began rummaging through my bag and that is when she turned to me. "Brown," she said softly. Her voice was vulnerable and her eyes alert. "Did you study at Brown?" she asked, her voice suddenly conspiratorial.

"I did my postdoc there," I said. "I am on my way to New York for a conference."

"I see," said the woman. She had a piquant face with coquettish eyes. "I went to Brown myself. I'm Patricia."

She was trying to cut off a little loose thread from her Miu Miu wool coat while I was staring at her crème Louboutin fuck-me heels.

"It was love at first sight," she said, her heels so high that she seemed to be sitting on tip-toes. "Isn't that what you want to ask me about? What happened in Boston?"

I followed the line of her legs with my eyes. Her own eyes were drawn to a tall well-dressed man who was just then walking past us. He was a European, my guess was Italian, and I noticed how her gaze rested on his expensive loafers and his large hands and feet. When she looked at me again, an innocent smile had settled upon her face. "Everlasting love," she said.

Just then, the gate attendants announced that the flight to New York was boarding, and Patricia followed me to the gate where we learned that we had both been upgraded to first class. This was an infrequent occurrence, which I attributed to the expensive air that hovered around this strange and new creature.

"I was waiting in the lobby of the Revere Hotel when I met him," Patricia continued. We were now boarded on the plane, seated next to one another. She said that she was afraid of heights and asked my opinion on whether she should sit next to the window. Her eyes were pleading. I suggested against it. "That's where I was when I met Khalid, I mean, the man who blew up the Prudential building."

Yes, that was the part of the story most people knew.

After the stewardess had given her the San Pellegrino she asked for, she said: "I had no intention of sleeping with him, although he was my type. He had that year-round tan that Middle Eastern men have. He was an Arab, born in the United States, but of course you already knew that. I could see that he was well-built under his Ralph Lauren shirt when he walked in, and he had those full lips that I love."

When Patricia's attention was directed away for a moment, I could not help but look for a reflective surface to take a glance at myself.

"Khalid was what us girls from Brown call a keeper. That means we date them for a year or so before we move on to the next guy. Of course, I had already started taking clients by then. That part is true."

Looking at Patricia, she had the sort of easy manner that people have who have always had money. In fact, this was not true of Patricia. She was the sort of woman who could engage in a conversation about mergers and acquisitions even though her grandfather had been a mere laborer, tapping rubber trees in the rain forest.

"People always ask me where I'm from," she said. "I was born in the United States, but my grandparents were from Brazil. I'm third generation. There are a lot of Brazilians in Massachusetts, the Boston area. I'm one of them." I thought I heard a nostalgic sigh then. "My parents had a restaurant and I used to work there nights when I was a girl. I always knew I would go to college though, and I always wanted to go to Brown."

"Did you always know you would enter this line of work?" I asked.

"I didn't go to Brown University so I could spread my legs for money, if that's what you mean." She laughed. "My full name is Patricia Patricio, by the way. Everyone calls me Tricia."

"That isn't what I meant," I said with a soft politeness, at least I thought so.

"I know," Tricia said. "I'm not in that line of work anymore. I won't ask if you've been to my shop, as you are a man, but perhaps you have a wife or girlfriend. She might like it, or you might pick up something for her. We sell expensive leather goods. Our handbags are particularly well-regarded because they have an old-fashioned flair to them, at least that is what I am told. But we also sell wallets, belts, things like that. We even sell leather saddles. Mostly because they sort of arrest your attention when you walk into the shop. They give the shop a certain flair and they are very expensive. A gaucho from Argentina stopped by the other day for a saddle. He was in Europe for a polo tournament. He was nice, very nice. He also bought a handbag for his wife, a Frenchwoman."

Patricia herself was carrying a Celine bag, a little yellow thing. And I could see the Brazilian in her: in the sun-kissed skin and the easy uprightness of her body, like tall uncut stalks of sugar cane. It was as if I was marooned with her in this field and the other passengers were those stalks of cane.

"Khalid approached me," Patricia continued. She playfully pushed her feet up onto her tiptoes and knocked her lovely knees together. They were smooth and fragrant, and she was not wearing stockings. "I was waiting for a man called Mr. Warrington and Khalid claimed to be a member of his staff. Lies, lies, lies."

There she was, sizing me up again. Tricia went on with her tale and I closed my eyes for a moment. When I opened them, she was telling me how she had arrived at Boston South Station from Providence that evening, a misty night in November. She had felt the cold air pushing her to the station, but she had not thought much of it then. The client she was to meet was swimming in it, so she awaited him expectantly.

I was not a prostitute or a call-girl. Mr. Warrington was what you would call a sugar daddy and I was his sugar baby. I tried to make him happy, and I believe I was good at it.

In reality, I needed these men, and I thought of them as sugar men, pouring their sugar all over me, leaving me happy and fulfilled. And I was happy. They paid off my student loans, but they also paid for my trips to Aspen, Los Angeles for shopping, Milan, or any other place I wanted to go. At our last meeting, Mr. Warrington had purchased a real Cartier watch for me. I still have it, but this, this is a

Chopard. On that November day, a day before Thanksgiving, I was giddily awaiting a weekend jaunt to Burlington, Vermont with Mr. Warrington, but I was a little tense too.

I was such a young girl back then. You don't really know what it means to be that age until it's gone. It was only six years ago but I have changed so much since then, at least I think so. He was a man and I was just a girl. But I needed his money. I wanted it. It was a beneficial relationship for us both. I had met with Mr. Warrington a few times before, and he was a good client, but then Khalid showed up. He had these big puppy dog eyes.

It goes without saying that I wasn't expecting him. Mr. Warrington was supposed to pick me up after his golf game in Newport. He had a house there. The Revere Hotel was easy to find from the station. It was even doable on foot.

I was the only guest sitting in the lounge, that's when this physical presence comes jaunting in. That's how I think of him, this sort of physical element appearing suddenly. And, he had this warm complexion, like a thousand summer days in Bahia, and this strong build. Well, what was a girl to do? I was looking at him with x-ray eyes. I saw him naked, lying on the bed. Perhaps waking up beside me.

Yes, I liked the idea of him. At first he didn't seem to be approaching me, but suddenly he was there. He offered me a drink. "Oh, Tricia, there you are," he said. Needless to say, I was taken aback.

All I could do was stare at him. "So you made it," he said. "I didn't think you would dare." I didn't know him, none of my clients were that young.

I asked him if we knew each other from somewhere and he said no, but then he said: "I am here to know you now. Mr. Warrington isn't coming. He had a stroke this morning."

I was in a panic. It was hard to find a client like Warrington. I also felt some apprehension. I had become used to this man's money and I kept thinking what I would do if I suddenly didn't have it. There was a girl that I lived with who had these brown leather Prada boots that came all the way up to mid-knee and I wanted a pair. I needed a pair. I had been hoping Mr. Warrington would give me the money, on top of the money he usually sent. But then I was suddenly afraid.

I should have known something was up as Mr. Warrington hadn't been answering my messages, but that had happened before. But I was afraid, somehow afraid of this man, this Middle Eastern man. I was afraid of him physically, but I was also worried about what he knew. Had he heard the messages we had sent to one another, Warrington and I? The sweet nothings? God, I hate that term – sweet nothings – but that's what they were. We were literally saying nothing to one another. What could I say to an old man and what could he say to a young intelligent girl from Brown?

We had nothing to say to one another so the words we said were nothings. Well, I wondered if Khalid had seen these words. Had he seen any photos? What if he knew about the dating site?

Mr. Warrington had two chauffeurs that I had met, and this man wasn't one of them. I didn't know much about Mr. Warrington's work, something to do with missiles and computers. He always seemed concerned about the wars overseas, especially in Afghanistan. Perhaps this man was an employee, but I hadn't met him before. I wondered if he was real. Of course he was, but what purpose would he serve in my life?

Well, Khalid, that was his name, he seemed pleased that I was taken aback.

"Don't worry, baby," he said. "I'll take care of everything."

"So you're his messenger," I noted.

"I wouldn't say I was his messenger, Trish. I am part of Mr. Warrington's security staff and I had a day free. He always talks about you and I was a little curious."

No, that last part wasn't it. He said: "I wanted to do this for the big boss. I thought I should. Once he's better, he'll reward me."

All I could muster was a pathetic: "Really?"

Khalid sat down next to me. I was sitting on a sofa in this lounge, this brown leather sofa that matched the warm wood paneling of the walls. The sofa had those shiny metal pins in it, to keep the leather down. It was very masculine that room. These expensive places were

Falling

all so masculine and young girls like me just loved it. And I had been sitting there when the most masculine thing of all stepped in, this Khalid.

So after all that talk Khalid sat all of a sudden next to me. I could smell his cologne, Fahrenheit by Dior. It was the same cologne that Mr. Warrington used to wear. All I could do was stare at this man's hands: they were large and had thick veins running down to the fingers. He had bruises on his knuckles, like a fighter, but they were beautiful hands: beautiful and strong.

And masculine. Yes, that too. Khalid wanted to book a room for the weekend and I whispered "Yes." My defenses were down. He was the sort of man I had fantasies about as I spent evenings with these men. Sometimes I pictured the soft touch of dollar bills falling on my body and other times I pictured a man like this. Now the opportunity had arisen. I didn't see any reason not to go with him if it was true that Mr. Warrington had a stroke. It was a once in a lifetime chance, and I was young and silly.

I grabbed my purse, a little black bag from Chanel, and just as we were approaching the elevator, Khalid said: "Let's go for a walk. Downtown Boston is beautiful in the fall," and it was true so I said yes. We walked around Boston like we had been lovers for years. At one point, we stopped in front of the Prudential Building and he just stared. "A real gem," he said. "An architectural beauty."

We went down Tremont Street and that's when he told me: "It's getting late. We should get back."

I had been enjoying myself but I was looking forward to that night. I wondered what his body smelled like, if he would like my body too.

We went back to the Revere and we soon reached the elevator. I got a notification on my phone and I said: "Khalid, is this from Mr. Warrington?" But the elevator had come. Khalid pulled me in and started kissing me passionately. My response was equally passionate. I was excited and ready. We reached the room he booked, which was near the elevator. I was standing behind Khalid as he pushed the key into the hole. I had slipped an arm around his powerful waist. No love handles there. I slipped my hand under his shirt and could feel the tough scratch of the hair of his abdomen. They were like so many little knives stabbing my forearm.

There was a bottle of Veuve Clicquot in the room that Khalid uncorked. The champagne foam got everywhere and I laughed. "It's the real French stuff," he said. He sounded a little common then, but I would wait until tomorrow to think about that.

"Have you ever had this before?" he asked.

He went off to the little kitchenette to get two glasses. Once he had a pair, he began pouring the champagne. "To us," he said. There was no thought of Mr. Warrington then. Our glasses clinked and we peered into each other's eyes. Mine are a dark green though people often think they are brown. After that, I returned to my phone where I discovered that Mr. Warrington had not put any money in my bank account like he usually did. Something was up. I don't know if it was the champagne or that I had not had much to eat that day, but I suddenly felt very faint. Vertigo, like the room was spinning, but I was also very happy.

I fell asleep, let's just say that, and when I woke up it was Sunday morning. My watch was on top of the end table beside the bed, and the time said it was well after 11 in the morning. That was when I heard the sirens. I had slept right through them. Sirens and even the voices of people on the street, though we were on a high floor. And then there were more sirens and more sirens. They were so profuse that I began to distinguish between the police siren sounds and the fire brigades. I remembered the previous night. I turned around and laid an arm where Khalid had been, to touch him, but my arm fell on an empty bed. I was alone.

"Khalid?" I whispered.

I went into a panic, that hysterical panic like when you lose your wallet. Something wasn't right. I decided to go outside and I got dressed. I was wearing a thin white chemise and this flashy coat: I was one of those pretty girls you see all dressed up and doing the walk of shame after a night out. Walking out of the hotel, I saw what had happened all over the news. The Prudential Building had been

Falling

blown up. I walked back to South Station and I was bombarded with story after story. It was all over the TVs in the stores, people were talking about it in the street and in the cafes. The waiters were listening to the reports on the radio. I began to piece it all together from all the TVs, and I knew that it was Khalid that had done it.

"Oh my god," I whispered. I must have looked ready to faint because an old woman approached me and asked if I was all right.

I didn't answer, and that's when I saw it. On one of the TVs they were showing CCTV footage they said had been be taken of the suspect from the night before. The suspect was said to have spent the night with a mystery woman. The image was of Khalid and me getting into the elevator at the Revere Hotel. Stupid. I just couldn't believe how stupid I had been. The footage was too blurry to see my face, but I was even wearing the same faux fur coat by Vera Wang that I had bought at Bergdorf's as I was walking through the streets of Boston. I was wearing it as I was watching myself on the television. "Well, so much for Tricia," I thought. Scatter my ashes at Bergdorfs. I am sure you know that line.

Stupid or not, now was the time to pull it together. I went back to the hotel and the police met me in the lobby. They asked me my name and if I had been staying in Room 311. I said that I had been. That was the room that Khalid booked. They wanted to take me to the station for questioning just like in the movies. Really, they wanted my statement. I don't think they suspected anything then. So I was waiting at the station for them to take me into that little room they use to intimidate people and that's when it happened. I started to cry.

The police didn't seem too interested in me at first; it seemed like they just wanted to take the statement and move on with the investigation, but as they were speaking to me it became clear that they were suddenly interested. They seemed to believe that I had known about the attack beforehand and they suggested that I should have told someone. But I hadn't known, how could I have? I told them I had never met Khalid before. I was waiting for some friends from Brown, which was a lie. Somehow they never verified that part of the story. I told them that I did spend the night in his room, but only that night, and when I woke up he was gone. The officers wanted to arrest me on a conspiracy charge. Fortunately, one of my clients was an attorney in New York, a big-time firm down on Water Street. His surname was first on the list of partner's names in the firm, you know what I mean? I immediately got in touch with him, and he had one of his attorneys sent over to the station. So this lawyer paints me as a young girl from a good school who got caught up with the wrong guy. I was in over my head. I was from a poor section of Boston, a charity case for a fancy school like Brown.

It worked, but when I got back to Brown I was shunned for a time, especially by that bitch with the Prada boots. I still bought a pair, and I wore them in front of her, with my Vera Wang coat. And I made sure that before I left for Providence I went back to the hotel to get the Chopard watch that I had left there.

I looked at Tricia then. She looked at me too.

"Someone very special gave me that watch," she said.

The plane had some turbulence after that, and the seatbelt light popped on along with the characteristic ding. The passengers shuffled back to their seats, occasionally bumping into Tricia on the way, and she continued her story in hushed tones.

The case was still going on, even after I was back at school at Brown. The professors droned on in their endless sophistry and we all pretended to listen. Some of us really were listening and others of us were not. I remember there was this tall guy with rich parents in my sociology class. When I came into the large lecture hall, all eyes were turned on me but I was looking around for him. I found him. He wasn't at all like Khalid, but he had that masculine energy too. He was wearing a shirt and skinny tie by Ralph Lauren and Burberry tweed trousers. I wanted to be a wife and he seemed like husband material, but I think I was off limits then. With all the talk going on, there was something dangerous about me. I was a girl gone wrong. But I still paid attention in my classes, if you can believe that of a call girl. Fortunately, Brown is sort of a finishing school for the rich, as you well know, and I was able to deal with frequent trips to Boston and reporters and still graduate on time. I took a full course load and

I still had time to go out once in a while, though it became harder with all of the attention. The trial came and went, but the reporters, they never quite went away. In fact, even now I still deal with them.

The reporters became really bad when I started doing the talk show circuit. I'm sure you must have seen me once or twice. I remember vividly one show I did here in Europe, in fact, this is how I ended up in Brussels. I did a show and the host, if you can believe it, kept asking me these leading questions, implying that I was part of some Arabian sex trafficking ring. He was going on about Middle Eastern princes, yachts, Dubai, Brunei. I don't know. All of these things I knew nothing about. I was really in over my head. I needed help and I didn't have anyone to help me. I had been prepared to be asked about bombs, conversations, people that I had never met, but not that.

If I handled that show poorly, it didn't seem to make a difference. Newspapers began to offer me money for my side of the story. The bombing of the Prudential Building was really big news. There was a fire, people jumping out of the building, all that. By that time I wasn't seeing my rich men friends anymore. It was too risky. Most of these men like to stay out of the spotlight. Most of them didn't even like it when I used their names on the phone or in texts. I used to have code names for them like Mr. Big, Aquaman, or Big Spender. But that was all in the past. I missed them. I missed their money. I was now in Europe doing the talk show circuit and men started to follow me. I mean, follow me around town, when I went on my shopping trips. Many of these guys were Middle Eastern men, convinced that I had a particular interest in them, based on the stories. You know how people are. Although I was frightened and I didn't like being followed, I was somehow enlivened. These men knew somehow.

"He was a rough, violent man," I had said on one of the shows about Khalid. "He had these big hands, like the type a strangler would have. Or a rapist."

The audience would gasp at those kinds of comments, and my stock went up. I would be booked on another show and I would say: "Khalid had the face of a monster, a killer. I could tell that he was dangerous, that he had the capacity to kill. But I was scared. He never told me anything, I just wanted to get away."

These men who followed me had heard all this, and I guess they thought I was a woman who just needed the right man. I needed a good screw and they were just the man for the job. I had said how violent and rough Khalid was on the show, and I had told the police the same story. I told them how Khalid had roughly grabbed onto my black hair, dragged me to the bed and pinned me down.

I continued doing the talk show circuit. I eventually opened my boutique and I started to be invited to talk about that, but the hosts always manage to bring up what happened in Boston. About Khalid. I suppose he is sort of a celebrity too, in his own way.

There was something frenetic and charged in the way that Tricia spoke. Sometimes she spoke very quickly as if she needed to get all the words out at once, and she frequently placed a hand on my leg or rubbed my shoulder. She would smile as she did this, and I could not help but smile too. She would frequently lean in close. It seemed she wanted me to want her, or at least wanted me to be under her influence, and I was.

I began comparing myself to Mr. Warrington and even to Khalid; perhaps it is natural for a man to do this, for us to see ourselves purely in relation to other men. That is the animal in us, I suppose. But in being an animal, perhaps I was not alone.

I wondered what she thought about how I was dressed. She said she had pictured Khalid under his clothes; did she picture me as well? I wondered what she saw there, what she thought. I had become the anonymous male.

"I ask myself what will become of me," Patricia said. "Will I spend the rest of my days as a shopkeeper, even if it is a high-end shop? That's a surefire way to end up penniless. You must agree with me there. What do you think?"

I chuckled softly, but I smiled. "I don't know," I said. "You have plenty of time to figure it all out."

"I don't think I do," she said. "Time goes by so fast. Boston seems like it was only yesterday, but it was six years ago. I will be an old woman soon enough. A spinster."

"No one uses the word spinster anymore," I remarked. "Fifty is the new thirty."

"Perhaps."

"I have just one question for you?" I ask. "Who was Aquaman?"

Tricia laughed, a slow one as if she had told this story many times before. She childishly took my San Pellegrino and finished the drink. "That was Mr. Spencer, a man with a very long yacht and very deep pockets. He had a house, a compound, up in Maine, not to mention his own island in the Bahamas. He was one of my favorites."

The plane came to a stop after that. Tricia glanced around, looking very claustrophobic with her wide-open doe eyes. She rubbed a hand on her white neck. I saw then her manicured fingernails, painted a dark color, like purple or black, and her Chopard watch.

PERSONAL EFFECTS

The driver must have lost his way. The road began off the interstate but then had weaved through houses scattered around a creek where a disused mill still stood; then the road had circled through to the town, casting behind us a view of the blue absence that we had just come through. The houses around the mill were separated from the town by a field that was flat, treeless, and which seemed without a purpose. It appeared blue in the sideways light from the neon streetlamps. Then the driver drove the pickup down the derelict main road, his snow tires digging through the heaped salt on the road and the remains of the snow. Most of the snow on the roads had summarily melted but there was another storm on the way. After stopping to talk to a man he knew at the intersection, the driver pulled the pickup up to the hotel, only it was the wrong hotel. He told me that we were there so I should pay, but I told him that he had brought me to the wrong place. This hotel had a different name and sat in the center of town. My hotel overlooked the shore. But eventually we made it to the right hotel, the one I had booked, and when we reached it the driver was smiling. I was smiling too. I barely noticed the man wearing the fox mask watching us.

 The front desk man closed and locked his office and led me to my double room after he had checked me in. I figured they couldn't get many guests here if he was able to do that. We took a long, drab hall to reach the stairs, passing along the way a courtyard that had sulci as from rivulets that had dried and covered with grass. There were only a pair of trees and they seemed to retreat from the space like curious, naughty ducklings. I told the man that I had come into town to visit my girlfriend's father. "Where's she?" he asked, and I told him that she was on her way. She should arrive by tomorrow afternoon. He gave me a knowing look, as if he understood what it meant to have a day away from one's girlfriend, and he said, "Remind me of your name again?" In case he got any calls for me. Sometimes calls came to the front desk.

"Nate Anderton," I said.

When I got inside the room, I set down my large camping bag and removed the small cedar box that I had brought from Harvard. My father had died a short time ago in the Cayman Islands, and the medical examiner there had sent me a box that he had been promising to send for weeks. The most present thing about the box was its scent. It had retained its new cedar scent onboard the however many planes it had taken to get from the Cayman Islands to Cambridge, Massachusetts. This is the scent that comes from the way woodcutting machines tightly and evenly grind the wood. Wood that has been cut with hand saws is generally less fragrant.

To the top of the box had been taped a square of lined paper that read: "A. Anderton: Goods, Personal Effects, etc." I unlatched the box, which swung open mischievously. Within were a blue tie with camel figures, cuff links, a pair of teeth, a ticket and a Piaget watch. The purpose of the ticket was to notify the holder of a safe at the Bank of the Cayman Islands that contained in excess of $450,000 as well as other things like jewelry, papers, etc. The items in the box were consistent with what I had heard: that my father had suffered a heart attack while cooking in his house in the Caymans.

In spite of the twin beds and the two dressers, the room seemed bereft of contents. A large window that overlooked the hotel courtyard loomed along one wall. The window was open a crack. The only other item on that wall was a painting of men and women hunting on horseback. They all wore black riding caps. After I set the box down, I glanced out this window and saw a strange image in the distance.

It was the image of a fox's head. It appeared to be a mask that a child would wear to a party; perhaps someone had left it on the grass. It had ears that were high sloping triangles, an orange face, and a fleshy, inhuman mouth.

"That hurts," I heard a woman say through the thin walls of the old hotel, interrupting my thoughts.

I heard some shuffling and then the woman said: "No, don't do that. Those are my stockings. I just bought them yesterday." There was something weak, vulnerable in her voice.

But then the woman laughed and I turned toward the sound of it as it bled through the walls. There was a bang, as of a man banging his knee against the table as he stands up, and when I turned back to the window I saw that the image of the fox's head now rest atop a man's body. It was a man wearing a mask. He was very near. The man was dressed in an immaculate wax coat and stood only a few feet away from the open window.

The lawn in front of the hotel was littered with foxholes. The foxes came and went but were never seen. Pris remarked on them as we waited for the front desk man to notice us, but I didn't think a foxhole was different from any other hole you'd find in the ground and I didn't attach any importance to them.

But Pris had already forgotten about the holes by the time we reached the room. She had gotten the extra set of hotel room keys that she wanted. She hung her faux fur coat in the closet and kicked her black riding boots into a corner. She was wearing a black Alexander McQueen pantsuit that hugged her figure tightly. Her hair was swept back in a bun. Her feet made a cute slap on the wood floor as she walked into the bathroom, and when she turned and rested her eyes on me her pupils were dilated. She fumbled in her clutch for her lighter. "My lighter's in here somewhere." she said.

I leaned back on the bed that I had sat on and sighed. I didn't want to meet Pris's father. I didn't want to meet any girl's father, but for Pris I had made an exception.

"It's pretty here," she said from the bathroom. "In this hotel. How did you find it?"

"It was the last hotel on the list I looked at on that website. And they had the best pictures."

"You'll get along with my father," said Pris. Her voice was provocative and precise, and I thought it sounded like that of a woman handling things deftly in her hands.

"Oh, I don't know about that, babe."

"He's old-fashioned, but in a good way. He's like a character from a movie. One of those old movies where the character's say things like, 'Look here, see. You're gonna put all the money in the bag, see.' Only he doesn't say things like that. You know what I mean? It's just that he has that old timey sort of accent, like Humphrey Bogart."

After Pris had lit her cigarette, she came and sat on the bed next to mine. I didn't know why she had to go to the bathroom just to light a cigarette. Her dark hair was almost black and with it up the jutting angles of her face were evident. She blew rings of smoke at me.

"God, that woman," she said. "Can't you hear her through the walls?"

Pris leaned forward a bit as she sat and her breasts separated slightly in her blouse. The breasts were a sixteenth birthday present from Pris's father and they had been so expertly done that it was impossible to see the surgical scars. That's because the scars were under the armpits.

"I'll have to thank your father later," I whispered.

"For what?"

"Oh, nothing."

"Anyway, that woman, she never stops."

When Pris was done with her cigarette, she put it out on an ashtray. Then she pulled out her compact and examined her teeth. She had lovely teeth: long, vulpine canines that formed a perfect symmetry with her long oval face.

That woman laughed again, the woman next door. She laughed like laughter was something you did to attract men. She laughed like she was trying to draw the foxes out of their holes. I imagined the woman sitting in a room that was much like ours: a grand space with two full beds spaced wide apart, two end tables, a small dining table, a tall mirror, and cheaply papered walls. But in her room there were bottles of Absolut and chardonnay. In her room there was also the bite of her Estée Lauder perfume as well as the musky scent from her body. Even though it was 8:30PM, the woman had just woken up. She hadn't bathed yet, and her legs and stockings still had their scent from yesterday. She was wearing her fur coat, like Pris's only hers was real mink. The woman sat while the men mostly stood. One of the men was sitting on the bed.

"Nate, I need to go back to the car," said Pris, fumbling through her purse again. "I left my Oxy bottle in there."

"Sure thing, babe," I said, and I handed Pris the keys to the Saab. They were her keys and she had asked me to hold them.

She wasn't gone long. When Pris came back, she was rattling the Oxy bottle in her hands. She handed it to me to open because she couldn't get past the child safety lock. She was silent for a time, but then she said: "God, I can't take her."

"Who?"

"The woman in the room next door."

She told me that she'd seen the woman on the way back from the Saab. The woman's door was open a crack and she could hear all the men in there. Pris said she had seen at least two men in the room, maybe three. The woman was laughing about something; she just never stopped.

"I think she must be a prostitute," Pris said.

"It's none of our business, babe," I offered. "Which bed do you want?"

"I want the bed farthest from that wall," she said. "I don't want to hear her all night.

The predominant sound in the office was of things fretting against the window and the sterile whiteness of the space countervailed my initial impression of Pris's father as a man who was very much entangled in an anachronistic time. His donnish grin when he spoke sprung from politeness. His eyes glared at you, which you didn't notice because of the gentlemanly manners. The office had the heft of a mid-sized apartment. The white floors shot up to white walls,

Falling

and the scattered, dismembered bodies of machines stood in stark contrast to the regularity of all else in the room.

When Pris and I entered her father's office, we saw that bottles of Saint-Bris Sauvignon and Orvieto had been sat upon the desk. The desk was like a 'C', being only tops and sides, so the skeletal legs of Pris's father in their gray trousers were visible to us. Pris's father wore a white lab coat though by Pris's report he was more than five years retired from Yale. There, he had been the chair of mechanical engineering. I didn't know what engineers needed white coats for.

"That's my favorite picture," Pris's father said, pointing to a photo on the wall. It showed an older man, himself, rubbing petroleum-based emollients onto a gigantic pump.

"Then we have those other photos," he went on. "That's a picture of me rubbing sunscreen on Priscilla's back in Montauk one summer. That's a picture of me when I received that lifetime achievement award in Denmark. That one's of Priscilla and me in Nice for the races."

"Monte Carlo," said Pris. "That one was from Monte Carlo. Remember, you wanted to race in the Longines Summer Invitational but it was too late to register?"

"You're right, darling."

From two hooks on the wall, the man had hung his olive green waxed cotton jacket and his fox mask.

"But things change," said Pris's father. "Priscilla left for Harvard as a gangly waif and now returns as a lovely girl with a gangly waif of a boyfriend. I think Priscilla is just swell."

I ignored the contumely and said: "I think she's swell too."

I didn't look at her as I said it.

"Daddy, don't be silly," said Pris finally. "Nathaniel is one of the good ones. He's not one of those you need to scare off talking like that. Like the others. Besides, he's not a gangly waif at all."

"I'm not trying to scare anyone off. I was only making a colorful remark."

After uncorking the Sauvignon, the man poured three glasses. He produced a cigarette from a gold cigarette case that he had been carrying. The gold case was gypsyish in the blare of the white office. It fought against the mechanical idea as argued by the haphazardly placed machine carcasses. Pris removed her red lighter from her black clutch and lit the cigarette. When she had finished with her lighter, she set the red thing on the surface of the table.

"You promised to quit," she said archly.

"I'll quit when you do," Pris's father remarked quickly. "This is a strange part of Connecticut," he said, resting his gaze on me. "This has always been a mill town but it didn't start to boom until about one hundred and fifty years ago. That's when everything abruptly changed. Most of the old traditions have died, but Priscilla wouldn't know anything about that."

"I have no idea what you're talking about," said Pris, looking away prettily.

"But Priscilla doesn't need to know everything. She's happy thinking only of Harvard parties, Jamaica Plain, and where her next pill bottle will come from. I never meet any of her friends."

The man was staring intently at me. The color of his eyes couldn't be made out because his thick glasses caught the glare from the overhead lights in the room.

"I don't bring people back to meet Father," Pris admitted. "And I certainly don't bring back men."

Pris looked at the metal parts on the floor and I thought she wondered what they made when they were all put together. Perhaps they didn't make anything and that's why they had been scrapped.

Pris didn't make any remark at her father's mention of pills and I looked at her. We were sat in two fragrant wood chairs across from her father's desk and she kept her legs crossed. She was mostly silent and nonplussed. Her white dress had a feathery sheath of a jacket that covered her shoulders. It was rare that she looked at me. She had this way of not looking at you, the way a duck or a swan doesn't look at you, and it was hard to know if this not looking stemmed from a lack of interest or if she tried deliberately to keep you in the dark as regarded her. She had lit a cigarette for herself too, and when she smoked it she blew out rings of mystification around herself and others. At times when I spoke to her I couldn't make her out because of the smoke hiding her face.

Pris's smoke couldn't obfuscate her father. The resemblance between father and daughter was more one of manner than of feature. Pris's manner of speaking was easy, but I could see now that she also had some of her father's superiority. Her chin pointed up ever so slightly and she sort of looked down her nose at you.

Pris stood up, looked at her platinum Blancpain watch and said: "I think I'll continue my cigarette outside."

Her father looked at her sweetly. "You do that."

Pris put on her coat and my eyes fell on the table, where Pris was forgetting her red lighter. It occurred to me that if she needed another cigarette she would have to return for it, or use the butt of the old cigarette to light the new one like old people do.

Pris's father smiled darkly and said: "It's good of you to come. I think it's good of you to date Priscilla too. Priscilla has this reserve that comes from losing her mother when she was a girl. A girl needs a mother, but I never remarried. I had no intention of marrying again. I suppose Priscilla's always been a lost cause."

"She's a beautiful girl."

"But she's like her mother. She has the makings of a slut. I think you're attracted to girls like that, Nathaniel. You can sort of tell when a girl is like that, I bet. That's the sort of girl you go after. The girl with the whorish nature lurking just below the surface, like a duck ready to have ducklings with any stray male. Just anyone. Priscilla is still a duckling herself now."

"I love her."

"No, you don't. You're being ridiculous. She beguiled you. And when she's done with you she'll move on to the next fornication. She's like her mother, moving from one fornication to the next. Of course, the question becomes whether the duckling is worth saving."

"I don't understand your meaning."

"You see, at this juncture, you know Priscilla better than I do. She's very thin. That's from the coke, isn't it?"

"OxyContin. Pris doesn't do coke."

"What do you think of her?"

I told him that I loved Pris and that I wanted to see more of her. And when he again broached the idea of whether the duckling merited salvation, I said: "It does, yes."

The town occupies a finger between the woods and the ocean. It has the sullen houses of a Connecticut mill town and the blank stares of people who know everything. It was once a one-street town before it became a suburb just like most of Connecticut has become a suburb, but it hasn't changed its character. Most people who come from outside stay for a year but not longer than that. You've come to this town because you've heard that it's a good stopping point to look out onto the shore and because it is known for its hotels. There is an odd hotel here that a woman named Zelda stayed at, the wife of an infamous writer, but many of the other hotels have been pulled down. The woman stayed here before she went mad. You've also come here because the place is close to the interstate and your girlfriend's father lives just outside of the town. This town is surrounded by woods and gaps between the woods, and littering the gaps between the woods are the holes. Animals emerge from the holes at night. The animals were once culled but they aren't anymore as the hunters have all died.

The town has a square like a giant pit right in the center of it. All of the main buildings in the town face the square but it is soulless, like something isn't there anymore. In former times something took place in the square but it doesn't take place any longer. At times the residents of the town all gather in the square. They stand and stare at its open space for a while and then they walk away. The only sound that can be heard behind them is the clang of the cobbler who still repairs shoes in the old way. He can take the sturdy leather boots that you've worn for ten years and put new Vibram or Dainite soles on them so they appear good as new. At times the hoot of the express train from Boston to New York can be heard but it only hoots if another train blocks it.

The hotel where Zelda stayed has the best view of the shore. The front of the hotel and the hotel parking lot overlook the ocean, which is usually still except for when the storms come. In the past,

Falling

the storms swept over the land and flooded the town, but then the residents built wooden embankments. The wooden embankments were built in colonial times and were replaced with stone during a war. You've heard that the stone embankments are the primary attraction of the town. The town has lost its place as an important source of lumber and paper, but the stone embankments still remain as do the descendants of the people that first settled the town. These people stand and stare at the square but they don't remember why.

The woman in the hotel room next to ours had been murdered, and when Pris and I returned to our room we were met by a detective who questioned us about our dealings with her. He was a youngish man whose trousers were a few sizes too big. His white collared shirt was baggy and one leg of it was sticking out of his beltline under his jacket. He scribbled in a notepad as uniformed men hovered outside in the hall. The farther reaches of the hall had been blocked by yellow police tape. The detective asked us if we knew the woman who was murdered and whether anything strange had happened that we had seen. Neither of us knew the woman. That is, we had neither spoken to her nor been introduced. Pris mentioned that we could hear talking and laughing through the walls, and she said that she had seen several men in the room the night prior. She denied that anything strange had happened, but admitted that she had heard some manner of thud late last night. "You wouldn't have heard it, Nate. You were asleep," she said.

This caught the detective's attention and he asked Pris: "Around what time did you hear the noise?"

"Around 11PM. Really it was closer to 11:15 because the show I was watching on my phone started at 11 and had been on for a little while."

"What sort of noise did you say it was?"

"It was a thud, like something falling on the floor. And then I heard a creaking sound."

"And how long did the creaking last?"

"For a few seconds. Less than ten seconds."

The detective left after that and I watched as Pris paced the room.

"The man at the front desk said the woman who was murdered had marks in her neck. Like something had bitten her," she said.

I saw when Pris walked over and opened the top drawer to the dresser, which was wide and stood conspicuously on the wall where the maw of the door was.

"This stuff wasn't here yesterday," she said.

She directed my attention to what sat inside the drawer, and I rose and joined her.

"It's a woman's watch and some teeth," I remarked. "A woman was probably staying here before and left them accidentally. A hunter. It's not a big deal."

"But those are human teeth. They might belong to the woman next door. The one who was murdered. And they were pulled because the root is still attached."

I told Pris that she didn't know that for sure and the right thing for us to do was to leave these things where they were and go to bed. Pris didn't say anything. She held her chin up a little and she looked at me ponderously but then glanced away. I regarded her as she changed out of her dress into her night clothes. She looked sylphlike in her gauzy white nightshirt with its wide belt. The wide belt washed her out. She had a cigarette, and when she was done she put it out and set her body down in her bed. She rest so airily that the stiff, ancient bed didn't let out a peep. Pris turned to face me then and I could see that she wanted to fuck, but it felt wrong as I wasn't sure if her father would be coming tonight to kill her or not.

A regular sound against the window in the night woke me. It was the sound of a branch fretting against the window but there were no trees in our part of the courtyard to do the fretting. There were other noises too but they fell glum onto the floor. I stepped out of the bed dressed solely in my boxers. The cold was biting as Pris and I had the misfortune of a room with a recalcitrant radiator, but I walked to the window. There I remembered how the shore weaved around a lip of land. The courtyard was beyond the window, and when I lifted up the clouded glass I saw Pris bolting frantically from one side of the space to another. She was near enough that I could see the pulsating artery

Falling

in her neck. As she ran, she clutched her head through her lovely dark hair with her hand and blood spilled through her fingers. There being no purpose for me, I shut the cloudy window and returned to bed, tripping over Pris's crème Jimmy Choos. I heard the slide of an Estée Lauder lipstick as it rolled off of the dresser and onto the floor, and atop the dresser I saw a red lighter and a woman's platinum watch by Blancpain.

BEHIND THE MASK

She was wearing Balenciaga boots and diamond earrings. I asked her if the earrings were from Van Cleef & Arpels and she said that they were. Her father had bought them in New York and had given them to her as a high school graduation present. He was a cardiologist. I could just picture her sleeping with all the boys in the dorm while wearing the teardrop diamonds her cardiologist father had given her. Perhaps she would just lose one of them, like in a Tennessee Williams play.

"I just want to thank you for bringing back my purse," she said.

She went on to tell me that her father had invented a new type of artificial valve, one that was very unlikely to form clots. Clots from the heart valves could travel to the brain and cause a stroke, she told me. Clots could also enter the venous circulation and travel to other parts of the body. Blah. Blah. Blah. I asked her if I could have her face and the answer was a curt "No."

I didn't take it personally. I had to admit that she was uncommonly beautiful and with that kind of beauty, self-assurance was sure to follow. Of course, it is a very great compliment when a woman admires the beauty of another. I think there must be a tinge to beauty that only a woman appreciates. A man either sees the physical attributes of the woman or the character, but a woman is able to see both at once, as if two separate dimensions had come to occupy the same space. I was certain there must be a law of physics that dealt with this. Some manner of quantum entanglement. Well, I knew this young woman possessed that rare beauty that indicates both perfection of form and purity of soul. She also had that infantile trust of others that children generally lose after the freshman or sophomore year of college. Perhaps this would be her undoing.

She asked me if I saw the storks conspiring in the park across the street from the cafe. I knew they were geese but I didn't tell her so. What I did tell her was that I was looking for a new apartment, which was true. I had been told the houses in the neighborhood were spacious and that I should have no problem finding a place with a large basement, which is what I wanted. We parted from one another, laughing at how we had both been so silly as to pick up the wrong purse at a party.

It was a short while later and I was knocking on the door of a house down the street from the cafe. It had a "For Rent" sign propped up in the window. The owner told me that a trio of Penn students was moving out in a week or two, as it was already May. He would have rooms available then. I could take one of the rooms or rent the whole house if I wanted. Although I wasn't working, I had money left over from an inheritance and I agreed to rent the house.

I thought the nicest part of the house was the front room because it had a large Victorian window that overlooked the street. I was sitting in this room when I first told Stan about the mask. Stan is short for Stanisław, which is a Polish male name. The room had a squat mustard-colored couch, which I had bought, and the television and telephone were by Bang & Olufsen.

"This is ridiculous," Stan said. This didn't bother me because Stan thought everything was ridiculous.

"But I have to do it," I told him.

"Why do you have to do it?"

"Because I do."

I knew that he would come around eventually and if he did not then I would find someone else. Stan was like an expensive coat that you wanted more than anything when you didn't have it, but after finally purchasing it you began to see it for what it was. It was just a coat. He was older than me and I had always thought of him as a sort of matrimonial prize, subconsciously, but I was beginning to see him in another light. Perhaps it was the change in setting. Perhaps I saw him through her eyes.

It was nice of the doctor not to keep me waiting long. He found me in the consultation room soon after I was announced by the receptionist. When I saw him, he was holding in his hands a sample of the fake skin that would be used for the mask. The skin had gossamer threads, like the underbelly of a spider's web. The doctor told me that the material could be altered to reflect any skin tone or shape.

"I'm glad that you came," the doctor said. "We only undertake this kind of project in very special cases. As you know, the cost of creating the mask is entirely covered by the laboratory. The subject does not have to worry about any of that. We only ask that you pay the small consultation fee if you are accepted as a subject."

"I understand," I said. "I only hope that you deem me to be a suitable candidate."

The doctor placed the skin sample in a tank of water by the window. There was a modern couch beside the tank and I was certain that it was an Erik Jorgensen because I tried to get one for the house. Stan talked me out of it because the couch would have to be shipped from Copenhagen.

"There is an important component of the mental state that I always discuss," the doctor said. "A facet of the mind. You see, I could give you everything you ask for and it still might not be enough. There are some individuals who will never be satisfied. Would you mind showing me your scar?"

I swept away a deep brown tail of my feathered hair. Wearing my hair this way was an old trick. The feathered hair hid the wrong side of my face. Sometimes I held the hair against my face to hide the wrong side. This was the left side of the face. I also learned to turn my head slightly when speaking to people, drawing their attention to my good side. At present, it was necessary to drop the parlor tricks. I held up the hair on the left side so the doctor could appreciate the long, thick scar that had paled from an enraged red to a less angry mother-of-pearl. It had been there more than ten years.

"How did it happen?"

I told the doctor that when I was a child in Poland I had been playing in my parent's house when I fell through a glass door. It was an accident. He nodded his head with what seemed to me like understanding.

"And the receptionist said you brought a picture with you?"

I had. It was a picture of a girl with long, lustrous hair. She looked like one of the girls from the front of the Revlon box. The box of hair dye. Her face was at once happy and proud. It is as if the young woman knows that she is pretty but doesn't want others to know that she knows. She's just thrilled with her new hair color. Thanks, Revlon. Now she can go down to the beach and fuck Chad or Tyler or Michael or whomever. And her nose, it's a cartoon nose: like Aurora from *Sleeping Beauty* or Bambi's mother. The girl in the picture has expressive, childlike eyes, like she's just waiting for the serial killer to capture her and she doesn't care.

"I wanted a small nose," I said. "I also wanted the eyes to be large and the forehead high and smooth. Like my own. My forehead is high like that. See?"

The doctor glanced at the picture that I gave him, an old Polaroid, then he glanced at me. The girl in the picture was pretty and delicate like a piece of Dresden porcelain. It seemed that if you dropped her she would shatter to pieces. I was similar though not the same. What the doctor thought as he looked at the picture and then at me would be known only to him, though I might guess at it. He wondered if the woman sitting in front of him would ever be satisfied with his creation. If she had the right sort of mind to be satisfied.

"My job is to restore that which is lost, not to create something anew," he said. "Although I am a surgeon who specializes in plastics and polymers, I am just as familiar with the mind as I am with molecules. I often meet subjects who want me to make them into something other than what they would've been had they not been in an accident. But my task is solely reconstructive. Someone who wants you to turn them into an entirely different person, some famous person, for example, well, that person would not be a good candidate. That person has a type of flaw that I cannot fix."

"I understand."

I thought I could hear the mask whipping about frantically in the fish tank beside the window.

"I'm not asking you to create someone new," I said. "My nose was broken during the accident and I know that it would have been smaller had the accident never occurred. See, my nose is enlarged," and I showed the doctor my face in profile so he could appreciate the bulbous tip of the nose and a wide bump on the upper bridge. "And I'm not showing you a picture of someone else, it's only me with some concealer. The mask would only cover my scar and restore the natural symmetry of my face. That is all I want."

"I see," said the doctor.

With that, the man rose from his chair and commenced to examine me. Using his nimble fingers, the doctor palpated my cheeks, focusing on my cheekbones. He also spent time on my chin and nose. Any pain that I felt was internal only; the doctor was very adept at his work. The pads of his fingers were soft and cold. Sterile. Then the doctor came to my scar. He bent down near to the skin and examined me closely, shifting his glasses to a better position with the tip of a finger. This unnerved me, this closeness, so I recited a mantra that I had learned as a child. It took me to a place far away, a foreign planet, Mars, where the trees had swaying trunks and their branches hungry mouths at the ends of them.

"Well, I think you would make a good subject," said the doctor when he was done. "I would like you to return tomorrow so that I can make a mold of the face and take some other measurements. It should only take about a half an hour."

He was smiling. He seemed quite pleased with himself.

I thanked the doctor and told him that I was glad to return tomorrow. I left the office with a joy that I hadn't felt in a long time.

Stanisław was waiting for me in front of the house.

"What are you doing?" I asked.

Falling

"We were supposed to meet for dinner at six, don't you remember? It's 6:08 now."

I told Stan that I had forgotten. I had an appointment and I forgot. I opened the door and suggested that he follow me inside. I made a pot of Ethiopian coffee in the kitchen and when I was done I carried two cups into the living room. There I found Stan sitting in one chair with his feet up in another.

"I saw the doctor today. He agreed to do it."

"You're crazy," said Stan. "How did you convince him? Really, you must be out of your mind."

"Perhaps you are out of your mind too."

"Well, did the doctor tell you anything?" Stan asked. "What did he say?"

"He told me that it was important to remove the mask every night."

"Well, that's obvious."

I reached into my purse and I showed him the picture. It was the Polaroid that I had shown the doctor an hour earlier.

"Where did you get this?"

"I found it," I said. "What do you care? You'll like me when I am beautiful. You'll see."

"And if I don't?"

"And if you don't then that's it. I'll find someone else. But you will, of course you will. Look at how the forehead flows seamlessly into the nose. See, Stan, you will love me then."

"Perhaps, but will you love yourself?"

"Now you sound like the doctor."

Stan laughed, a rare thing these days. We were only twenty-five and twenty-seven but we were already like an old couple. "You've created this elaborate fantasy for yourself and it will never come true," Stan was saying in his usual laconic manner. "The whole thing will come crashing down. Then what will you do?" When Stan was done saying this, he gave me a long, self-satisfied look.

At times I wondered if I had made a mistake in dating him but it's helpful to have a boyfriend. It sounds a little opportunistic, but a woman with a boyfriend might attract a better man. Somehow having a man gave this hypothetical woman a confidence she didn't have before. And considering my scar Stan was a catch. I was pretty, with magnificent Eastern European bone structure, but the human eye was trained to catch anomalies and other people always noticed my scar, no matter what lengths I might take to try and hide it. So Stan would have to do. For now. He had a good job as an assistant architect at a large and well-known architectural firm. He had gotten his bachelor's in Europe and his master's in architecture in New York. In fact, his credentials were impressive for someone his age. He had a good income and he was tall. He wasn't exactly what you would call handsome but there were enough good things about him that people usually said he was handsome anyway.

"Well, there is the luncheon at work tomorrow," Stan said. "You promised to come."

"I can't," I said. "I have to go back to the doctor's. He has to do a mold or something and then he'll get to work on the mask."

Stan shrugged and then he left without saying anything.

The doll was waiting for me in the doll's room. That's what I called the spare bedroom in the back of the house. The house was rather small: just big enough for two or three people. It had a front room, kitchen, and dining room on the first floor. And then there were two bedrooms on the second floor. One of these rooms I had set aside for my dolls. I had once had many antique dolls: fancy little girls with turn of the century miens. They had large heads and eyes that lolled about. They had small, pouty lips like a silent film star's. The hair was the most striking aspect of the dolls and at one time I had combed all their heads on a rotation schedule. At present, there was no need for a schedule. I had repaired all of the dolls and given nearly all of them away. They had been my orphans and they had all been broken at one time. They came to me that way. One was missing an ear, a few had chipped faces. One had a whole patch of hair that had been pulled out; this necessitated new hair to be sewn into the scalp. I had fixed each one of them on my own, teaching myself how to do it, and I was proud of my work. Now there was only one antique left.

I thought this particular doll was the most like me: a prissy thing with real human hair and gray-blue eyes. She was wearing a high-waisted, white Edwardian dress. This was Katarzyna. I had given away dozens of dolls and Katarzyna was the only one left. I couldn't bear to part with her. Besides, she wasn't finished.

I returned to the doctor's office on Tuesday and on Thursday they called me. My heart raced at the thought that the mask had already been completed but I soon discovered that the office had actually called about something entirely different. The receptionist was on the other end and she asked me to hold for the doctor.

"Hello, Ms. Dembrowska," the doctor said. "How are you? I'm sorry to call you, it's just there's a slight problem. I think you left the wrong check at the office on Tuesday. The name on this check is Małgorzata Stepska. You might have left it here by accident."

"Oh, no, Dr. Kyo. That's the right check. I had to transfer some money around so someone else had to cover me for the fee. I hope it is all right."

"Oh, I see," the doctor said. And then, after a pause: "It's fine, Ms. Dembrowska. I just wanted to confirm. Have a good day."

"And you as well, Dr. Kyo."

The first thing I bought was a pair of Balenciaga Knife Boots. They were over a thousand dollars and it was frivolous of me, but the mask made me feel like a new woman. The skin of the mask was translucent and it appeared even more so on my face. The material was so thin that after ten minutes I forgot I was wearing it. When I looked in the mirror, I saw that my forehead was high and aristocratic like I wanted and the area around the eyes had a seductive, feminine quality. Shortly before I picked up the mask, I had gone to the hairdresser's and dyed my hair chestnut brown so now my hair color was the same as the girl's in the photograph.

I didn't have to use tricks to hide my scar when I went to the shop to buy the boots. The workers were unusually kind and helpful. They were swept up in the storm of my beauty and I'm sure they assumed I was rich.

In fact, my financial situation was dire but I would deal with that later. There was no time to think about it now. As I walked back home, cutting through the Penn campus, I thought how far I had come. In Poland, I had been part of a program for young women scientists and I was already picturing how impressed the Penn students would be with my advanced knowledge of physics. I had been keeping up to date on advancements in quantum entanglement theory and I was sure that I knew more than the other students did. They would be baffled when this beautiful woman suddenly appeared who knew more than they did about everything. I hope you understand my meaning. I hadn't been accepted at Penn but *she* was a student there so I would take her place. That night I would fall asleep in my black Balenciaga Knife Boots, picturing their astonished faces.

Things were certainly falling into place, the only thing I had to think about was Stan. Should I dump him now or should I wait until I found someone else? Naturally, it would take time to find the right guy, I probably wouldn't find someone decent until well into the next year so it made sense to keep Stan around for the time being. I could keep our dates to the bare minimum to hide my changing feelings. The truth was that I could barely hide my growing repulsion.

"I'm too good for someone like Stan," I said to myself. I was walking into the doll's room.

I walked over to Katarzyna and took her into my hands. "What should I do?" I asked her. Although I rattled her gently, Katarzyna was defiantly silent. Even her gray-blue eyes seemed to be looking away. "Hm, what should I do?" I gave Katarzyna a wet, sloppy kiss on the cheek. She's very childish so she likes this.

Then I heard a voice clawing its way out of the basement.

"Ignore her," I told Katarzyna. "Look," I said, and I took my driver's license out of my purse. "That's me."

"Please," a distant voice cried from the basement. "Please!"

The girl was growing bold. I hadn't fed her in three days and she still had the energy to scream. I laughed and tossed Katarzyna onto the ottoman. Then I thought better of it and decided to take her with me.

"Please," said the voice again as I neared the basement doorway.

"Be quiet," I said as I slipped a key into the locked basement door. "You know better than that. I could stop feeding you altogether. Is that what you want?"

I had to descend the stairs slowly as the light could only be switched on at basement level. The last thing I wanted was to slip and rip the mask on the first day wearing it. The light switched on with a loud click. "Please," said the girl. With the light on, I could see that her hair was stuck to her face from several weeks' worth of dried sweat and blood. I drew closer to her so that she could get a better look at me.

"What did you do?" she whispered.

I thought this was a little melodramatic and I couldn't help but laugh. The laughter only seemed to anger her and she announced that there was no way I would get away with it. Ever. That's what she said. "You'll never, ever get away with it." I told her that I already had and I called her a silly bitch. Then I showed her the Polaroid. I told her that the girl was me and no one would be able to say otherwise. Ever. We were even the same height, give or take half an inch.

It was too miraculous to be a coincidence. We could have been sisters, mask or not. Even the doctor hadn't noticed that the woman in the photograph and the woman sitting in front of him were two different people. And the girl's parents were from Gdansk, where I was born. I reminded her of that, which was a mistake, as she then proceeded to go on and on about how her parents were sure to find her. But I informed her that I had left her parents several misleading messages so I was certain that I could delay things for a few months. School was out, I could just say that she was staying at a friend's summer house.

That was when she gave up, looking at me with eyes that were pleading and defeated.

"That's a pretty doll you have," she said in a pitiful attempt at conversation. "What's her name?"

"Her name is Katarzyna," I replied. "She's my favorite doll but I won't have her for much longer. I found a home for her, just like I did for all my other dolls. I want to go on a road trip and I can hardly take her with me. And God knows I can't leave her here alone. A few more dabs of paint and she'll be fixed. Someone wants to buy her."

She groaned and looked away.

"Well, I can't stand here talking all day, Małgorzata," I said. "I'll come back tomorrow."

"I'm not Małgorzata. I'm Agata."

"Not anymore, Małgorzata. I'm Agata now."

"But I'm Agata."

I told Małgorzata that I had been planning on bringing her something to eat but as she was being kind of a bitch, I had changed my mind. She didn't like that, but it didn't matter. I hitched Katarzyna under my arm and marched back upstairs. I took her into my bedroom, sitting her atop the bedside table. Then I sat in a chair and raised my calves to get a better look at my footwear. "Do you like my boots?" I asked Katarzyna, but she just glared at me. I sighed and got into bed. I just didn't have the energy to try to get them off. This might be something Stan could help with but I wasn't in the mood for a lecture so I didn't bother calling him. Besides, there was something sexy about going to bed in a pair of high heel boots.

So I laid myself in bed, atop the covers, and closed my eyes for a moment. Although I couldn't see myself just then, I did feel a sense of impenetrable calm at the thought of how beautiful I had become. It was like suddenly being girded in armor.

"What did you mean when you said you found a home for me?" a small voice asked.

I sighed again. I didn't open my eyes.

"I meant just that. I will hardly have any time for you, Katarzyna. It won't be like before. These people, whoever they are, they will be much better for you. They are a husband and wife, although I don't know much more about them than that."

"What are their names?"

Falling

I couldn't remember their names and I told her that. Katarzyna was from Poland too and I think she was trying to figure out if her new parents were Polish. "Katarzyna, I'm going to tell you a story then I want you to go to bed."

I don't know if she followed my advice but I certainly did. I had a night filled with pleasant dreams and I awoke elated to start another day. Things were already very different from before. I had a brief moment of panic when I realized that I had fallen asleep in the mask, but when I touched the left side of my face I felt the familiar ridge of the scar. Katarzyna must have taken it off.

"Katarzyna, what did you do with the mask?" I asked.

I turned and noticed that she was no longer sitting on the table beside me. I also didn't see her as I walked down the hall to the bathroom but I figured I would find her there. She had to be there.

"Katarzyna?"

She wasn't in the bathroom so I began a thorough search of the house, calmly at first, but soon my calm turned into frenzy. I couldn't seem to find Katarzyna or the mask anywhere. I inspected Katarzyna's room and she wasn't there. There seemed to be a void in the place on the ottoman where she normally sat. I searched every room and nook in the house, including the kitchen cabinets that I knew were empty because I never cooked. I even went down into the basement where I found Małgorzata sleeping, all curled up on top of her chains. "Katarzyna!"

I searched the backyard. She wasn't there either. That only left the front of the house, facing the street. I opened the front door, feeling greatly overwhelmed as I stood there. My throat had become dry as a desert and I thought I would faint into a heap on the front steps. Just as I was pulling myself together I noticed something pink rising off of the smooth surface of the asphalt in front of the house. They had just repaved the road and that pink thing might as well have been a screeching piglet that had wandered into the street, it was that obvious. It was the mask and it was lying limp right in the middle of the road.

As soon as I realized it was the mask, I caught the sight of a green BMW barreling down the street. The driver saw me too, but he honked his horn and drove over the mask, completely flattening it. I heard a happy squeal escape from the bones of the house, the giddy squeal of a child. I looked up and there was Katarzyna standing by the window.

METAMORPHOSIS

His name was Brian, and I met him in the fall of 2008. Brian was not his given name, but more on that to come. You have been to my office in Boston, or "in the trenches" as I like to call it, but you perhaps do not remember my office in "the woods"; that is, my office in Lebanon, New Hampshire, not far from the Dartmouth-Hitchcock Medical Center. It is a small practice, but there were enough upper class folks concerned with the preservation of their skin that I had plenty of clients capable of paying their doctor's fee. Indeed, I refer to it as preservation as sometimes I felt akin to the mad scientist in the Sci-Fi movie: pulling skin like plastic back over an octogenarian head. But Brian wasn't one of these; at least I didn't think so.

My office occupied the lower floor of a three-story Federal building worked in Flemish bond. It was about sixty feet long from front to back so I had plenty of storage space, three patient rooms, and even an office for the nurse. From the street, one entered the hall and through a door was the walnut-paneled waiting room. When I was a boy, I had seen a movie where all the Wall Street bad guys met to plot their evil deeds in a walnut-paneled room so I always hoped I would have one of my own. There was also something about it that suggested money, like vacationing in the Austro-Hungarian Empire, and I wanted my clients to spend as if they too lived in such a place. Like going to see Dr. Freud.

Brian was sitting with his long fingers tensed unnaturally in his lap when I walked into the patient room. The fingers remained that way until I examined him, aside from frequent bouts of fidgeting: grabbing the fingers of one hand with the other and such. He was also wearing dark sunglasses. Brian, whose real name was James Brian Mulder, was a tall, athletic man with the sort of olive complexion I associate with Southern Europeans, the people of the Alps, and the Welsh. He was a handsome guy, preppy-dressed in a thick, gray Shetland wool sweater over a plaid shirt and black New Balance sneakers, and I was expecting a consultation on the topic of "how to stop thinning hair in a man of 21," even though the nurse had scribbled "black skin" on the chart.

"What's her name?" I asked. It was the sort of question I asked to put young male clients like these at ease.

"I don't know what you mean," said Brian, and he forced a smile.

"The name of the girl who made you come in about your hair," I added.

"Oh, no," said Brian, and he chuckled uncomfortably. "I'm not worried about that. It's my face."

"She could have asked you to come about that too."

"There isn't any girl," Brian said, but his tone told otherwise.

"You can tell me later," I said. "It isn't good to keep secrets. They attract these critters that burrow under the skin and then they lay these eggs. It's pretty nasty. They can travel up to the brain."

Brian sighed. "I see you're gonna be *that* kinda doctor. Like my pediatrician."

"Just breaking the ice. And I'm certainly not your pediatrician. So what are you here for?"

"My skin is turning black," said the young man, and he took off his sunglasses.

I sat on the chair across from Brian, who was sitting on the examination table with its noisy, shiny paper, and I took his hands into my own. Methodically, I turned them over and examined them, including the space between the fingers. I pulled Brian's plaid shirt sleeves up a little to take note of his wrists, and then I moved to his face and neck. Brian's face was clearly darker than his neck and hands, yielding a diagnosis that I was very familiar with.

I took a quick look at Brian's strong, barrel-chested torso which was shirted, and then glanced, briefly, downward, and then he said: "Don't worry, Doc. I don't think we'll need the stirrups for this one. In addition to my face, I have some spots on my legs."

"All right," I said. "Why don't you change into a gown and I'll be back in a few secs."

I left the room and used these unexpected free minutes to venture into my research space. My wife, your mother, described this space as something out of a Gothic horror story, with specimens of all types preserved in jars, but it was of great use to me. I had another case of a man who had a particularly virulent basal cell carcinoma requiring a skin graft, and I was researching how small skin grafts from cadavers could be stimulated to grow with electricity and without the need for rejection medicines. In one bottle, a skin graft had twisted itself and was floating in a bluish sea with something like sea foam on the brim of the jar. It looked like a squid changing shape into something else, or taking a black shape from something which it had been previously.

Brian was undressed when I returned. "I'm ready, Doc," he said.

"Is that a Charleston accent or a Savannah accent I hear?"

"You're pretty good," said the young man. "It's Charleston. I came up to Dartmouth for college, much to the disapproval of my family, my mom in particular."

"Does she have a part to play in your skin problem?" I asked. I noted that the most obvious issue for Brian was his darkened face, but that he also had black lesions on his legs, some of which had yellow edges and poorly-defined borders.

"My mother does have a part to play in all this," said Brian. "It was at her house that I met the man who started it."

"You want to tell me about it?" I asked.

Brian told me his father built a new house his senior year in high school; that's where he started off. "My father built this house, which seemed silly to me as I would not have long to live in it," he said. The house had been built over a Negro graveyard, a slave graveyard,

Brian went on, and his mother said any house built upon that land must be cursed, though she had been smiling when she said it. There were many demons in that country, Brian intimated to me, and I understood him to mean secrets or unfortunate tales that were passed on for generations, like stories of masters who did unspeakable things to their property.

But the Mulders were a happy family by all accounts. Perhaps too happy; too happy and too rich, just the sort of thing to make a big, popular guy like Brian go running into the lap of the first colored girl ready to have him. "And that's exactly what I did," said Brian. Here, now he was getting to the heart of the story. Brian told me that he came across a poetry website where young women, like a certain Lavinia Ford, uploaded their work for the enjoyment of others of their ilk.

So Brian ran away from the house built upon the slave graveyard, over the wooden bridge that spanned the canal, through the woods where slave hunters had tortured and hung slaves that had tried to run, and made his way to the creek. Brian's father had built his holiday house far outside of town so there was always a long way to go to get anywhere: past this landmark or that. Brian's favorite landmark in the area was the creek, and it turned out this was Lavinia's too. As Brian approached this place, he saw Lavinia bobbing up and down upon a swing. "There was this old swing hanging between two oak trees," said Brian. "I saw her from the back, and it was like she pulled me right into her body." He said he never thought of being a couple with Lavinia in the way that his brothers were coupled with their wives; all he knew is that he wanted her in the worst possible way.

"Of course, I knew she was a poet," Brian told me. He had first come across the poetry website when he had gotten an email about a contest, to which he promptly replied to the sender "Bullshit!" but he clicked on the link anyway. That is where he read a poem by Lavinia, which was accompanied by her photograph. The photo revealed Lavinia to be a buxom, dark-skinned girl with what Brian described as delicate features on a black face. But he knew that that face belied a brick house body, a body that he would spend nights ruminating

Falling

lustfully over just like one might expect from a man of that age. Brian particularly enjoyed a poem in which Lavinia imitated the romantic style of the 19th century, describing the modern day South Carolina football player as: "an ambulating line of muscular flesh. Beautiful. Achilles burning upon his pyre. The last explosive testament to youth that must be destroyed so that other, wickeder men might live."

Brian did not understand what Lavinia meant by most of that, but he formed the impression that this pretty colored girl seemed to fancy White football players, or at least he thought so, and it was sort of interesting that she was unlike the other girls in the area, who were about as sharp as toilet paper on the roll. So he met Lavinia upon the swing: he walked right up to her as the sun was setting and sat down beside her without a word. This was a good tactic as Brian was a tall, dominating man who inspired fear in some. Lavinia looked at him. "You're not like I expected you to be," she said.

"You're exactly what I expected you to be," said Brian.

"What do you mean?"

"You're beautiful. I mean, you have a pretty face."

Lavinia laughed, Brian told me, and then she said: "Do you even like poetry?"

"I do," Brian lied. "I like Henry James and Tolstoy, in particular."

Lavinia laughed, though she didn't realize that he wasn't joking. Brian really thought these two names he had pulled out of his jock hat of discombobulated information were actually poets. He told Lavinia that he had seen her before, in Charleston, when he was having brunch with his parents one Sunday. Lavinia asked if Brian lived in Charleston, and he said that he did, but his father had just built a summer house out there in the country and that's where they were staying. He told her his family was old and known in the Charleston area, and that one of his great-great-grandfathers had been a general, but he immediately regretted it as soon as he said it.

"But you like poetry?" Lavinia asked. "You write it yourself?"

Brian said that he did. He told her he didn't think you needed rhyme, meter, and cadence to formulate an idea, but poetry was a reflection of the particularly human capacity to create, why, anything at all. In reality, Brian thought poetry was "for women, hippies and sissies; basically, San Francisco types," which he was sure to tell me as I listened and continued to examine him. Lavinia seemed to admire that Brian was a man of contradictions, which, in fact, he was not, and she told him that she thought her poetry credentials had been what had gotten her accepted early into Dartmouth College, where she planned to start in the fall.

Lavinia told Brian she wished to recite a poem for him. "She looked at me with eyes that were trusting and hopeful," he said.

The twain had now settled beneath an old twisted oak hanging with Spanish moss. The only witnesses to this fleeting moment, in which a young girl recited a poem to a young man, were the impossibly-distant crickets who hissed feverishly, as they are known to do in South Carolina. Brian told Lavinia to go ahead and recite. He still recollected her words.

"Love wounds like the hurricane,
Upturns the levee until there's nothing
To remember or to forget.
Nothing at all:
No contrition, no limbs to carry
The bales of cotton to the sharecropper,
No livers;
No cracks in the roof to be impregnated
by the downpour of moss, mosquitoes and the lynch-man's lies;
No ancestors, no air,
Only black bodies bruised by the rain carried up
From Santo Domingo.
Only black bodies.
Nothing at all."

When Brian reached home, he heard the booming voice of his father and the heady laughter of his mother. His father was the eldest son of a strict Baptist preacher, and as free of an independent thought as one would expect of such a person. His mother was different. But then Brian heard the deep voice of a third person and something like the tap of a cane upon the pinewood floors. "Oh, Mr. Manchester," said Mrs. Arabella Mulder. "We do so enjoy when you come round."

Brian walked into the dining room and saw the man. He was Mr. Manchester, the former governor of Alaska who had to flee to the Cayman Islands on some scandal and now was back in the States. A mirror's reflection revealed him to be a towering pale man with a stooped back and pomaded black hair. He was even taller than Brian. "And there is the boy," the man said when he saw Brian. Brian said the man's lips smiled though his eyes did not.

"Brian, walk Mr. Manchester to his car. It's the Mercedes parked out front," said Brian's mother.

The two men left the house and as they walked to the car, Brian told the man that he had heard many untruths about him.

"Untruths?" the man asked. "What are untruths? Perhaps one man's truth is another's untruth. If I told you that the world exists for the man who is able to take from it what he can without thinking and without looking back, is that an untruth?"

Brian looked at the man, but he didn't know what to say. But the man said: "I think you'll go away to college." Then he touched Brian's hand, and it was like a thousand fleshy centipedes crawled upon Brian's skin, digging through the integument to the sweet flesh beneath.

"It was him that did this to me," said Brian.

So though his staunchly Southern parents were aghast, Brian applied to Dartmouth College and was accepted. He had let Lavinia lead him there, deciding that he would follow her wherever she would go until the inevitable happened. Brian should have taken a spot at Erskine College, the local school where he might settle into his natural place as King of the Jocks, marry one of the local bimbos, and have children who would also one day take their own places in one of these two roles when they came of age. But Brian had followed Lavinia to Dartmouth where they might "live like heathens," as Brian called it.

It was a blessed heathen life, if it must be called that. It was a life comprised of long walks down unpaved wooded paths where other young souls had tread: beneath maple trees and in the shade of collegiate buildings that wealthy donors had somehow, magically, imbued with palpating, puerile life. Lavinia ignored Brian at first, but then she seemed suddenly to see him: her South Carolina Achilles burning upon his funeral pyre. Brian still had to win her, as she was a pretty Black girl in a place where there were certainly very few of those. She did not respond to his messages, and it was only when they ran into one another at a raucous fraternity party that they finally connected.

Lavinia seemed more interested in keeping Brian as an admirer, realizing perhaps that he wasn't really a poet, and thinking that there might be more apt men for her in this fertile ground of trees she didn't know the names of and young men looking dapper in their snug Levis. But then common acquaintances began describing them as a couple, and Lavinia did not deny it.

They would see Brian and Lavinia sitting beneath trees burnt in the multi-hued fall colors that can only be found in the Northeastern United States; certainly not in steamy South Carolina, a place almost licentious in its heat. They saw Lavinia reading to Brian while his head was nestled on her bosom in the most gentlemanly way that such a pose could be. Lavinia's friends would have known that she majored in English, and they would have heard her recite the following line from a play by John Webster:

Though in our miseries Fortune hath a part
Yet, in our noble sufferings, she hath none:
Contempt of pain, that we may
call our own.[1]

Seeing the pair as naught other than two young lovers, Lavinia's friends were surprised when she began showing up to classes wearing a black dog collar around her neck, but they didn't attribute this attire change to Brian, not at first. In fact, it had been Lavinia who had asked Brian what he liked after they had made love, like heathens, for the first time. She said she wanted to please him, or so Brian told me. He told her he liked submission during love play; he framed it poetically, though he might regard the poetic art with derision.

The changes wrought upon Lavinia would be slow. She would remain the laughing girl who fancied attention, dressing in outfits that well framed her figure and wearing her hair up to accentuate her startling bone structure. But once Brian got to work on her in earnest, Lavinia began to show the effects of the dark engine of Brian's unconscious designs. Indeed, what Brian did, as he related to me, was to chip away at Lavinia's identity. He told me this as if it was something entirely out of his control. It had merely happened. It was no different than the slave master giving his ship-borne property a new name after they arrived on the plantation, and beating him if he resorted to the old one. Brian destroyed Lavinia and created a new woman, one fashioned in the fantastic image of his mind.

Brian told me he started to call Lavinia "whore" playfully, and then one time he convinced her to let him write the word on her body with a black marker. He framed it as a game. Once Lavinia accepted that, and began to want it, Brian proceeded to make demands upon her sexually. He would only "breed her," as he called it, on the floor. Once they had gotten into the rhythm of doing that several times a day, Brian told Lavinia that he needed to know that she wanted to be bred, that she was grateful for it. When he was ready for the act, he would stand over her and that was her cue to say: "I am ready, Master. Please breed me like the whore that I am."

"It was when Lavinia showed up to a poetry reading with a bandage on her arm that I got into trouble," Brian told me. "Lavinia and I had been cooking together in her dorm. Spaghetti. She got burned by a boiling saucepan turning over when I bumped into it and she told people that I branded her."

I would never know if Brian really did brand Lavinia, but it was the night of Brian's expulsion from Dartmouth that he noted the color change on his face for the first time. Brian showed his dark spots to a friend who said it was surely just nerves. Brian had two small circles on his cheeks: dime-sized, flat patches of tan on an otherwise white face. And Brian didn't tell his parents right away about his expulsion.

He had an allowance from his father, and he used the money to obtain an apartment of his own in the sleepy town of Lebanon as he could no longer live on campus. Eventually he would have to get a job but he would worry about that later. "Everyone expected me to go back home," he said. "They probably would have still let me into Erskine, even with what I did, but I didn't go home. Perhaps I still wanted Lavinia."

He joined a local football club made up mostly of townies, but with some Dartmouth alums too. In this way, Brian kept his drive and his sanity in the midst of it all. One might say that Brian was of a similar character to his forebears. They had been tall, proud men who might be said to suborn the needs of others into their own. He told me that his mother was a descendant of Confederate general Bedford Forrest, well-known in the South for fighting in America's Great War and for creating an institution designed to reenact the violent status quo of a former period, where masters had bred their slave women and sired ill-begotten children upon them.

Brian told me that one day he was getting dressed for a football club game and he started to think about Lavinia. "I missed her smell. She had this spicy smell that was unlike any other girl I had been with. The others had all been White girls. Being with Lavinia was like being John Carter and meeting Dejah Thoris on Mars. She was like the hills of Mars, the Martian earth, the oxygen-thin air. She was something else and breeding her was like nothing I could describe."

Brian did not seem to appreciate how his words might sound to someone not of his ilk, but he was so accustomed to being among his own kind that he could not really understand. I had no desire to wonder about whether such a young man should be forgiven, as I was hardly the Grand Inquisitor, and I decided that I should focus on his skin. And that's what I shall do here.

It was the events of this particular football game that brought Brian into my office. Brian seemed to forget that he was playing football and not hockey, and at one point during the game he embarked on a shouting match with an offensive lineman from the opposing team, leading both men to remove their helmets. It was the sort of intercourse a man initiates when he wants to start a confrontation. The men drew close to each other, and it seemed only a matter of time before one of them launched the first shot. It was Brian who took this role, head-butting the other player, though Brian alleged that the player had muttered something about his mother and "combat boots." I never did understand why athletes were always so concerned about whether or not their mothers wore such footwear. Brian was removed from the game and made to sit out the remainder of it, which his team inevitably lost.

Long after the other players had gone, Brian was changing on the field when he noticed something strange. The dark spots were no longer solely on his face. Now they were on his legs, too. Three large spots were on his calves, even larger than the ones on his face. Even the dark spots on his face had grown and darkened.

"You asked me what brought me in, well here it is," said Brian. "When I went home that night I lie in bed, tossing and turning. I felt an excruciating pain. The room grew dark and started to spin. I thought I had meningitis or something. I was really losing it. The pain grew worse and I felt an intense heat. I closed my eyes and as I opened them again I heard a splash. *My water had broken.* Yes, as a woman's water breaks, and a motile black placenta had revealed itself beneath the covering of the sheet, between my legs. I let out a silent cry, a cry of total devastation. I saw a black thing lying on the foot of the bed. Some devilish abortion that I had given birth to. I tossed off the covers and saw a wave of black crawling up my body.

"I stood up, but was so weak that I crashed to the floor. I lay there crying, sure that I would die that night. I managed to crawl back to where I had slept, and the bed seemed to swallow me whole, drawing me into a deep, dark space. To my amazement, I did wake up. When I awoke, the skin on my legs was darker. Some of the spots were so close I thought my whole leg might turn black. My face had darkened too, as if spreading out from the first two spots."

Brian's words still pulsated with panic and terror. "Now, I'm here," he said.

"Brian," I began. "The diagnosis is simple."

I walked toward the window of the room. I pulled closed the heavy blinds. "It's exceedingly simple, really. You are turning into a Black man."

"Sir?"

"It might be more correct to call you a mulatto: the man who is half Black and half White, and who springs from the union of a White and a Black. They commonly resulted from the union of a White slave master and a Black female slave."

Brian gazed at me in utter bafflement.

"I call you a mulatto as you still have a bit of white in you. Are you familiar with the Fitzgerald scale? You have a Fitzgerald type IV complexion, making you more prone to turning into a Black man. Actually, this type of complexion is more apt to develop melasma than other skin types."

"Then, then," Brian stammered. "I have melasma."

Brian no longer inspired fear. He had suddenly become old, as if the last representative of a people so ancient that the lands whereupon they had formerly dwelt were now deserts. His expressive eyes were sullen and averted.

"What you have on your face is called melasma, and it is treatable. But the spots on your legs I shall have to check out."

"And it's contagious?"

"No, Brian. Lavinia did not give this to you when you bred her."

"And what about this Mr. Manchester, the man who touched me?" Brian asked.

I sighed. "Well, in terms of this Manchester person you spoke of, you see, we have a name for this in medicine. We call it magical thinking. It's no different than believing in vengeful spirits, voodoo, or leprechauns."

I could not help but chuckle.

"I don't think it's funny," said Brian.

"I'm sorry, Brian," I said. "Neither do I."

Brian smiled uncomfortably and muttered to himself. "I am not turning black. You're joking. It's ridiculous."

Brian left that night and later returned for an excisional biopsy of three different lesions, including two that had highly irregular and discolored edges. Brian was diagnosed with malignant melanoma and was prescribed an aggressive course of treatment but he later died. He never reached his twenty-second birthday, and he never attended Erskine College like his parents wanted. But that night, as Brian left, I was reminded of something else that John Webster had written. I never told Brian but I, like Lavinia, had also studied English at Dartmouth. This particular line was from Webster's play, *The Duchess of Malfi*, the same play that Lavinia had quoted to Brian beneath the multicolored Dartmouth maples.

Whether we fall by ambition, blood, or lust
Like diamonds we are cut with our own dust.[1]

I closed the office that night and had the nurse reschedule my appointments for the next week. I used that time to travel to Central New York to pick apples with my wife, your mother. We basked in the autumn colors, the rain and the silence. We drank wine like Europeans, and seemed far away from New Hampshire, South Carolina, and even Earth. Perhaps we had settled upon Mars. I gave my wife a bag of so-called Empire apples, very delicious I was told, and I felt pleasure when she looked at me in appreciation. She smiled, and I saw that she had lines around her eyes and around her mouth. I took her hands into mine, her frail white hands, and I noted the signs of age that had already taken root in them: the lax skin and the liver spots. She was turning into a crone like my mother.

1. Webster, John. The Duchess of Malfi: A New Mermaid Edition (New York, NY, 1965)

ACQUIRED SITUATIONAL NARCISSISM

Tommy lives on Colburn Street in a house that used to be a brothel. The house is right outside Hanover and I can see him going into it from my car. I'm parked across the street. My guess is Tommy doesn't know I'm back at Dartmouth, if he remembers me at all. He doesn't remember how I used to wear my curly hair long. Now I've cut it frantically short, as if cutting the hair away scissors the past. When I reach my house in Lebanon, which I've never been in before, I walk past a row of mirrors – one after the other – and it's like I'm seeing myself for the first time.

 When I reach the clinic, I give my name to the receptionist who instantly sends me upstairs to see the doctor. She smiles and seems eager to help because of my baby face. Butter wouldn't melt, as they say. It's at night, the night of the very day that I returned to New Hampshire from rehab in Pennsylvania, and so the waiting area is empty when I get there. The light bulbs flicker in the hall and the color of the space is brown: brown from the dim light and the drab, peeling furniture. I'm seated in a stiff-backed chair that has clumps of a synthetic orange material spilling out of it from a small hole in the rim. The material makes the chair soft when you sit against it. I hear a man's happy laughter as it bleeds down the hall and then I see

Falling

a small blue fish whip in the fish tank by the elevator, across from where I'm seated. I didn't notice the fish tank before.

I get up and walk to the sound of the laughter. There is a man in a room, muttering softly. The doctor. The door to the room is ajar and I think the doctor must have seen or heard me because he suddenly stops muttering. "You can come in," he says. The doctor is sitting in a swivel chair and his back is to me. I take a seat. I look down at my hands, which until recently hadn't been put to good use. I used these hands to handle baggies of things, to move white powdery substances around on mirrored surfaces.

The doctor swivels around and I see that he's wearing a Lyndon B. Johnson mask. It's the sort of mask that you would wear to a Halloween party. It's cheery and horrific. The mask is large for the doctor's face. He introduces himself as Dr. Burke, and I can see the brown and silver placard on his desk that reads: Dr. Thomas Burke, supportive psychotherapist. The doctor is smiling but only because his mask is smiling. I'm dreading that he'll ask me the usual *So tell me about yourself?* So I decide to get things started.

"I don't actually have a diagnosis," I say. "Not a real one."

"I see."

"I'm only here because I had to come. Therapy was recommended after I finished rehab last week."

"It says here," and the doctor flips through the pages of a manila folder. "Acquired Situational Narcissism."

"Yeah, but that's not a real diagnosis."

Outside, the tree branches slap against the window. We're up on the second floor. A woman yells at someone on her phone and a car alarm booms. Dr. Burke sits silently for a moment but I believe he's actually laughing underneath his mask. On the desk there's a box of old Nintendo cartridges and on the wall hangs a tall mirror.

"You're right," Dr. Burke says. "It's not a real diagnosis. A doctor in California made it up."

"That's a diagnosis they give to child actors after they've grown up and completely lost it," I note, suddenly feeling like the doctor had taken me into his confidence. "No one knows what to do with those kids anymore. No one knows what to do with me. Not even my parents."

Dr. Burke stares at me from behind the eerily human plastic of his mask. He has steely gray-blue eyes and it's like they're drawing me onto a shared plane with him. I wonder what he thinks of me.

"Acquired Situational Narcissism. That's not me. I don't see how that has anything to do with me."

"Perhaps it doesn't have anything to do with you," the doctor says. His voice is even and pleasant, maybe a little too pleasant. "At times we run away from things. That can be problematic too."

I can tell that Lyndon B. Johnson doesn't run from things.

"It's my task to help clients accept those things about themselves that might be difficult," says Dr. Burke. "To own them. You might, for example, have a murder fantasy. That's okay. Most clients find that seeing me in the mask helps them."

The Lyndon B. Johnson mask continues to grin.

"You can wear a mask too if you'd like."

"No, it's all right."

"Fine by me."

"I saw Tommy when I came back," I tell Dr. Burke.

The way I frame it, it seems that Tommy has something to do with the cocaine that got me to rehab in the first place, but Tommy represents an entirely different dimension from the tormented place where I originated and this is something critically important. I tell Dr. Burke that Tommy and I were on the diving team together at Dartmouth but ever since I went to rehab after sophomore year I haven't kept in touch with any of the kids from the team. A year has passed. I barely knew Tommy anyway. He's like a Polaroid that you keep in your wallet. The Polaroid represents something that occurred a long time ago. Something that only has meaning to you. He was a situational thing, like the narcissism.

"So you saw Tommy and then what happened?" the doctor asks.

"Nothing happened. I saw Tommy go inside his house off campus, and then I drove off and went to my own house."

Falling

The house I'm staying in is my mom's idea. She doesn't think that living on campus is good for me because she sees the giddy, fast life of a college kid surrounded by other giddy, well-off brats as somehow wrapped up in the Acquired Situational Narcissism. She doesn't comprehend the inherently artificial nature of this diagnosis or the fact that my attorney only used the diagnosis as part of the plea deal that prevented me from doing any time. The house is large and silent like a tomb. It's two stories and I'm the only one living there because my mother decided to rent the entire house just for me. No distractions. Every night she calls and asks me if I'm taking my medication. The medication I'm supposed to take for the condition that isn't real.

At the restaurant, Camille slides into my booth seamlessly. "Why didn't you let me know you were back in town?" she asks. I'm tempted to tell her to go fuck herself since I know she already knew I was back in town as my dad, naturally, would have told her. Camille has been tight with my parents since they met her freshman year, my dad in particular. Now she spies for them, even though she's bipolar and significantly more disturbed than I am. But she's pretty and rich and everyone loves her and she's never been to rehab.

Camille's smile is predatory and she says: "I missed you, Kyle. You know that."

We're seated by the window and I can see the cars driving by on the road with their high-beams on. It has begun to rain, a rare, ugly New Hampshire late summer rain.

"I'm trying to get away from the things that I was doing before," I say.

"You weren't doing them with me."

When my food comes, Camille sticks her fingers in and brings the curl of shrimp to her lips. She licks her fingers when she's done, teasingly, and then she glances out of the window. She's trying to bring me in like a fisherman's reel. "It's so hot in here," she says.

The waiter comes and I push my bowl over to Camille. She can keep it for all I fucking care. I order a tempura platter and I can already smell the characteristic crisp of the tempura. It's strange to me that you can toss batter on a slaughtered creature and turn it into an entirely different dish. I see when Elin comes in and Camille whispers: "Don't even think about it." Camille was my first girlfriend at Dartmouth but after I broke up with Camille I moved on to Elin. Elin was actually the one who got me into doing coke big time. She's a dealer too, like I was, but she's so far managed to elude the cops with her bottle blond, good girl act. Her blond hair is so pale it's almost white. The way her hair frames her face, you can't see her ears and she looks like a sleek, dangerous animal. "Don't even think about it," Camille says again.

"I heard you the first time. Are you saying that I can't even look at her?"

"Yes. That's exactly what I'm saying."

I see a kid with a green windbreaker jacket walk in to the restaurant out of the corner of my eye and I turn to look because I think it's Tommy. It's not. The diving team wears these green windbreakers with white lettering on the back. It turns out I know this kid. Cameron, or Cam for short. He glides up to the bar, smiles at the worker and grabs his takeout. He nods my way as he walks out.

I return to Dr. Burke's office, narrowly catching the security guard before he leaves. "You got ten minutes," he says. In the waiting area on the second floor, someone has dropped a copy of *Cosmopolitan* in the fish tank and the little blue fish are doing pirouettes around it. I see that Dr. Burke's door is still ajar as I approach. He hasn't left the clinic yet. He also hasn't told maintenance to fix the lights. They still crackle their forbidding, brown light. "You can come in," Dr. Burke says as I approach but at that point I am already pushing open the door.

Atop the doctor's desk, there are several client folders. Dr. Burke is inscrutable behind his Lyndon B. Johnson mask. "You're back," he says.

"I wanted to talk about something."

"About the diagnosis of Acquired Situational Narcissism."

"No, about something else," and I tell Dr. Burke about how I had met Camille and Elin at the restaurant. I don't expect Dr. Burke to

Falling

understand. Seeing Elin brings back the old life of dealing and using that I'm trying to abandon. Elin taught me to test cocaine by putting a dab on the roof of your mouth with your finger. Good cocaine melted on the roof of your mouth if you put it there. Buttery.

"So you want to talk about that?" Dr. Burke asks. *Yes, Dr. Burke. I'd like to talk about that.* He smiles but then again he always smiles. The part in Lyndon B. Johnson's hair is white, as if the gel has dried.

"I want to talk about Camille," I tell the doctor. "She's my ex-girlfriend but my parents have her spying on me. She even followed me to the fucking restaurant today. Do they know what it's like to not have one second of peace? Not one second? Rehab was bad enough but now I have a girl that I'm not even dating following me around and it's my own parents that put her up to it."

Lyndon B. Johnson stares at me with serene deliberation. It's really a high quality mask because you can't tell that the blue eyes staring back at you are not Johnson's. I wonder where the mask was made and how the company managed to ship it without ruining the skin integrity.

"Well, you know what to do," Dr. Burke remarks archly. "If this Camille girl is bothering you, why don't you just kill her?"

I watch the methodical swing of the ceiling fan in Dr. Burke's office. It blows around stale, dusty air.

You have a desire to dissociate from the mundane routine of your daily life so you might be in the market for a rubber mask. Our rubber masks are designed for all facial types, ages, and weights. Rubber masks are perfect for fancy dress parties, psychoanalytical group sessions, bank heists, and run-of-the-mill surprises. A mask permits you to show a face to the world while hiding the true visage beneath. Our masks are manufactured from the highest quality Indonesian rubber and are hand-painted with synthetic polymers that have been carefully tested on oceanic wildlife. This means that they are perfectly safe for you. Because our masks are manufactured in Indonesia, Vietnam, and other Southeast Asian countries, we are able to provide you with the finest quality masks on the market for reasonable prices that rarely exceed $16.95. Our masks are known for their soft, realistic feel, and they have been carefully packaged and shipped to ensure that the characteristic, buttery touch of the mask is maintained when it reaches you. Concerned about the handling of the mask once it ships to the retailer? Consider ordering our rubber masks directly from the factory. There's no middleman. Our company maintains direct relationships with all of the factories that supply our masks.

I'm in the market for a mask I can wear to fulfill my wife's murder fantasy. Do you offer a wide selection of masks? How many different types of rubber masks do you have?

Chad, 24

Billings, MT

Those are great questions, Chad. We like to believe that we have the widest selection of original rubber masks currently available on the American market. Many companies can offer you a Britney Spears mask or a Boris Johnson mask, but none can offer you some of the better known selections from our catalog. We currently have more than 300 different rubber masks for sale, all of which can be viewed on our website or in our print catalog. Below is a list of some of the more popular masks from our 2019-2020 production line (with prices).

Ariana Grande mask	$13.95
Colonel Sanders mask	$13.95
Donald Trump mask	$13.95
Jean-Claude Van Damme mask	$13.95
Lyndon B. Johnson mask	$13.95
Aung San Suu Kyi mask	$16.95
Guy Fawkes mask (realistic)	$16.95
Crucified Jesus mask	$16.95
Stevie Wonder mask	$16.95
The Darkness (Legend) mask	$16.95
Thulsa Doom mask	$16.95
Your own face (special order)	$16.95

Falling

After driving to Tommy's house and sitting in the car a few minutes, I go to Monica's for takeout. Monica's serves the largest cut of rib-eye in the area: a bloody 3.5 pounds made to order. My wait time is a cool half an hour, pretty good considering the prize, and I take my steak and potatoes and drive back to my house in Lebanon. The house stands on the scythe cut of land between the road and the woods. Because of the conformation of the ridge, the houses fronting the road are all of different heights. Some houses are higher above the road, some lower.

I have only early classes that day, a Tuesday, so by the time I make it home I am done for the day. I pass a hand over my face, but when I look in the mirror app on my phone it's still my face staring back at me. I walk up the steps to the porch, noticing the girls watching me from the house next-door. Townies. They have permed hair. They aren't bad looking.

It's a few hours after I get home that the hooker shows up. "I prefer the term streetwalker," she'll tell me later and laugh. I have never seen her before. She knocks on the door, asking to use my phone, and I let her in. No one knocks on doors asking to use phones anymore. They only do that in the movies. "This is a nice place," she says. She isn't wrong. It is a nice old house, but it isn't a good place to live. The house gives you the impression that many people have lived here before. They've all made memories here and they've all died, but the silhouettes of the memories are still here. The house seems simultaneously filled with things and empty. The house hasn't been renovated but it's well-made. These twin realities coexist in the house.

"I'm Lily," the woman says. She is a woman in her forties and she's beautifully dressed. Her platinum blonde hair is frizzed in a short, provocative cut. She could have been the frontwoman for an '80s band, like Blondie or something, and she seems somehow right for New Hampshire. She follows me into the parlor.

"I'm Kyle," I tell her.

I don't ask her why she came, why she followed me from Tommy's, but I do offer her a refreshment. "I've got orange juice, Pepsi, and water," I say.

"I'll take a Pepsi," Lily says. "No, give me a water."

"One water coming up."

When I return, Lily is sprawled kittenish on the coach. The couch is old and gray, and it probably hasn't seen a woman like this in forty years. It came with the house. I hand Lily the water and she immediately sets it on the coffee table. She doesn't touch it or look at it for the rest of the night.

"Did you hear about that woman who got murdered? It was all over the news. I'm terrified," she says, and she shivers but the shiver only makes her seem more sexually available.

"No, I didn't hear about that," I lie.

"Her name was Camille something. She was a student at Dartmouth apparently. It's weird, you never hear about these things happening to students. That's why it was all over the morning news. They wouldn't stop talking about it. It was in the paper too."

"No one reads the paper anymore."

"I do," says Lily. "I don't believe anything I hear on the news. The TV news. I only go by what's in the paper."

"How'd she die?"

"Stabbed in the neck. They found her body wrapped in a clear white sheet. Like the type of sheet you would cover the walls of your house with when you're renovating."

I'm sitting on the uncomfortable chair on the other side of the coffee table.

"Can you imagine killing someone?" Lily asks. She looks at me expectantly.

"The murderer really carved that girl up, apparently," and Lily glances down at her fingers. "There weren't any pictures or anything, but I heard people talking about it downtown. It's a small town in New Hampshire. People talk."

I straighten the framed picture of Tommy that sits on a corner of the coffee table.

Falling

"Who's that?" Lily asks.

"That's a friend of mine. We were on the diving team together when I first came to Dartmouth."

"So you're a student too. That's what I thought when I saw you. You're very good-looking. That's why I followed you. I hope you don't mind. You look like the guys they used to have in these catalogs back in the day. They used to come in the mail. The International Male catalog. I'm certain you've never heard of it."

"I have."

"You have that look. That sort of blond surfer look. A surfer wearing a suede vest with tassels." Lily laughs with sudden warmth. It's a heartfelt laugh that rolls whorishly on the floor. It climbs up the wall. "Are you from California?"

"No," I answer. "I'm from Boston. My parents are anonymous rich people. They're very, very rich and when you're that rich you sort of forget that you have children."

"Or what it means to have children," Lily says. "I completely get it. I wasn't always like this, you know. Does your father own a company or something?"

"Or something."

I don't get the impression that Lily is the chatty type. She only gabs like this because I'm a prospective customer and she needs to hook me.

"How about I invite someone over?" I suggest.

"You could invite your friend Tommy."

"Right."

"And if that's the case," says Lily, "I can invite another girl. Don't worry, I know lots of girls. There are some really nice girls up here. You'll like her, you'll see. And if you don't like her, we can just get rid of her," but Lily never clarifies what this means.

Lily reaches for my hand and I give it to her. She squeezes it and smiles at me. Then she shrugs. Her hands are thin-skinned and blue-veined. "Oh lookie here," she says, pulling her mobile out of the front pocket of her black leather jacket. "I guess I do have my phone after all." She wears the leather jacket over a form-fitting blue dress.

When the other girl arrives, she's prettier than I expect: a tall redhead with an attractive meekness and a thick regional accent. I wonder what Dr. Burke would do to these girls if he had the chance. If he'd let them live. It seems the best thing to do is to see where things lead. Whatever happens, I can talk about it with the doctor tomorrow.

"So where's your friend?" the new girl, Joyce, asks.

"Oh, he's on his way," I say. "He's just running a little late."

"That's good."

I get up to begin the long walk to the kitchen, which is down the hall at the back of the house. But before I leave the parlor, I turn round in the doorway and say: "I've got to check something out real quick, I'll be back."

"I'll come with," says Joyce, and she grabs her pocket book and follows me out.

"So what's your real name?" I ask Joyce when we reach the kitchen.

I'm sure I saw a bottle of wine stashed in the cupboards somewhere. It's probably a leftover from the last tenant that the landlord didn't remove.

"My real name? Oh ho ho, that's gonna cost you," says Joyce.

"Can I pay you in Monopoly money?"

"No."

I glance into Joyce's eyes and I find therein the image of Tommy. I see a tall kid with closely-cropped strawberry blond hair who wears a green windbreaker jacket. His back is to me through the aperture of Joyce's irises then he suddenly turns around. In many ways, Tommy is like me. Boston. Altar boy. Parents from the Southside who stumbled into money. But Tommy is more me than I myself am. He's the *me* that should've been.

The doorbell lets out a high-pitched ring and I say: "That's Tommy." Before leaving for the door, I look in one last cupboard. "There it is," I say, grabbing onto the neck of the white wine bottle.

I reach the door where a kid wearing a green windbreaker is standing facing the street. I can see him through the glazed glass

Falling

in the middle of the door. The door swings open and the kid turns around. "Kyle," he says. It's Cam.

Cam dusts off the soles of his shoes on the welcome mat and follows me into the house. We talk about old times for a few minutes and then he leaves, promising to give me a call in a few days. At this point, I understand that Tommy isn't coming and I decide to send the two girls home. I march into the kitchen, thinking I'll find Joyce there, but the kitchen is empty. Joyce left the tap in the sink running and I hear the methodical splashes of the water against the metal basin. I hear the sound of a woman's laughter and I return to the parlor. The parlor is in disarray. A lamp has been knocked onto the floor and the coffee table is overturned. In a corner, Joyce is down on her knees and Lily is strangling her.

As I leave the parlor, I notice a card on the floor. It must have fallen from Lily's pocket book. It reads, "Dr. Thomas Burke, supportive psychotherapist," and below the name and title is written in red ballpoint pen: "Lily, call me whenever."

When I reach Dr. Burke's office, I quickly walk in and take the elevator to the second floor. The security guard has left for the night and the door is unlocked. I pass the fish tank, where an issue of *Elle* floats among the guppies and goldfish. This time I find Dr. Burke's door shut when I reach it. I knock before I enter. Inside, Dr. Burke stands in front of a gurgling coffeemaker. He still wears his Lyndon B. Johnson mask but from this angle I see that he's got the tail of a serpent.

"I'd like to know your true name," I say.

"It's not important that you know my name," the doctor says. "Coffee?"

I tell Dr. Burke that I'd love some coffee and he pours out two cups of black coffee in small porcelain cups. When he's done, he walks over to the desk and hands me my cup. It's warm. He glances up at me for a moment and our eyes meet.

THE RAVEN

Allen was forty and probably a dentist. He lived alone in Baltimore and his apartment was haunted by the memory of someone, or of many people. He had fantasies about women who were out of his league, edited articles about imaginary islands near the South Pole on Wikipedia, and maintained a kind of savage discontent with the world and everyone in it. He had a sister whom he loved dearly and incestuously, and it pained him that she seemed to have written him out of her memory. A crow followed him.

He was fairly certain it was a crow. The beady black eyes and smug demeanor were a giveaway. The jaunty, deliberate way in which it walked made him want to boot it hard in the ribs. Allen decided that it was a harbinger of death, most likely his own, and that if he was wise he would find a way to get rid of it. He believed this because it was more grimly satisfying than any other explanation he could think of.

It was an explanation that satisfied his friend Anna, too. She was the new receptionist in his office and a worse receptionist was hard to imagine. But she was shy about her crooked teeth and she was sort of amused by the lecherous old boss so she stayed. Allen wasn't sure but he suspected that he didn't own the dental practice. It was presided over by a Dr. Lutz, a burly man with large hands who looked like he should be carrying heavy things around rather than sticking his hands in people's mouths. He was sort of shaped like a Clydesdale. No one else seemed to notice.

As Dr. Lutz saw most of the patients, Allen was never quite sure what he was expected to do. He spent most of his time standing by Anna's desk, surveying everything with a kind of disinterested contempt. It wasn't that Allen was a contemptuous person, but rather that he didn't have much to do and this sort of disdainful look he had adopted was a way of keeping curious people at bay. Eventually, he stopped pretending to care. The incompetence of everyone surrounding Dr. Lutz was extreme, and legendary, and no one seemed particularly concerned about him.

Well, at least until the crow showed up. It perched on his window ledge every morning and watched him with interest as he readied himself for the day. Then it followed him to work. The first few days, he had been sure he was imagining it. But then one day he turned round to look at the bird and he noticed something: the same black, beady eyes that he had seen on the very first day. It was the same crow. Whether the bird truly was the herald of his death or just the carrier of an avian pestilence Allen didn't know, but he knew enough to keep the thing outside. That didn't stop him from talking to Anna about it, in their downtime.

"Top of the morning," Anna would sing when Allen came to work. "How's the long, slow road to the grave treating you?"

"Horribly, thanks," was invariably Allen's reply.

"What are we dying of today?"

"Bone cancer."

"Osteosarcoma, I see," said Anna.

"Or osteomyelitis. One of the two."

Anna didn't care about the fax machine, she didn't care about answering the phone, she didn't care about correcting the language in the memorandums, and there was something refreshing about the sunny, lawless way she would laugh at the details of his twenty-first century nightmare that made Allen seek out her company. If she noticed this, she kept silent about it.

Anna named the crow Qouth, which she thought was funny. She had taken to composing short verses of poetry in its honor. She had a degree in English literature, but she hated children too much to teach. This included adolescent and college-age children. So she worked in offices. She used to temp, but after Dr. Lutz had offered to make her temp assignment in the dental office a permanent one she left her days of temping behind. But she continued to write poetry in her spare time.

"It's a symbol," Anna informed Allen one heinously long afternoon.

"A symbol of?"

Allen was seeing how long it took to fill a page of Microsoft Word with profanity. Anna was sitting on his desk, and he pretended that her way of sitting and meditatively eating grapes was a source of great personal suffering to him.

"Of your humanity," said Anna. Her eyes flashed through the horned rims of her glasses.

"Shouldn't it be a puppy or something," said Allen. "Or an owl."

"You don't like puppies. You'd try to kick one." She laughed. "I kicked a pigeon once. It didn't go so well."

"It flitted away?"

"It didn't anticipate my commitment to pigeon-kicking."

He didn't see himself seriously being committed to wounding the crow with a kick, but the way it followed him made him feel like the hounded man in a gothic novel and he was sick to death of it. He was morbid as it was. He was intelligent in the least useful ways. His friends had given up talking to him about women. His mother had quietly set all her hopes for grandchildren on his younger sister. Socially, economically and genetically, he was a cul-de-sac and he knew it. The last thing he needed was a flea-ridden blackbird of death flapping around after him. It was tacky and beneath him entirely.

Anna still thought it was funny though – Anna with her train-wrecked dreams and not-quite-appropriate-for-work clothing – and her Poe pastiches had come very, very close to making Allen laugh on more than one occasion. One night, harkening back to her whimsical

Falling

suggestion that he train it as a minion, he had lured the creature close to his apartment with an outstretched piece of toast, and, to his dismay, it was easily coaxed into hopping onto his arm. It perched like it had been born to perch there. The idea of breaking its neck had occurred to Allen. He fed it more bread instead.

"Now you've become the protagonist of a gothic novel," Anna commented when he told her about the crow's new trick.

"Well, I've already got an antagonist," said Allen darkly. "She's shredding my paperwork."

Anna shifted her weight, contritely. "Next, you train him to go 'caw' whenever he thinks you're angry. Oh, and buy a cloak, that's important. Stand on rooftops a lot. On moonlit nights…"

"Don't you have actual work to do?"

"Not in the slightest. I gave Lutz my notice yesterday."

Allen looked up from the piece of paper he had been slowly turning into origami.

"That way my last day'll be the day of the Christmas party and I can act like it's all on my account."

"Good."

There was a Secret Santa for the Christmas party, of course. Ignoring the name he had drawn from the hat, Allen bought a length of red ribbon and tied it onto the now-docile crow's neck. Somehow it looked more wretched than it had before.

"You're a terrible symbol."

Croak.

"And a terrible present."

Anna wasn't there when Allen got to the party. She'd been there, Lutz said, eyes straying repeatedly toward the crow, but then she'd disappeared. Aware that he was garnering a great deal of unwelcome attention from the staff, Allen left the office and climbed the stairs. He wanted to go to the roof as Anna had told him once that she like rooftops. He had been pretending not to listen.

He found her with her eyes settled far away from the door, like a girl waiting for the killer. She was wearing a dress, and she had an uncharacteristic quiet in her long, akimbo limbs. Only her legs seemed well-proportioned but this balance was thrown off by new heels. The crow on Allen's arm made a hoarse noise and Anna turned sharply. The beast raised its wings as Allen lifted his arm to wave. Anna waved back.

"Listen to this," said Anna, pulling up a story on her phone. "Woman murdered in downtown apartment building. Foul play believed but no suspects in custody. Do you think it was the crow?"

"Probably," Allen said.

Anna crossed in short steps to join Allen in the center of the roof. He told Anna that he was spending the first week in January at his sister's house and if she wanted to come she could. He gave her the address and they both looked up at the darkening sky, where the rainclouds had gathered but not broken. Allen thought he saw acid rain or chem trails up there, but he didn't say anything. They watched the storm gather for a few more moments and then Allen walked away.

He walked right into the arms of his sister. A stranger's arms. At least that's what he told the crow on the ride up to Orange County. "I barely know her," he said. "Not anymore." The crow flitted in its wicker cage while the taxi driver looked back anxiously at them from his side of the divider. The ride from the airport should have been a short one, but the cab's slow, unconfident stride made the journey long and deliberate. Allen didn't mind.

He was coming home. Well, it was his sister's home now. She had inherited the two hundred acres of horse farm after their father died. Their mother had remarried and moved to Colorado, renouncing any share that she should have had in the property. That had made it easier for Allen's sister. Now she could have the horses to herself. Now she could have the dreary solitude and snowy winters to herself. She could live there alone and be murdered when the time came for the murderer to ferret her out and kill her. That's what she had always wanted: to die in a dramatic way. To die in the middle of the dance floor. Or at 4AM on the horse farm with no one else around.

"I hope you don't mind the coffee, we're out of Earl Grey."

Berenice knew that Allen only drank black teas, but she was out of them so coffee would have to do. Allen would like that since he looked like he wanted to stay up and talk anyway. She got up from the table and put the coffee on. The kitchen was right next to the dining room, where they were sitting, so she shouldn't have any problem hearing its wail.

"You heard what happened to Barbara," Berenice remarked.

Berenice really was a beautiful name. Allen and Berenice. It was as if their parents had invested all their good genetic material in her and left Allen with the remnants. She was tall and statuesque; she had hair that was both red and brown at once. She had high cheekbones like a Russian Tatar and a long neck like a goose. High cheekbones like Anna Akhmatova. Zygomatic!

"I don't know any Barbara," said Allen.

"Of course you do. She used to live in the house behind us, that brick house with the overgrown garden in front. Well, she's dead. Murdered." Berenice chuckled. "You certainly chose a good time to come back home. Now the police will put your name on their list of suspects."

"That sounds about right," said Allen. "I always look suspicious to law enforcement."

The sound of the rain striking the window was not quite enough to obfuscate the sounds that the crow made as it flew and peered through the French doors. "What is it?" asked Berenice. "That black thing?" Allen told her it was the crow and that he had brought it with him from the city. Berenice said that she thought it was a crow, she had majored in natural resources at Cornell after all, but she could hardly believe it. There seemed no logical reason why there should be a crow on the farm all of a sudden. It was the winter and they didn't have any clients renting the horse stalls because they were all at their vacation homes: in Maine, Virginia, New Hampshire. The clients had taken their horses with them. There were only their own horses left on the place, and Berenice hoped the crow wouldn't be a nuisance and agitate them. That was the last time the crow came up in conversation.

It wasn't much of a conversation, really. Allen wanted to say a great deal but ended up saying nothing. He wanted to say: "I know you're seeing someone, Berenice, why don't you just come out and say it?" He also wanted to say: "If you were fair, you would have sold the farm and split the money with me after Dad died, but you're pretty, you've always been pretty so I forgave you." For her part, Berenice didn't know what to make of her brother. He wasn't exactly ugly but he wasn't handsome either. He was tall and had a narrow waist and long legs so he looked all right from far away, but when you got close you suddenly noticed the hawkish, expectant expression and the grim brown hair, and soon you wondered how you had ever imagined that someone like that was handsome.

"I asked someone over," Allen spat. "I hope you don't mind. She's a co-worker and a friend."

"I don't mind at all. Why would I? I hope she likes riding because I wanted to take a pair of ponies out tomorrow. A neighbor moved away and left them to us."

Berenice loved to do that: to speak of *we* and *us* as if she and Allen were in it together. They weren't. She lived in the big house in the valley, overlooking the stream. She got all the profits from the horse farming business. She owned the rental building on Van Houden Street in a non-descript Orange County town. Allen got nothing, had nothing and was nothing. But he still loved Berenice.

The next day, Allen and Berenice rode those ponies along the stream. They rode them right onto the neighboring farm but the owners lived in Manhattan and didn't farm anyway. Besides, the ponies couldn't be expected to know which land belonged to whom. The crow circled above them, curious about it all, but Isolde didn't notice because she had never seen it in the daytime and it was too far away for her to tell it apart from the peregrine falcons that hovered in these parts. As they rode the ponies on the gently undulating land, introducing them to the territory, Berenice would always cast her eyes back to a shack that straddled the line between her property and the neighbors'. Allen thought it was probably a hunting cottage belonging to the neighbors but when he went back to inspect it after lunch he saw that it was lived in. There was lamplight burning inside, spied through a window, and there were cigarette butts in the grass. New ones. There wasn't anyone there now but someone lived there.

"Why won't you tell me who he is?" Allen asked Berenice at dinner, finally.

"Why don't you get a job?" Berenice rejoined.

"I have a job."

"Well, why don't you get a decent one? That way you wouldn't have to worry about the farm. You wouldn't have to worry about me." Berenice lit a cigarette at the table and began to smoke. That was the giveaway. She had never been a smoker before; that man had introduced her to cigarettes. "So when is this girl coming?"

"I don't know. She probably won't be here for a few days. She just left the job, she quit, so I assume she's traveling around for a bit."

"So she's like you then."

A vagrant. A vagabond.

"No, she's clever, quick-witted. You'll like her."

Berenice shrugged as if to say: *I'll do anything but like her.*

And Allen would do the same. He would do anything but like the man that Berenice was seeing. Of course, Allen wasn't seeing Anna, not yet, but they were close. Allen thought of this as he neared the shack that night. It was four in the morning, the perfect hour for clandestine intercourse, and he knew he would find Berenice there. He wore his country boots as he called them, high Burberry boots that crunched the grass proudly like grapeshot fired over a field, and Allen thought they were the perfect attire for discovering someone in. They went well with his muted green trench coat and flannel shirt.

He heard them before he saw them: their sweet nothings grotesquely mumbled in the heady hours of the morning. He saw the sinful shape of his sister's body as it squirmed in the man's arms. He saw the supple curve of the left buttocks and the surprised look of a still buoyant breast. Dr. Katzenberg had done Berenice's breasts. He was good, that Katzenberg. Perhaps Berenice was having sex with him too. Perhaps she had gotten a discount: two breasts for the price of one.

It was already night when Anna arrived. He knew it was her. He saw the swirling high beams of her rented car as she hesitantly came up the driveway and he heard her clear her throat before she rang the doorbell. As he neared the door to open it, Allen heard her shout and step out of the way quickly; he knew that was the crow. "I'm surprised you haven't figured out how to get rid of that thing yet." Allen gingerly took Anna's overnight bag from her freshly-manicured hand and invited her in. He turned back to smile at her as he led the way to the day room. This was a sunny room filled with ferns attached to the back of the house. Looking at her in the fresh, new light of this room, Allen would realize that Anna had recently gotten a chemical peel.

"I tried," Allen said when he reached the room. He poured Anna a cup of tea.

"You tried what?"

"I tried to get rid of it," said Allen. "I even fired a warning shot. That didn't work."

"I wouldn't expect it to," said Anna. "A bird like this you just have to shoot. No warning shot. And you'd better do it soon. Do it for me. I don't want him to be a witness to all our crimes."

Allen, who had begun to walk toward the kitchen, turned to look at her, but then he realized she was joking. "Where's your sister?" Anna called from the day room. Allen could barely hear her over the running water of the kitchen sink. "Oh, she's missing!" he cried.

When Allen returned, he was unnerved by Anna's alarmed expression. "What do you mean she's missing?" she asked. "I hope she's all right."

"Oh, she'll be fine," said Allen. "She does this. She finds a guy she likes and then she disappears for a few weeks, sometimes a few months. She can do that because she's independently wealthy. Well, not wealthy, wealthy, but wealthy enough. The house is paid for, she gets rental income from a building she owns in a town not far from here."

Anna nodded as if in understanding but she could hardly relate. Her parents had come into the country as illegal aliens. "I like it here," she said. "This is Orange County, right? Not rednecky at all. Well, not like I was expecting."

"No, it's not so bad."

Anna gazed at Allen for a moment, at his gray-blue eyes and his fuller-than-you-would-expect-for-his-age brown hair, and then she said something. "I missed you."

"Very funny. What, did you run out of grapes or something?"

"No," said Anna. "I missed having someone to talk to. Someone to be strange with."

Allen laughed and then they sat silent for the rest of the hour: she watching a television playing softly in the background and he drinking his fourth cup of Earl Grey. After Berenice was taken care of, Allen had taken her car into town to buy a tin of the stuff. There was a place in town that sold gourmet teas in these old-fashioned, British-looking tins. Allen had gone to junior high school with the owner and his wife, but they had forgotten him too. Just like Berenice.

As the night began to wear on, Allen decided it was probably best to show Anna to her room. She would take his old bedroom, which was at the end of the hall on the second floor. It wasn't a large room, but it was perfect for guests because it had dramatic exposed brick along one wall and a high cathedral ceiling. After giving Anna some time to settle in, Allen returned with a warm blanket and some toiletries for the morning. The nice kind, from that store L'Occitane that Berenice always raided whenever she went to New York. Anna fell quickly to sleep, even though she was jobless and her money was running out; these things had been worrying her over the last few days. She forgot all about the crow.

She forgot all about money too. The next day, Allen and Anna went riding on the ponies, and when he laughed in shock at how quickly the ponies took to her, she shook her head humbly. Then she laughed too. They didn't ride to the property line where he had ridden with Berenice a few days before. No. Instead, they took the stream the other way: to where the land terraced steeply up to a ridge. There were caves under that jutting land, for those who liked spelunking, and on top of the ridge was a house with a crooked tower.

They stopped their ponies at a bend in the stream. Allen's parents had put a commemorative bench here many years ago and they sat on the obsidian top, obscuring the melodramatic passage with their butts. Anna made sure that she was close to Allen. He reached for her hand and then she leaned in for a kiss.

Before they knew it, it was growing dark again. They had spent the day with the bleary-eyed ponies and the encroaching cold air. It bit their faces and made Anna's nipples hard. The air seemed perfectly at home in this unpeopled place. When they got back to the house, Allen immediately went to work at dinner. The Cornish hens were already thawing and the Riesling was being chilled. It was impossible to fuck up a Cornish hen. All you had to do was thaw it, season it and stick it in the oven.

"You have to do something about that crow," Anna said as they sat down to dinner.

It was hardly dinner talk.

"Shoot it for real this time. It's evil. It probably *is* responsible for all those murders. Maybe it takes the shape of a man when no one's looking. Or a woman. A really maleficent one."

Allen didn't want to talk about that so he went to work on his Cornish hen. It was pretty good, if he said so himself, and he made sure to tell Anna that. She agreed. She had never had Cornish hen before. Was that something that rich people ate, she wondered.

They walked solemnly upstairs to Anna's room when they were finished. They didn't clear the table or do the dishes. They just left their unfinished food where it was, as if the people who had been eating dinner had suddenly died. The door creaked as Anna opened it. It was as if the door hinges knew that something important was about to happen, like at the end of the gothic novel where you know the crazy woman is about to burn down the house. Everyone knows it. Anna sat on the edge of her bed and Allen joined her. "Let's not talk about the crow," she said. "Let's not think about it."

Agreed, thought Allen. He lowered the straps of her dress and saw that her breasts were young and upright, like Berenice's. But Anna's hadn't come from the surgical table of Dr. Katzenberg, or from any other doctor for that matter. These were her own God-given breasts. And Anna's hair was a golden brown, like the golden coat of a Karabakh horse. They made love and then they fell asleep in Anna's bed. Anna slept through the night. Allen didn't. He woke up in the early hours and walked to the old, spotted mirror that hung in its bronze frame in a corner of the guest room.

Allen looked in the mirror and he saw the image of a man who was probably a murderer. Not probably, certainly. And it wasn't worth the continued charade to attribute all of the bad things around him to the crow. These things had started before the crow had entered the picture. I knew that as well as he did. I tapped my beak against the window and flitted about anxiously. Allen didn't turn to look at me; he was very much in another world at that moment. I tried to get his attention. I made a sound, finally mastering the tenor of the caw.

A SECOND COMING

The war was a longstanding one. The house was at war with the wolf gods and wolf mothers that inhabited the place, and our father was at war with us. He didn't have any particular reason to be at war; that was just the sort of person he was. He had come home from Afghanistan with the fight still in him and since there were no Taliban opium dens here we must be his targets. We, the people, you might say. We, the people, in order to preserve familial peace and justice, do hereby shoot our father in the back and toss him into the lake. We were both thinking about him as we drove away from Princeton in Zach's Mercedes. I told Zach not to look so excited.

"It's hard not to," Zach says. "We're leaving Princeton to spend winter break with our father: Pol Pot."

"He's not Pol Pot," I said, turning the radio to something other than classical music. "Pol Pot was from Cambodia."

"Well, Pinochet then."

And then Zach asked me if I brought the list of things Dad wanted.

"No, I remember them by heart." And I just couldn't help twisting the knife. "One of us actually deserved to get into Princeton."

Zach is older than me by a year but I started Princeton earlier because Dad sent him to military school in Virginia for two years while I enrolled on time. Dad said that Zach needed to be toughened up. We're legacies because our father and grandfather both attended Princeton.

Zach laughed and told me that if I knew what was good for me I'd stop that line of talk. He might just have to show me what he learned in military school. I stop because I like Zach and, to be fair, I need Zach as an ally. Zach was more like a father than our actual father was. Aside from the years he spent in the Persian Gulf and Afghanistan, when Dad finally did return to the States he spent more time at his corporate office in New York than with us: his wife and children. Well, his office in New York and the various sluts he played with in that office. Our father is the chairman of a military defense company.

"Is she coming to the lake house?" I asked Zach.

Zach didn't have to ask who I was referring to. "God no," he replied. He said that Mom would probably hire an Argentinian gigolo to pretend to be her boyfriend just to make Dad jealous. We both agree that that wouldn't work.

"What's on that list?" Zach asked. He was trying to figure out if we should go to the ammo shop before getting on the turnpike.

I told Zach that he should get on the turnpike and take the earlier exit home because most of the items on the list are fishing things, and the bait shop was nearer to our house than to Princeton. Zach groaned at the thought of spending hours alone with Dad on the lake and I suggested that maybe Dad had changed.

Zach didn't have to say anything to that; the icy glare he gave me was more than enough. "Look at this attachment he sent me yesterday. It's a personal ad from a woman he went out with last week. He's bringing her to the house."

Zach handed me his phone and I read the ad aloud.

"Australian belly dancer seeks businessman for long walks on the beach, elk stalking in Wyoming, and tantric sex. Prefer gentlemen that are married or widowed."

Zach said that this pretty much summed up Dad because if Mom hadn't agreed to a divorce he probably would have hired a hitman to take her out. That would make him a widower, like the Australian belly dancer wanted. And if the hitman botched the job, Dad would find a way to convince Mom to come back. You see, our father has this way with women. Maybe it's the money or maybe it's just this general impression that he's the sort of person that always gets what he wants. Dad says that half of success is simply looking and acting like a successful person. And he always looks at me when he says it as if he's already given up on Zach.

For his part, Zach has always managed to maintain a stiff upper lip. I admired my brother and I thought a lot of my admiration had to do with the way he kept trudging along, even though our father treated him like he was the tadpole that never should have made it to the egg. He just wormed his away along and somehow got to the finish-line instead of one of the other, more deserving tadpoles.

Zach certainly didn't look like a tadpole when he came down to dinner that night dressed in all black. After stopping at the bait and tackle shop, we reached the lake house and promptly took showers and changed into more suitable dinner wear. All of our father's friends were wealthy and we were used to having to look the part so we assumed that we should treat this Australian belly dancer as if she was just more of the same. That is, an ordinary part of our father's social set and not the catch of the day. Obviously she wasn't a part of Dad's set and the aging man was going through some sort of midlife crisis, but it wasn't worth showing up in khaki shorts and sandals and risking Dad breaking Zach's nose.

The showers were quick. Zach and I were close so he didn't have to turn the water off when he was done, he just got out and told me it was my turn. By the time I was finished and came down dressed, Zach was already seated at table. We were looking at one another when the sound of the key turning in the door reached us. Dad had ordered catered food for dinner and it was waiting in metal containers on the granite island in the kitchen. Zach had made sure to set the dinner table before we had taken our showers.

"There are my boys," our father said when he saw us.

"Good evening, Dad," I said.

"Good evening, Dad," Zac said.

Falling

"I know you boys like crab so I wanted to treat you today. Lobster tails, melted butter and Maryland blue crab."

Dad took a seat at the head of the table.

"But you said Maryland blue crab was only for special occasions," Zach remarked.

Dad tells us that it is, in fact, a special occasion. He's decided to get married again. I glance at Zach, Zach glances at me, and then Dad, who had briefly sat down to talk, gets up to bring the trays of lobster tail and crab to the dinner table. "I know it's sudden but you boys have to meet her," he said when he returned. "She's a special person. She gets me."

"You're referring to the Australian belly dancer," Zach noted.

"Is that what she called herself in the ad?" Our father chuckled to himself. "Yeah, I guess that's her. We didn't talk about anything having to do with belly-dancing though. I guess it makes sense."

"I didn't realize that Australia had a belly-dancing tradition," said Zach.

"Oh, it has the best tradition, I'm sure," Dad said. Only the best for our father. "Are you boys gonna eat this or do I have to eat eight pounds of crab myself?"

Zach and I both open our individualized containers of crustacean, which appear surprisingly warm and fresh, with a perfectly oceanic blue tint to their claws. Their eyes were still bulging. "Boy, I'm not sure this one is dead," I say, and then I pick mine up and shove it in Zach's face. "Brody, you're making a mistake!"

Zac sighs but Dad chuckles. "I get it, Brody, even if Zach doesn't. Sebastian the crab. Brody, you were always a joker but I think Zach's got more comedic talent than you do. It's just hiding under that Stoic, juiced-up exterior."

Zach banged a fist on the table and my eyes darted over to him. He was seated beside me and he hadn't touched his food. Zach had a temper, I knew that, but we had always gotten along so well that it never was an issue for us. I knew it was the testosterone he was taking.

183

Testosterone was one hell of a drug. Zac had been taking it since high school and by his freshman year at Princeton he was really a massive guy. I thought he took steroids so he could set new PRs in the gym, but our father told me that one of Zach's testicles had to be removed when he was in junior high so his test level was naturally on the low side. I was always a little disappointed that Zac never told me this himself but waited for Dad to say something. "As usually happens in these cases," Dad told me, "Zach is prescribed more than he really needs so that's why he looks like the Russian amateur bodybuilding champion." Students at Princeton thought it was weird that this huge guy was always in the library buried in his computer science textbooks, but I think they'd cut him some slack if they knew the kind of family we came from.

"What's going on, Dad?"

It's Zach who asks this.

"Is that why you banged your fist on the table?"

"Maybe," said Zach. "You tell us you're getting married and then you're being unusually nice. What's going on? Are you going to prison?"

"Perhaps I'm just happy to see my two boys."

Zach snorted and looked away.

After a brief silence, our father said: "All right, you got me, I *am* being especially nice but it's because what I have to tell you is something that pains me. Deeply."

I put down my anti-crustacean utensils and glanced over at Zach. The look in his eyes was a mélange of ire and terror.

"I told you I was getting married," Dad began, "but I didn't tell you about everything else that goes along with that."

With that, our father rose from the table and walked to one of the front windows. This house, the lake house, was originally a manor house in England that our grandfather purchased for a song. He bought it from a peer crushed by the weight of the infamous British inheritance taxes, thanks Lloyd George, and rather than adhere to his verbal promise to maintain the house as he found it, and where he found it, he had the manor dismantled piece-by-piece and shipped to the United States. Grandfather didn't want to live in England, our father told us. And since Granddad had the money, why shouldn't he have the house rebuilt where he wanted it? Detailed architectural diagrams allowed the Jacobean house to be rebuilt stone-by-stone in Delaware, where we lived. The front double doors of oak sat between two wide dormers, and the two towers of the main wing cast shadows over the front of the house, shrouding everything in dark. But there isn't much to see anyway as the house sits about two thousand feet behind an electronic gate. Our family has a 400-acre property.

Our father stood silently by the window, looking out at the alley of trees, and then he turned around and finally told us what he meant. He told us that he was disinheriting us. It had been a hard decision, but he had been thinking about it for a long time and had reached the conclusion that it really was the proper thing to do. He would still pay for our Princeton degrees, even though he had considered leaving us to figure out another way to finish school, and he would even consider continuing Zac's car payment. But as for leaving us some of his fortune, estimated by *The Wall Street Journal* at over $260 million? Those days were over.

"You son of a bitch," Zach whispered.

Dad laughed and the look in his eyes told me he was back to his old self.

I could see that Zach wasn't taking this well, and I was sure that I was less annoyed about it than he was. Perhaps I didn't see cause to worry because I assumed I would always have Zach as a partner in crime. Zach clearly didn't see things that way. I glanced at him and I watched him push his chair back as if he was about to rise from the table and walk out of the dining room. That's when I changed the subject by asking: "So when is the Australian lady coming?"

"She should be here in a day or two," our father replied, glancing briefly at me.

Zach asked if we could be excused and when Dad agreed we left the table. Zach went to his room, which overlooked the lake, and after about an hour in my room I decided to join him in his. I could hear the scratches of static on his Army radio as I neared the door. He started talking to me in tune to the radio's metronome. "I'm calling the Orlovski twins," he said. The Orlovskis lived at the scrapyard about a mile up the road from us. Their dad owned a scrap metal business and they were our nearest neighbors, that's how isolated we were by the lake. I told Zach that I thought it was a bad idea. Once we got them talking, the Orlovski twins would never shut up. We'd be on the radio with them all night. But I could see that what our father said had upset him so I didn't protest too much.

"Wolf's Home to the Orlovskis," said Zach. "Dan and John, do you read?"

"Copy. This is John."

And that was the beginning of hours of idle chatter, just like I had anticipated. It was only much later interrupted by strange sounds from the attic. It must have been about two in the morning. Zach asked me what I thought it was and I told him it was probably just Dad rummaging through old papers. But Zach said our father had a bad back and we would have heard him struggling to make it up the steep attic stairs. Zach stood up and I noticed for the first time that he had a gun sitting in his waist holster. He took it out, handed it to me and told me to follow him. When we reached the steps up to the attic, we saw the whimsical rays of a flashlight whipping around first this way and then that. I followed Zach up the stairs, silently, and there we saw a man bent over a large box of papers.

Zach told the man to stand up and then Dad said: "God, I knew you boys would still be up."

Zach asked what he was doing and Dad told us he was looking for Zach's birth certificate. And when I asked why he said: "Because Zach isn't mine, that's why."

I didn't say anything to that but then Zach said: "You're lying."

"Am I?" Dad asked. "It was the late '90s. Your mother was doing blow and waking up God knows where every night. I went to the Persian Gulf in '99 and you were born eleven months later."

"That's a lie."

"Believe what you want," said Dad.

Falling

We approached our father in the darkened attic and the sounds of the insects crawling between the walls were like the blare of the sirens at the prisoner-of-war camp or the hush before the British dropped their bombs on Dresden. It seemed we had always been at war. Us boys. Our father. "I meant everything I said," said our father. "I'm not disinheriting you because I don't think you're mine. You need to learn to survive. I'm just teaching you how to live."

Dad picked up a box of old photos: pictures of Zach before his first day of school, pictures of Zach in his little league uniform. He took the box and carried it to the window, straining under the weight even though he was a big man. Heavy as it was, Dad didn't seem to think twice about tossing it all way. I raised the gun but Zac couldn't see me because I was standing behind him. Dad turned the box upside down with difficulty and then I pulled the trigger. I had shot him: hitting him in that vulnerable spot just below the shoulder blade on the left side. An expertly-done sniper shot. Dad staggered for a minute, clutching the wide plank window frame. Before he fell out of the window, more than forty feet above the ground, he turned to look at his two boys.

Zach never asked me why I shot Dad. He never talked about how we would get our stories straight when the police came: why did we come upstairs, whose gun was it, which one of us had shot dad, why. He didn't say anything. He just ran downstairs (I followed), and when we reached Dad's body on the macadam he checked the pulse to confirm he was dead. He was. The only discussion we had on the matter was what to do in the immediate aftermath. Zach suggested that we bury Dad in the thick woods that bordered the state land, but I said that because the ground was so cold it would take forever to dig a suitable plot and Dad's girlfriend might show up before we finished. I suggested that we tie some of Zach's dumbbells to Dad's arms and legs, and toss him in the lake. We could bury him after Sheila had come and left, and Zach agreed.

The lake seemed to agree too. Its only answer to our sin was a few feeble bubbles that rose to the surface as Dad's body sank. Even the fish seemed to turn their backs on us. Even the wolves. There wasn't a single animal in sight. Zac returned to the house after that, about a thousand feet back from the lake, and he didn't notice that I didn't follow him. It was early morning and I rejoined the road.

I suppose I just needed to clear my head. They didn't teach patricide at Princeton, at least not anymore. I didn't know where I was going. Part of me expected to hitch a ride with a stranger, maybe a trucker on his way to West Virginia. I might have some sort of adventure. It didn't occur to me that in the age of Uber and Lyft, drivers were unlikely to stop for someone walking on the road no matter how vulnerable you looked. No matter if you looked like the heir to a military defense fortune, with your brown hair parted in the middle like Richie Rich.

I did eventually reach the town, more than ten miles away. As soon as I stepped on the smooth concrete sidewalk, I seemed to know what to do. I walked down Main Street for about a quarter of a mile and then I turned off onto one of the side streets. This particular street was where all the seedy stores were: the brothel that masqueraded as a day-long arcade and the antique shop where the hippie owner sold meth by the ounce. *Her* shop was in the middle of the block.

"We're closed," the woman said as the bells hanging from the door chimed.

I heard the slap of her tarot cards against the table. When I reached it, hidden in a private nook in the back, I saw she was just then turning over a card. It was the Devil: a red creature with a man's face, angry wings and the terrible image of a goat's hairy hooves. "I said we're closed," she remarked.

"I'd like to see you."

"I don't do readings this early." She must have noted how I watched her at play with her cards because she said: "Some things it's better to keep out of."

I sat in the paying customer's chair.

"I didn't come for a reading. I need your help."

"What did you do?"

My sigh was lazy and long.

"I'd like to fix the damage I've done. I want to appease a potentially vengeful spirit. Well, a definitely vengeful spirit. I'd like to make things right."

And after a pause: "I killed a man."

"Who was the man?"

"My father."

The woman rose from her chair and walked over to a row of shelves hanging from the wall. They were like shelves from a house built in the '70s: cheap factory-made material painted white. And she didn't look at me as she rifled through them. She was searching them with calm and collected irritation as you would when looking for the last can of Vienna sausages. She was a woman wearing a curly black wig with jewels of jet about her neck and hanging from her earlobes. Her brown skin was a like a hundred endless summers and it was impossible to tell her age. On her head was a wicker crown from which hung the skulls of rodents: rats, ferrets, stoats. "What sort of person was he?" she asked. Her back was to me.

"Avaricious," I said. "Cruel. He played with the minds of people. He told my brother that he wasn't his son and I'm still not sure if it was some kind of sick joke."

The woman returned a few minutes later with a figure made of sticks bound together with twine. The twine looked like strips from tree bark. "Take this man and wrap his body in a large bill: a fifty dollar bill or a hundred," she said. "Walk around the house three times, holding the figure in your hands. When you have done, bury it in sacred ground."

I took the figure from the woman's hands and thanked her for her aid. I asked what I could do to repay her and she said that I could go from her shop and never come back. So that's just what I did. As I left, I turned round to look back at what I had left behind, like Lot. The sign in the window read: "American Indian Sorceress. Tarot Readings & Celestial Aid."

That night, Zach and I were sitting in the living room dressed for dinner, just as we had been when Dad had come the night before. We listened to the howl of the wolves and then we took showers: Zac left the water on and I stepped in when he stepped out like always. Zac was reading *The Wall Street Journal* that our father had brought and he was engrossed in a certain article. He told me about its contents. It explained that restaurants were still questionable investments but creating a food company that services prisons continued to be one of the best business ideas in the US.

"What are we going to say if she asks us what happened to Dad?" I asked Zac.

"I don't know."

I buried my head in my hands. I was still sitting like that when we heard the sound of the door opening and a woman walking in.

"I met your father on an Alaskan cruise. It's not true that I met him from that ad about belly-dancing. It's just a funny story. I met him before that. I was on the cruise with my boyfriend at the time and your father was traveling alone. I thought it was strange for a man like him to be without someone. As soon as I saw him it was like I was hit by a bolt of lightning."

When I saw her, I understood why Dad was marrying her. She had an easygoing way that was perfectly suited to manage his intractable one. If he was the sand, she was the sea. Perhaps the warm summer waters of the Bering Strait. Mom had never understood. Sheila was wearing a fox fur coat and black Louboutin shoes.

"I had a feeling he wouldn't be here when I arrived," said Sheila. "He gave me an extra key."

"He should be back soon," I said. "I think he went to Baltimore for a meeting."

Zach shot me an impossible to misinterpret S*top talking, Brody* look.

"I had a horrible time on that cruise," Sheila said. "Most girls love a cruise, even to Alaska, but I kept thinking that if I got thrown overboard who would save me. My boyfriend couldn't swim."

I could hear the regular thud of footsteps as she spoke.

"I think I should have gone to the Yucatán instead. Get lost in a henequén forest. You know, my last husband was the half owner of a henequén plantation so I know all about plant fibers."

Falling

"I don't think Brody cares about any of that." That was Zach. "He's more interested in proving that Romulus and Remus actually existed."

"You should explain who they are, Zac," I said.

The footsteps we heard before drew very near.

"It's all right. I know. Romulus and Remus were the twins who sucked at the teat of the she-wolf. After killing Remus, Romulus went on to found Rome. I know about things besides belly-dancing, you know. Oh, there you are," said Sheila, rising from her seat and petting the face of the fox around her neck. "The boys said you wouldn't be back today."

"I surprised even myself," said Dad. "I went for a swim and I didn't think I'd ever come back."

Sheila embraced our father and brushed away some plankton that was stuck in his hair. Dad took his seat at the head of the table, across from Sheila who returned to her seat at the foot.

"You know, it's easy for a man to underestimate his children. Well, until they shoot him and drown his body in a lake," said Dad.

"What an odd thing to say," Sheila noted.

"Why don't we bring out dinner," and Dad walked into the kitchen to fetch the trays of food. He had ordered catering again.

"I hope it's seafood," said Sheila.

"No, it's lamb," said Dad. "The slaughtered offspring of a sheep. You know, I've always wondered how the parents of the lamb felt about that. If they were glad that the lamb was gone. If they suspected what it might one day do."

"My family were shepherds," said Sheila. "I always hated living on a farm. All that bleating. That's why I became a belly dancer."

Dad returned with several more trays, and when he had set them down he removed the metal covers. He personally distributed the food, lamb along with various kinds of vegetables and mashed potatoes, and then he returned to his chair. Just as he sat down, one of his eyeballs popped out of his head and began a circuitous roll on the parquet floor.

"Oh, honey, look," cried Sheila. "One of your eyes came out of the socket. I'll get it."

"Thank you, dear."

When the operation was completed, that of putting the eye back in its proper place, Dad sat down again. "Sheila's been reading the Kamasutra and she's planning on teaching me some new moves," he said. "I'd invite Zach to join but he only has one testicle."

Zach slapped his hand on the table. "Dad," he said, but quietly. I could see that the ongoing war between us, the war of two brothers and their father, had exhausted him.

ESTRANGULATA LAETA

No one ever thought they would turn on her. As soon as you entered Darlene's office you were met by them, all these plants, and I always thought they gave the impression of desolation, as if the woman surrounded herself with all these things because she herself had already died. Of course, I had heard about her before I made it to her office on that November day. It had been Professor K. who told me that I should leave class to see her. And as I left, Jack Jones, a 135-pounder on the wrestling team, told me: "Be careful. They say she murdered her husband. He's been missing for four months."

Well that was clearly a fascinating bit of information, but Darlene herself was not a particularly interesting person, something that I knew without the necessity of having to meet her. There was something in her name, Darlene Brown-Racine, that made me think of a lady who spent long nights alone doing rote tasks, something along the lines of knitting, translating old books, or gardening, and when I met her this turned out to be the case, although there was more to her than met the eye. In fact, Darlene was to become an important part of my life, albeit for a short time. Her face was ordinary – somewhat round with the beginnings of a double chin – but her eyes were beautiful. They were large and a bright brown, like upturned soil that had partially dried. I found myself drawn to her, like one of her plants. I do not know what attracted me; perhaps it was just her availability, but I do know that she toyed with me, as she did with many other young men, and when she was done with me she cast me aside.

But I wasn't thinking of any of this as I approached Darlene's office. Vice Dean Darlene Brown-Racine's office was on the first floor of the Chemistry building, that is, down the hall from the lecture room where I had until recently been bored to death by one of K's lectures on the literary beginnings of the English Renaissance. This class was mandatory for all English majors, and we all looked forward to it about as much as the enlisted men look forward to the Army's twice yearly hernia exam. The man had had a problem with me from the moment he caught me falling asleep in class. In my defense, I was seated all the way in the back and I had no reason to believe that he'd see me with those telescope-lens-thick spectacles of his. He had given me a solid C on my first essay and now this: directed to meet with a woman whose purpose, I was sure, was to tell me how much of an ingrate I was.

When I reached the Vice Dean's office, I heard a soft chatter and then watched the door swing open. I glimpsed a room filled with a profusion of verdant green plants and then a young man stepped out, who I could only guess was a graduate student. At the time, I was more surprised by the student coming out of the Vice Dean's office than I was by the appearance of the office itself, mostly because of the guy's looks. The student, who looked like he stepped off of the set of a Merchant-Ivory film about the British Raj, grinned at me. He was square-jawed and of average height, had a medium brown complexion, black hair parted on the side, and was wearing a '20s style Oxford-Cambridge' suit. His hair made me think of men of the South Pacific islands who were said to rub their black hair with plant juices every morning.

"Is that Jason?" I heard a woman's deep voice inquire from inside the office.

"Yes, it is," I said.

"Ah, Jason, come in."

I entered the office and was directed to sit between two ferns, which I later learned were split-leafed philodendrons.

"As you know," the Vice Dean began, herself taking a seat beside a tall poinsettia, "I have recently come into this position due to the untimely electrocution of former Vice Dean Munro."

Her voice was deep like Kathleen Turner's.

"No," I remarked. "I did not know that."

"Yes, so sad," said the Vice Dean, and then she cleared her throat. She picked up an arrangement of oleander flowers and castor bean stalks that she had on her desk. She picked a little bit here, a little bit there, and then she promptly set the arrangement down again. "So tell me, Jason, what are your strengths?"

"My strengths, madam?"

"Madam? Is that how you address me?"

I caught a brief glimpse of three-inch black pumps beneath the Vice Dean's desk. Into these pumps two extremely pale feet had been squeezed.

"Your Excellency?"

"Oh, Jason," the Vice Dean laughed. "I am not an archbishop! You can call me Darlene. All the young men do. How about this? Why don't you tell me what your goals are?"

The Vice Dean did a sort of dance under the table with her feet, and I remembered where I had seen her before: on her bicycle riding to the English Department in her high heels.

"My immediate goal is to pass Professor K's class."

"I meant your long term goals, Jason."

"I'd like to do my PhD on the poisonous plants of medieval literature," said I.

"In the Department of English?" Darlene asked.

"Yes, madam. I mean, Darlene. I'm thinking of writers like Chaucer, Ariosto, Boiardo. Perhaps go a little into the Elizabethan and Jacobean periods. John Ford, Shakespeare and the like. But mostly Ariosto because I think he has been overlooked in the bourgeois modernism of the present day. I am worried that my lack of Italian language skills might impede me."

Darlene's laugh was short and curt, the sort of laugh you'd expect from a clown who was actually intending to belch. "Oh, you won't have any problems there," she said. "I can barely speak English and I am the vice dean of education at Princeville University."

"Princeton."

"That's what I said. Princeton." Darlene sighed. "Well, I wonder if you have the right stuff to pursue that sort of training."

"I may not have the right stuff now, but I am only a sophomore. Actually, I don't understand why you are all giving me such a hard time. This is supposed to be Princeton. What happened to the grade inflation?"

My 19-year-old self thought that was a good joke, but Darlene didn't seem to agree.

I actually let out a little gasp, like a little girl, and the Vice Dean sort of shook herself, as if she were awaking from a dream. "I'm sorry. It's this new bra. It's like my breasts are being shot into the stratosphere. Well, what were we talking about?

"Poisonous plants."

"Poisonous plants, right," Darlene echoed. "Plants are a good line to follow as they allow you to sort of explore the intersectionality of science and English. Chemistry and biology. Yes, I like biology. I am actually a devotee of making flower arrangements, but that is a story for another time. I know a lot about plants, mind you. I prefer mixing reds with blues. Purples, too. Of course, there are greens, but most plants have a bit of green. But that isn't what we're here about, is it?"

"What are we here about, Darlene?"

"It's your grades, Jason. They're just abysmal. I mean, they're all right if your goal in life is to be a sperm donor, but you didn't come to Princeton for that, although I'm sure they'd pay a lot more for yours than they would for Joe Delaney on the corner there."

"Darlene?"

"Don't look so serious, Jason. I am not only the new Vice Dean of Education. I am also the Chairwoman of the Water Department of Princeton Township."

I had difficulty seeing how one was connected with the other, either in a professional sense or a cognitive one, but Darlene was the Vice Dean of Education, not I.

Falling

"Now where are we?" asked Darlene, again losing her train of thought. "Yes, what to do with you. I have to admit, Jason, I find you attractive and I'd like to invite you over to my house to discuss how we might salvage your career in the English Department. I just buried my husband... Excuse me, divorced my husband four months ago so I'm free. I'd like to invite you over to talk. I'll have some coffee on the pot, you'll dress yourself in something nice, something that shows off your youthful figure, you know, a tight pair of jeans or something, and we'll figure out how to get you writing about, who was it? Pavarotti?"

"Ariosto."

"Ariosto that was it!"

When Darlene ushered me out of the office and closed the door, I found myself consumed with fits of laughter. I just laughed and laughed, bent over with the stuff, until the venomous looks of Darlene's secretary helped me to remember where I was, which was either the Office of the Vice Dean of Education or the Department of Water of Princeton Township.

As I approached Darlene's house in my car all I could think of was what would happen to all her plants if there was a war. Her lawn was overflowing with them. I recognized azaleas, Jerusalem holly, and several types of Arum. I only knew these because they were common ornamentals and an old aunt had introduced me to them. Perhaps when the bombs finally did fall, it would be the people that died and the plants would live on. At least until the atomic dust blotted out the sun.

But that was the farthest thing from Darlene's mind as I sat with her in her double-height living room. She had met me at the door in her high heels, red this time, and she was already nursing a glass of sherry. She must have caught me eyeing the drink thirstily because she said: "This is for me, sweetie, not for you. You're just a child." I wondered what would happen to Darlene if the neighbors caught her hosting 19-year old students late at night while wearing garters and stilettos but I didn't get the impression that it was Darlene's nature to worry about tomorrow, so why should I? I needed to be more like the sturdy Tibetan bamboo that I saw planted beside the coat rack in Darlene's foyer. I needed to suck up all the water while I could, remember what I was (a bamboo shoot), and worry about tomorrow when tomorrow came.

And so I followed Darlene into her living room, mesmerized as much by the sights around me as by the irregular clack-a-dack-dack of her heels. I suppose she was already in the early stages of getting drunk. "I have a meatloaf in the oven," she remarked on the way, and I wondered whether I should remind her about it on the way out or just let her burn the house down.

We reached the living room, which had twenty-foot high windows that looked out into the garden. In fact, I think the windows were that high in order that the plants inside could be suffused with the light they needed to grow, even in the winter time. I knew very little about exotic plants then, but Manoj would tell me later that the strange plant with the reddish fruits was called *Ximenia caffra*, or the large sourplum. It could be found in Southern and Eastern Africa. There were many different types of Ficus and there were plants that I could only call ferns, as I did not know what they were. But these were not ordinary ferns. Many were well over six feet tall, and they gave you the impression of getting lost on a trek through the center of a tropical island, especially with the bright flowers that were placed beneath them like in an understory. What all these plants had in common was that they gave the impression of flora that had naturally assumed a tropical arrangement, as if by accident, and they also gave a suggestion of things that could be eaten.

After Darlene sat down on a red leather chair, I watched as she reached over to a potted plant on a nearby table and began picking off little leaves. Using her chubby fingers, she picked these and placed them in a tea cup. "You aren't going to make a drink with that?" I asked.

"Don't worry," said Darlene. "This is to make a tea. It's mint."

I nodded and looked around some more. That was when I noticed *it* for the first time. It was an unusual plant, to say the least. Not quite a Venus Fly Trap, but unusual enough to me. It looked like a short pine tree because it had what I thought at first were needles, but they were actually very small leaves. In fact, closer inspection would reveal that it was a shrub or a vine that already seemed to be sending out feelers. There were also small white flowers occasionally sprouting from the branches.

"That's a vine," Darlene told me. "People call it a brushwood, but it's actually a vine. It comes from the Indian subcontinent, but it was known to the Romans. How they knew about it only they could say. They're all dead now so they're not saying anything. All the people who knew."

My gaze drifted outside where I noted a number of interesting trees. One very tall one looked like some sort of sequoia or pine; Manoj revealed to me that they were deodars and they grew to be extremely tall. They were the objects that he noticed most on her property, perhaps as they were a reminder of home. Of course, I didn't really know Manoj then but we would become familiar in time.

"But we won't have any tea now," said Darlene, returning to what was by then an old point. "Tea will be for later. It's certainly past tea time. Oh, I'm so tired!" And she yawned. "I really could use another drink."

Darlene leaned back in her chair and closed her eyes for a moment. It was then that I saw the unusual brushwood stretch out one of its feelers. It grew longer and nimbly wiggled around like a limb. That limb out and ready, the plant looped itself around the bottle of sherry on one side of Darlene, sent another loop around the glass, brought the two intoxicating articles together and poured the brown drink into the glass. It was almost like magic. The plant deftly placed the glass on the table beside Darlene who, almost as if on cue, awakened herself awkwardly and noticed the now-full glass. "Oh!" she said with a smile. "There it is! Thank you, Jason!"

I heard the distant beep of an oven timer and so I said: "I think the meatloaf is done."

"What?" asked Darlene, finishing off her drink. "Oh yes, that meatloaf. You know, I really didn't want to take this job at the water department but I thought if I don't take it, they'll give it to somebody else. Some long-legged bimbo who could get any job she wants. A nice high-paying gig in New York probably. But I like Princeton. I don't know how long I'll keep this vice dean thing."

I looked at her then and I thought she looked pretty in that light, with her dark hair down and her face all made up. That was when Darlene remembered that she had a meeting with her cycling group tomorrow. The group was entirely composed of women, but she liked to break the droll monotony of a bunch of middle-aged women talking about books that they had half-read or movies they hadn't actually seen by inviting a young man, a student, to join them. I wondered how many male students she had invited and what they looked like.

I told Darlene that I would not be available for her group, even though it would be nice to finally see Einstein's house, where the cycling tour was to start. I said I had a meeting with a professor, which was a lie; the truth was I just didn't see the use of getting up that early. I left soon afterward, as Darlene kept falling asleep, but I did remember to take the meatloaf out of the oven.

I returned to Darlene's house the next day, just as her cycling group was getting back to its headquarters, her house, and when they finally departed I waited to see what Darlene would do. She wasn't expecting me, but I wanted to pick up where we left off as last night had not brought the conversation that she had promised, but I think I was also curious about her. I didn't have the courage to knock on her door and so I watched from a bench across the street as she brought a tea kettle and a cup out of the house and poured herself a cup of tea in the garden. I assumed the leaves were the mint she grew in her arboretum-style living room. I was just about to leave when I saw something flash by. It was the young Indian man I had seen coming out of Darlene's office that first morning. He was riding a fancy Schwinn and, sure enough, he cycled his way right to Darlene's house. He was very irritating with his confident handsomeness, but he was entirely oblivious to my presence. I think he heard Darlene in the garden because he left his bike on her steps and walked around to the back. I changed my vantage point so I could watch them better.

All I heard at first was the sound of laughter. Darlene's was unnatural, as if she was afraid of making a bad impression, while the student's was deep and self-assured. I assumed Darlene was uncomfortable standing in the grass in her heels as she stepped out of them, but then she must have noticed her splotchy feet as she stepped into them again. The traffic passing by the road died down so I heard when Darlene remarked that *Breakfast at Tiffany's* was the greatest American novel of the twentieth century, which gave me the impression that she probably never read it. She kept mentioning Lady Windermere, which I was sure was a character from Oscar Wilde and not Capote.

After the student left, I stepped a little closer to Darlene's side of the street, I just couldn't help myself, and that's when she saw me. Her smile beckoned me to come closer although I thought her eyes held a look of disappointment. "Jason, you shouldn't be here," she said when I was only about ten feet away from her, but she smiled still. "The nostrils of the lioness have caught the scent of a superior stag," she said, but I had no idea what she was talking about. Finally: "I will send you an email when I am interested in seeing you again."

That email came later that afternoon, right as I was returning to my dorm from a group session with another student. She wanted to meet that evening, close to eight, and I made sure that I squeezed myself back into the tight jeans like Darlene wanted even though I was sure she was going to dump me.

When I reached her house, the plants seemed more overgrown than ever. There were the tall ferns that made the house seem like an abandoned cottage on Anguilla and below the red hibiscus was in bloom. There was clematis creeping up the walls and all sorts of other plants I didn't know hanging from chains both outside the house as well as in. When Darlene met me at the door she was holding a tea cup this time, not a sherry glass. "It has brandy in it," she said. "I was going to make a hibiscus tea but I didn't feel like putting the kettle on. All I do is boil water, like an old spinster. Boil water and eat meatloaves."

I wanted to ask Darlene if she had any children, but I knew she did not so I didn't say anything. I watched her sip the brandy in her tea cup as she traipsed along to the living room again. When we reached it, I noticed she had several flowers spread out on a table that she had moved to the center of the room, I assume for the purpose of arranging flowers there. She had a yellow hibiscus that I knew because it was a relatively common flower and then she had some seeded plant that looked like cardamom and something that I thought was foxglove but I couldn't be sure. Darlene sat down in her chair again and arranged the hibiscus, cardamom, and foxglove into what looked to me like an attractive arrangement. I glanced around and noticed that the brushwood with the tentacles and the white flowers was no longer in its place in the living room. Playing on the record player was a song by the English boy band *Take That*.

"I feel myself falling

I'm feeling happy now-

I feel myself falling,

we'll live forever now"

"Jason, we need to talk," Darlene said in a funereal voice. It was as if she finally decided to drop the facade. I decided not to look into her face.

"I think it best that we don't see each other anymore." She said it very dramatically as if she was reciting a line from a Jane Austen novel. Darlene looked out the window, at the deodars. "You are not interesting enough for me. Not like Manoj. You are like an old pair of sneakers, a pair of faded Reeboks. As you see, I wear high heels. These are Manolo Blahniks. Do you know who he is, Jason?"

I went into the kitchen and turned on the faucet. Someone had to make tea and if Darlene didn't want to I didn't see any reason why I shouldn't. I didn't know enough about the different types of plants in the house to make a tea from them so I searched through her cabinets where I found a pack of Lipton. I didn't like the cheap stuff but I didn't want Darlene to hear me rifling around her cabinets so I put the Lipton tea bag in a cup. When the kettle reached a boil, I poured the water into the cup and went outside where I stood on the steps for a few minutes, drinking. I saw a hibiscus flower right near my foot and I squashed it beneath my Timberland boots.

When I returned, Darlene was passed out in her chair like the middle-aged academic she was. In fact, you could hardly call her an academic. She was really just the chairwoman of the Water Department. I returned to the kitchen to dump out the rest of my tea. I put the cup in the dishwasher rack but thought it might be rude to leave it like that so I ended up washing it. As I walked back to the living room, I noticed that Darlene was no longer at her place in the chair, which I thought was strange as I had not heard her heels tripping on the parquet floor. I saw an open door at the end of a hall and there Darlene was, lying on her bed. I wondered how she had gotten there but then I saw the brushwood vines retreating down the hall, back to wherever they had been hiding.

Darlene was arranging flowers on her lawn when I went back to the house on Saturday morning. I walked right up to Darlene and Manoj and joined them, Manoj even shaking my hand. This time I knew that one of the flowers in the arrangement was foxglove while the other two looked like pokeweed berries and jimsonweed seeds. Manoj was sitting in a chair across from Darlene in a pair of short shorts that showed off his muscular brown legs. He was reading from the book *Heat and Dust*, which Darlene had told me was her favorite, although she said it had been written by E.M. Forster, which I knew to be false as I had been forced to write a paper on E.M. Forster before I came to Princeton.

Darlene took breaks from her flower arranging to occasionally caress Manoj's leg, which he didn't seem to notice. He just kept on reading in his scholarly, mature accent. One minute he was speaking in a British accent and then the next he was speaking in a thicker Indian one, I suppose imitating this character or that. Darlene seemed to be thinking of the wrong book because she kept making remarks about Pakistan and Manoj would get these puzzled looks on his face. Darlene wore a loose sweater over some tan jodhpurs. She was wearing the sweater inside out so I knew it was an Alexander McQueen as I saw the label. She wasn't wearing a bra so I figured she was tired of feeling like her breasts were in outer space while she was still here on Earth.

Darlene occasionally placed a hand on her chest, as if she was having heart trouble, but then she would laugh it off even though she was uncomfortable. I suppose that was like her, to be overly concerned with appearances.

"What is *that*?" Manoj asked at one point, looking at Darlene's brushwood with the white flowers that had a habit of appearing suddenly in the semi-tropical environment.

"Oh, that. That's *Estrangulata laeti samenti*," said Darlene.

"The happy strangulating plant," Manoj laughed. "I see. That is the one that the Romans wrote about."

"Yes," said Darlene happily, and the look she turned on me was icy. "Some students are handsome as well as smart."

As we sat there, I wondered if this fresh patch of lawn was where Darlene had buried her husband.

Manoj eventually left and that was when Darlene put down her flower arrangements. We sat there across from one another for some time, soon turning to watch as the sun set behind the deodars, the jimsonweed, and the ferns. It suddenly felt very hot, as if we were somewhere other than New Jersey, like Southern France. Darlene leaned towards me, and her breasts sort of hung forward giving the impression that they were very large. I was suddenly attracted to her again and I braced myself for a remark from her about how she told me it was over and why did I come back. But she didn't say that. She simply leaned forward with her large breasts, looked ahead of her at a point somewhat past me, and then sat back again. She began to talk about the book *Thérèse Desqueyroux*, which she said was about a man who poisons his wife although I knew it was the other way around. She took a sip from her tea cup; the heart palpitations reared their ugly head again but just as soon as they had come they were gone. Before I left, Darlene slapped me hard in the face for stepping on one of her hibiscus flowers and when I went home and looked in

Falling

the mirror I had small reticulated lines going up and down my right cheek where she had slapped me, like veins on a leaf.

Two days later, it made the news that the Vice Dean of Education at Princeton had died mysteriously in her home that morning. She was found by her housekeeper who only came once a week, but because the Vice Dean had reported to work the previous day it was suspected that she must have died sometime between leaving work and when the housekeeper came at 8AM. Everyone in the English department knew about Darlene's penchant for flower arranging and most also knew that she didn't know as much about flowers as she led people to believe. Everyone suspected that she had accidentally poisoned herself with all the deadly plants she kept around her and the report from the medical examiner confirmed that suspicion.

When I ran into Manoj in the hall of the department he told me that he didn't doubt that there was poison in her system but he didn't believe that this is what had killed her. He admitted to me that he had seen a very strange sight one evening when he came to Darlene's house. He said he saw a large sprouting plant with vines and white flowers walking away from her lawn as if on legs. The plant appeared to be going for a stroll. I asked him if he had perhaps seen several different plants and mistaken them, but Manoj was sure that it was the same plant and it had moved. He followed its egress into the adjoining property and then it disappeared into the shadows of the adjacent house.

"I'm certain that plant strangled her and then escaped," said Manoj.

He didn't tell the police because he didn't think they would believe him. He also said that he didn't trust the police and he didn't want to get deported, but I knew that rich people never get deported in America and Manoj was very rich even if his family's wealth was in rupees and not dollars. I looked him up on the Forbes list and apparently the family had made several billion dollars in the thirty years since they left their rural backwater of Mirzapur. I could hardly imagine how much that must be in rupees.

Made in United States
North Haven, CT
01 December 2023